Loose Ends

Kill

Bob Doerr

TotalRecall Publications, Inc.
United States of America
Canada and United Kingdom

All rights reserved. Printed in United States of America, Europe and Canada, simultaneously. Except as permitted under the United States Copyright Act of 1976, No part of this publication may be reproduced, stored in a retrieval system, or transmitted in any form or by any means electronic or mechanical or by photocopying, recording, or otherwise without prior permission of the publisher.

Exclusive worldwide content publication / distribution by
TotalRecall Publications.
1103 Middlecreek Friendswood, Texas 77546   281-992-3131   281-482-5390 Fax
6 Precedent Drive Rooksley, Milton Keynes MK13 8PR, UK
1385 Woodroffe Av Ottawa, ON K2G 1V8

Copyright © 2011 by Bob Doerr

ISBN: 978-1-59095-718-9
UPC #   6-43977-47180-2
This is a work of fiction. The characters, events, views, and subject matter of this book are either the author's imagination or are used fictitiously. Any similarity or resemblance to any real people, real situations or actual events is purely coincidental and not intended to portray any person, place, or event in a false, disparaging or negative light.

Printed in the United States of America with simultaneously printings in Canada, and England.

1   2   3   4   5   6   7   8   9   10

FIRST EDITION

Acknowledgements

With the printing of my third book, LOOSE ENDS KILL, I would like to thank all the people who have helped me make it this far. Foremost, I thank my family. They have been more helpful than even they could imagine. Secondly, I need to extend my deep appreciation to Bruce Moran for taking a risk early last year with a new, unknown author. Third, I need to pass along my sincere gratitude to Sharon Cornehlsen, Jim Fitzgerald, Dallin Malmgren, Bill Mannecke, Shelba Nicholson, Elaine Hutchinson, Steve Polk, Pat Stokes, David Swiger, and the San Antonio Writer's Guild. Finally, I shall always enjoy remembering Rhonda Swiger, Sherry Green, Susan Mannecke, and Suzy Fitzgerald for their fabulous and unique rendition of "Paperback Writer." Thanks to you all!

Author Bob Doerr

Bob Doerr grew up in a military family, attended the Air Force Academy, and then had a career of his own in the Air Force. It was a life style that had him moving every three or four years, but also one that exposed him to the people and cultures of numerous countries in Asia, Europe and to most of these United States. In the Air Force, Bob specialized in criminal investigations and counterintelligence gaining significant insight to the worlds of crime, espionage and terrorism. In addition to his degree from the Academy he also has a Masters in International Relations from Creighton University. Bob now lives in Garden Ridge, Texas, with his wife of 37 years and their pet dog.

To find out about new titles, release dates, book signings, speaking engagements and other appearances visit

www.bobdoerr.com

Prologue

She was still in bed, although it was nearly noon, and he had been gone for an hour. He had been especially good this morning. She wondered why she treated him as poorly as she did and then laughed to herself. She treated them all poorly didn't she?

A key rattled at the front door of the condo, and she thought she heard the door open and close.

Pulling the sheets up around her, she sat up in bed. She stopped herself just short of asking, "Back again so soon?" After all, it could be someone else.

"Hello, who's there?"

A person appeared in the doorway carrying a grocery bag.

"Well, I didn't expect to see you today. I thought you were supposed to be out of town until tomorrow. Come over here and tell me about your trip." She patted the blue satin sheets on the bed next to her as she spoke, the top sheet on that side of her falling to her waist.

The person took three steps toward the bed and stopped. She thought something about her visitor looked odd. The facial expression wasn't quite right. Maybe it was the eyes.

"What's the matter?" she asked.

The response was a hand reaching into the bag and removing something that she didn't recognize at first. Recognition came too late. Her killer had already aimed the pistol at her from the end of the bed and pulled the trigger.

She was dead before her body collapsed back onto the pillows.

Only then did the killer come around and sit next to her on the bed; staying there for a full five minutes, feeling sad for what they had done, before getting up to leave. The key that was used to enter the condo was returned to its place in the kitchen drawer. Departing quietly, the killer locked the front door from the inside and pulled it shut.

Chapter 1

The call came in at seven in the morning. I was awake but not yet up. Chubs, my ever obedient dog was asleep on my feet at the end of the bed. He knew I didn't allow him on the bed but had also figured out that if he waited until I was sound asleep, he could usually jump up, and I wouldn't notice until morning. At that point I would yell at him, and he would jump down, feigning sorrow until the next night when the process would be repeated.

"One of these days," I threatened Chubs as he jumped off the bed. He knew my threats were about as sincere as his look of remorse.

I reached for the phone. "Hello."

"Is this Jim West?" a woman with a sultry voice asked from somewhere inside my phone.

"Yes, can I help you?"

"Mr. West, I'm with the law firm Caruzzo and Dilbert here in San Antonio. Do you know a Randy LaMoe?"

I paused for a moment. Randy LaMoe. Now that was a name I hadn't heard in a dozen years.

"Yes. What's up?"

"Well, Mr. West, Randy has retained us to handle his defense in a police matter. He's also asked us to contact you and request that you come to San Antonio. He has something urgent and personal he'd like to discuss with you as soon as possible."

"Why? What's the problem?"

"I am not at liberty to discuss the matter over the phone."

"Why doesn't Randy just call me?"

"It's not as simple as that."

A light went on in my head. "Is he in jail?"

"Yes," the voice paused. "We'll gladly cover the travel expenses."

"We can talk about that when I get there later today. What's your name, and how do I get in touch with you or Randy?"

"Cynthia, Cynthia Rich. It would be better to talk to us about this when you get here. We could fill you in with much more detail at that time."

She provided me with the law firm's contact information and said that someone would be at the office until around seven that evening. If I was going to be there later than seven, she suggested I wait and call in the morning.

I let Chubs out back and sat there on my patio drinking a cup of coffee and watching Chubs do his routine yard inspection. It was still cool and the concrete pavement felt cold on my bare feet. I enjoyed these mornings in New Mexico.

I hadn't seen or talked to Randy LaMoe since we were both in the Air Force and assigned to Ramstein Air Base, Germany. Randy was a pilot, and I was a special agent with the Office of Special Investigations (OSI). Randy and his wife Julie were neighbors and good friends with my ex-wife and me. We played golf together, and the four of us were part of a larger group that frequently hung out together. The last I had heard he was flying for one of the airlines.

After my coffee, I contacted my neighbor to see if one of their five children could watch Chubs for three or four days. Two of them volunteered. I went back to my house and, after doing a few last minute chores, packed. I figured I would be gone two nights, possibly three. There was nothing on my calendar until next Tuesday.

I had second thoughts about making the trip to San Antonio. It wasn't that I didn't want to help Randy; it was just that I had done my twenty years in the military, and when I had returned to New Mexico my plan was to take it easy. I had my Air Force pension, and my goals were simple. Do a few lectures to earn a little extra money and improve my golf game. The last time I went out to help a friend I nearly got killed. That one trip did more damage to my body than it had experienced in my prior forty years. My hair was even trying to turn grey now.

But there was no way I could say no. Against my better judgment, I knew I had to go and at least try to help him. Plus, the trip would give me a chance to check out my new black Mustang convertible on a long drive.

The trip to San Antonio was uneventful. West Texas usually is. I watched the dust in the farmers' fields turn into large dust devils between Lubbock and Big Spring. From Big Spring to San Angelo I tried to count the giant windmills and lost track somewhere around a hundred. The only noteworthy event was my purchase of a copy of the San Antonio Express News at a gas station in Junction. I leafed through it in the station and found the article I was looking for.

Man Arrested for Murder of Wife was the headline in the Metro section. It went on to say that Randy had been arrested and was being charged with his wife's murder. I quickly scanned the rest of the article before throwing it in the back seat of the Mustang on top of the gym bag that was serving as my suitcase for this trip.

I arrived at the city limits around six. I contemplated calling the Law Offices of Caruzzo and Dilbert but decided to first find a hotel room and get cleaned up. My sandals, jean shorts and

Jimmy's Gym t-shirt probably wouldn't make a good first impression. I took the interstate all the way to the heart of the city before getting off on Market Street and heading to the River Walk to find a hotel. It was a Wednesday in September, so I didn't think finding a room would be hard.

There was a new Hyatt hotel on the river so I gave it a try. No problem. For a hundred fifty five dollars a night I could have one of their standard rooms for as long as I wanted. I called the law office as I was undressing. Cynthia answered on the second ring.

"Hey, Cynthia, this is Jim. I'm in town and would like to meet with you if possible. I'd like to know what's going on."

"Where are you right now?"

"I'm at the Hyatt on the River Walk. Do you want to come here or should I come to your place?"

"We'll come there. I believe there's a nice lounge in your hotel on the main floor, close to where you checked in. I can't think of the name of it, but we'll be there in about fifteen minutes."

"Okay." I figured that would be sufficient time to shower and get downstairs.

"If I have your hotel mixed up with a different one and there's no lounge, we'll just meet you at the reception desk."

I hung up and got into the shower. Too bad she wasn't coming alone.

Chapter 2

I made it to the lounge in just under the fifteen minutes allotted me. I didn't see anyone who looked like they were looking for me, so I took a stool at the bar and ordered a Shiner's. I had put on a pair of brown slacks and a yellow golf shirt and at the time wondered if I should have brought something a little more formal. Looking around the lounge and the reception area, I realized that everyone else was wearing either shorts or jeans. After all, this was San Antonio.

The beer was good and cold, and I had just about finished it when two women walked into the lounge and look around. They met my gaze and, assuming correctly, approached me at the bar.

"Jim West?" the taller of the two asked.

"Yes. Are you Cynthia?"

"Yes, and this is Nita Ybarra. She's also an attorney with Caruzzo and Dilbert."

"Nice to meet you both. Would you like to grab a table here or go somewhere else?"

"Here is fine, Jim, perhaps over there in the corner." Cynthia suggested, pointing to the far point of the room away from the other patrons.

"Lead the way."

I followed the two of them through the scattered tables and chairs. An interesting duo, I thought. Cynthia seemed to be almost as tall as me, six feet, and Nita was barely more than five.

Cynthia was blond, her hair short and curly, and Nita had long jet black hair. Cynthia had the build of an athlete, while Nita was thin with more delicate features. Cynthia probably had a Scandinavian background and Nita was obviously Latina. Despite the extreme differences, both were attractive in their own ways.

When we arrived at the table I realized there was a fourth person in our little parade. He didn't join us as we sat down.

"My name is Enrique. It will be my pleasure to be your server this evening. May I get you ladies a drink?"

"A vodka martini for me, please," Cynthia requested.

"House margarita on the rocks, please," Nita followed.

"And I'll have another Shiner's."

"Jim, I hope you don't mind us having a drink. It's been a long day," Cynthia commented, as she looked around the bar.

"Not at all. Is the stuff with Randy keeping you busy?"

"No. Our office management, that is the partners that own the firm, announced some downsizing steps and personnel cuts during a meeting this afternoon. Luckily, except for having to sit through the drama of the meeting and follow on sessions, Nita and I weren't affected. As you can imagine, there were a lot of tears and anger. Some good people were let go. It was quite stressful."

"Cynthia, Jim isn't interested in all that," Nita interjected. "Actually, Jim, we haven't had a lot to do on the LaMoe case. He was arrested early yesterday afternoon. We've talked to him, and to the police, and have had a private investigator follow up with the police. It looks pretty bad for him."

"I can't believe he would murder Julie. They were always such a happy couple when I knew them. That was a number of years ago, but still…"

"How many years has it been?" Cynthia interrupted.

"Oh, it's been about a decade since I spent any significant time with them. I've run into mutual friends on a couple of occasions since who had seen him more recently, but I haven't."

"Are you aware of any marital problems they may have been having?"

"No, not at all."

Nita joined back in. "We believe she was having an affair, perhaps more than one. If that is true, would it have been sufficient cause for Randy to have killed her?"

"No, I don't believe so. It's hard enough for me to believe she would have had an affair. It's even harder for me to believe Randy would kill her if she did. We've known other couples that broke up because one spouse was having an affair. I can't recall a single occasion where Randy made a remark or gave me any other indication that he would kill Julie if she had an affair. It's too out of character for him."

Cynthia took over the conversation again. "We've arranged for you to see him tomorrow morning at nine. Is that all right?"

"Sure."

"It's important that you let us know what he tells you, Jim. He told us he wants to meet with you alone. We're not sure why he doesn't want us there. We advised him we should be there but he says you're an old friend, that he can trust you. Can we?" Cynthia stared straight at me as she asked this.

"Depends how many martinis you have."

"Not funny, Jim." Cynthia may not have thought so, but I was pretty sure I saw a slight grin try to form on Nita's face. "Can we trust you to let us know everything he says?"

"Yes," I lied. I certainly would pass on anything pertinent, but I would decide what was pertinent.

"Good," Cynthia responded. "There is no way we can provide him our best if we don't have all the facts. If he admits to killing his wife, we need to know that."

"Do either of you think he did?"

"Yes," they responded in unison.

After a short pause, Cynthia spoke up. "It looks bad for him. He was seen going into the condo complex around noon and then leaving in a hurry minutes later. However, in fairness, no one saw him enter the actual residence. Shortly after he left, the police received a call from one of the owners who thought he heard a gunshot coming from the vicinity, within the building, of Randy's unit. The police, along with the complex manager, went door to door throughout his wing and the one above. Just so happened someone was in every other apartment the police went to - we're just talking about six units - and facilitated the search. However, when they got to Randy's and rang the bell no one answered. The police claimed they could hear a baby crying inside so they had management open the condo. The baby was next door, and I think the police knew it. They just used it for justification."

A good one, too, I thought. No one was going to fault the police for going into an apartment seemingly empty except for a crying baby. They would get ridiculed for not doing so.

"Inside they found Julie. Shot once in the heart. Died instantly, I believe." Cynthia stared at me, waiting for a response.

"Did they find the weapon?"

"No, other than the dead body, nothing seemed out of place in the apartment. Her purse, with over a hundred dollars in it, was undisturbed on the kitchen counter. She still had her wedding ring on. A matching ruby necklace and earrings were on the bathroom sink."

"Where did they find Julie?" I asked.

Nita answered me. "In bed, naked. We were told that it

looked like she had recently had sex with someone."

I felt like asking, "How does one look when they've recently had sex?" Instead, I remained quiet.

"The police are working the DNA angle. Their theory is that Randy showed up at the condo, found her in bed nude, knew that she had just screwed someone else, and killed her on the spot. They believe Randy had been waiting outside the building for her lover to leave. He then went immediately inside and killed Julie."

"If that were true, why wouldn't have Randy killed the lover, too? I mean, if he was waiting for him to leave, then he needed to know the lover was there."

"We don't know the answer to that. Maybe he planned on killing the lover later."

"What's Randy's story?" I asked Nita.

Cynthia answered for Nita. "Would you mind us not telling you? We need to hear what he tells you."

I looked at them both for a moment before responding. "Which one of you is in charge of this case?

"I am," answered Cynthia. "But please understand that you can speak to either of us at any time. We frequently work as a team. Nita is a genius. The partners and I consider her invaluable. It's just that I have her by four years with the firm."

I wondered if she said this for me or for Nita.

Nita smiled. "She is just saying this to reassure me, Jim. The other two lawyers in the firm from my year group were let go today. But do understand that anything you tell me will be shared with Cynthia."

"And vice versa." Cynthia added.

"Well, don't worry, I won't pick favorites."

They remained in the lounge for another ten minutes assuring me they had Randy's best interest in mind but that they needed my help in corroborating the story he told them. They promised they would be more open with me after I talked to him. It made some sense.

I learned that the firm of Caruzzo and Dilbert had practiced law in the San Antonio area for a little over ten years. It consisted of three partners and seven other lawyers. Up until today it had been ten other lawyers.

I offered to buy them a second drink but they declined. Cynthia paid for their drinks, but not mine, and said they expected to hear from me after I talked to Randy. Before they left, they both gave me business cards that included their cell phone numbers.

Moving back to the bar, I caught our server's eye and beckoned him over. His name tag did, in fact, say his name was Enrique.

"Enrique, can I get something to eat in here?"

"Sir, may I recommend the nachos supreme? They are very good."

I ordered them and ended up spending another half hour there eating the nachos and chatting with Enrique. Business had slowed to a crawl, and he was as bored as I was at that time in the evening. Enrique told me he was working at the hotel to help pay for college. He was in his final year at the University of Texas at San Antonio and lived at home with his mother.

It was nearly ten when I finally went back to my room. I had a hard time falling asleep, not necessarily because of anything bothering me. In fact, with the limited information I had about Randy's predicament, he wasn't even on my mind. I kept wondering about Cynthia and Nita. An interesting couple, I thought. I had noticed neither one was wearing a wedding ring. I did my best not to let my imagination get too carried away and finally fell asleep.

Chapter 3

I awoke around seven thirty and decided to walk along the River Walk before heading off to see Randy. It was already warm outside but not very humid. The sidewalk along the San Antonio River was quiet except for the occasional jogger and other walkers. Nothing was open yet, however, there was activity at a number of restaurants and small businesses as employees were busy getting ready for another day. It had been a while since I visited San Antonio, and I made a mental note of the restaurants where I wanted to eat during my stay in the city.

I returned to the hotel just long enough to get a second cup of coffee before jumping into my car and heading west on Commerce Street out of the city center. The drive to the Bexar County jail was a short one. I arrived in plenty of time for the nine o'clock appointment Cynthia had set up for me. Once there, I found the big "Visitors Report Here" sign and followed it into the large brick building.

The visitor reception area was already crowded, and I began to worry if I was going to be seen by anyone before nine. I had only stood in line for about a minute when I felt a tap on my shoulder. I turned around and was greeted by Cynthia and Nita.

"Come with us, Jim. We have everything set up with the staff here." Cynthia pointed to a side door as she spoke.

I followed the two of them into an office that held three desks and chairs and not much else. Two of the desks were occupied by deputies in uniform, and the remaining desk was occupied by a heavy woman in civilian attire with thinning brown hair. One of the deputies with jet black hair - too black for his age, I thought - stood when all three of us were inside. He looked at Cynthia and asked, "Are you ready, ma'am?"

"We are," she replied.

"Follow me," the guard instructed. He turned to a door in the wall opposite from where we had entered, punched in an access code and led us into an interior hallway. We walked along the hallway for about twenty yards before coming to another door also requiring an access code. Once we entered the room I could see that we were in one of the administrative offices facing the prison proper. The room had large glass windows that allowed the staff to see into a large interior common area one level below. The common area was surrounded by walls and bars.

"Joe," our guide addressed one of the uniformed guards in the room, "these people are here to see Inmate LaMoe. I believe he's already waiting in one of the visiting rooms."

"Yes, he is," replied Joe. Then, looking at us, he said, "Please follow me."

"At the moment, it will just be Mr. West who will be going to see our client. If you don't mind, my partner and I will wait here." Cynthia's remark was quickly followed by glances at the two women from the four other male guards in the room.

"That'll be fine," answered one of them.

As I followed Joe out of the office I could hear a guard offering the two attorneys some coffee.

The room in which Randy was waiting for me was only a short distance from the admin office. A guard stood outside the room. He barely gave me a glance when I walked by. Inside, I noticed the room was only furnished with a small wooden table and two chairs. Randy sat in one chair, sporting Bexar County Jail prison attire and a pair of handcuffs. He looked years older than I would have ever imagined.

He stood when I entered and said, "Hey, Jim, thanks for coming." Then he started to cry. He tried to stop crying but it took him a few seconds.

"It's all right, man. Please sit down." I sat and looked at him as he composed himself. In that moment, though, I knew without a doubt that this broken man did not kill his wife. The Randy I knew was a proud person who flew fighters in the Air Force and who could always take what was dished at him. What was happening to him now was something he had never expected, and it had overwhelmed him.

"Sorry, Jim. I've handled myself just fine until now. I'm glad you came."

"What's going on, Randy?"

"Someone killed Julie. Shot her, I assume, since the police have asked me repeatedly where the gun is. The cops who questioned me claim Julie was having an affair and think that's why I killed her. I didn't do it, and I find it hard to believe she was seeing someone else. You know Julie, Jim. Do you think she was fooling around on me?"

"No, I find that hard to believe myself."

"Even if she was, I wouldn't kill her. I'm not sure I'd even leave her. Not if she promised it was over and she would never see him again. We've been together twenty years. No kids, just the two of us. We're joined at the hip. Sure, I look around and flirt all the time. She does, too, but it's all innocent. I know it, she knows it, and so does everyone else."

"I know it. Look, we've hung around a lot in the past and there were many times when the four of us had a little too much to drink. Never, sober or not, did I ever suspect Julie was hitting on me or on anyone else."

"Thanks, Jim. But say she did fall for some other guy in the last few months. It could happen, I guess. But if she did, I didn't know about it and certainly wouldn't have killed her if I'd found out about it."

We were both quiet for a few moments. My mind had turned to my own failed marriage. A line of thought I tried to stay away from. It still hurt.

Randy must have sensed what was troubling me. "Julie never gave me any reason to believe there was another man that broke up your marriage. And she would have known. She talked to your ex a number of times after you all split up. Julie would have told me."

"It's not important, Randy. Let's focus on getting you cleared of this mess."

"Can you help me, Jim?"

"I'll try, but you need to tell me everything you can remember about your activities two days ago and everything you can think of about Julie's over the past several days. I'll also need access to your house, the condo, your cars, computers, everything."

"I imagine the police have everything under their control right now."

"I'm sure they do, but as soon as I can I'll need access to them too. I imagine your lawyers can draft up the proper documents identifying me as an agent for them, but they'll want your okay before they do so. That will give me some legal status in doing all this and save you some money in the process. I imagine I'm a lot cheaper than the PI's they're using now."

"Jim, the last thing I'm concerned about now is the expense. I'll pay you whatever you want."

"No charge, Randy. If I can get you out of this fix, maybe I'll let you cover my expenses. I'm not here for the money."

"I know, man. I'd be there for you, too." Then he grinned as he continued, "Although I have to admit, if I could've remembered that other agent's name, you know, the crazy one, I probably would have called him."

I smiled, too. I immediately knew who he was talking about. "You mean Ratskowski."

"Yeah! Whatever happened to him?"

"I don't know. I lost track of him after he retired."

Randy and I talked for another half hour before I left him to his guards. Despite the circumstances, it was good to see him again. On the short walk back down the hall to meet with Cynthia and Nita, I thought about good old Ratskowski.

He was an old school agent from the Viet Nam era. Already in his fifties when I met him in Germany, Ratskowski wasn't enthralled with all the rights and niceties being given to the criminal elements in society. The incident that endeared him to a lot of us there in Germany dealt with his handling of an all around, really nasty guy. I couldn't remember the bad guy's name but I recalled that he had been involved in a number of violent beatings in which the victims refused to press any charges because of their fear of him. We also suspected the rotten creep had committed a couple of rapes.

On the day of "the incident" Ratskowski responded to a call that a young woman was being beaten up and possibly sexually assaulted in an apartment complex located near the air base. Ratskowski happened to be in the apartment complex parking lot when the radio call went out and was first on the scene. When he arrived at the victim's apartment the bad guy was just leaving. Ratskowski blocked his departure and pushed him back into the apartment. Inside there was a lone female, maybe twenty years of age. She was crying. Her nose and lip were bleeding and her skirt was torn. Ratskowski saw her panties on the floor.

"What happened?" Ratskowski asked the girl.

The girl just stared at the two men in shock.

"Nothing happened to her, or to her little sister." The jerk spoke loud enough so his victim would understand the not-so-veiled threat.

What happened next was never really proven, despite the official inquiry. But what I personally believed is that Ratskowski somehow provoked the bad guy into pulling a knife on him. He probably stuck the knife close to Ratskowski's throat, at which time, Ratskowski grabbed the guy's knife hand and jabbed himself in the chin. I wouldn't be surprised if he'd simply held the knife still and hit it with his chin. The wound to his face was superficial. But it served its purpose. Ratskowski simultaneously fired one shot into the jerk's groin with his government issued .38, effectively neutering him.

The perp later yelled and screamed that he hadn't stabbed Ratskowski, but the crime scene photos of Ratskowski's bleeding face were accepted as sufficient evidence to justify the shooting. Ratskowski already had a reputation, but after that incident we all used to joke about calling him to help us resolve our unusually tough cases.

Cynthia and Nita were still where I left them, but a few more male guards and staffers had found their way into the admin office. I imagined word had gotten out that two attractive ladies were there. The entire group was engrossed in a conversation about the Spurs' chances this year. The Spurs had won the National Basketball Association championship a number of times in the last decade and, understandably, had quite a fan base in San Antonio.

Both ladies looked up as I entered.

"Everything go okay?" Cynthia inquired.

"Yes, for now. I'll need to talk to him again after I've checked on a few things."

"Let's go somewhere and talk," suggested Nita.

One of the guards escorted us out to the reception area that was now even more crowded than before. From there we walked outside.

"That's one busy place," I commented.

"Visiting hours don't usually start until noon, but the last couple of weeks they have been experimenting with the earlier start. Not sure it's making any difference," Nita responded.

"Where to?" I asked.

Nita looked at Cynthia and suggested a place called Tres Leches. I knew that was a name for a cake but wasn't familiar with a restaurant or café by that name. She also offered to ride along with me to help me find the place. We would meet Cynthia there.

Chapter 4

Nita was wearing a navy blue skirt with a white blouse. The skirt showed off a nice pair of legs while I held her door open and she climbed into my car. I tried not to stare. Once I got behind the wheel, she immediately began giving me instructions. Turn left, go straight, turn here – the usual stuff. It only took us five minutes and we were pulling into the small parking lot of a small diner. Cynthia was already getting out of her car as we pulled in.

We followed her into Tres Leches. The sign at the entrance said "Please Seat Yourselves," so we followed Cynthia's lead and headed to a table in the middle of the small restaurant. We were the only customers there.

The place looked old but clean. The dozen or so tables were covered with red and white checked plastic table cloths.

"Since this place is usually busy, we are obviously in between crowds," remarked Cynthia. "So, Jim - and it is Jim right, not James?"

"That's right, never been a James."

"So, Jim, what did Randy say to you?"

Before I could answer, a young man came up and took our orders. Three coffee's, two potato and egg breakfast tacos, and one cinnamon roll. Mine was the cinnamon roll. Once he left I started my debriefing.

"I don't think Randy killed her. He said he didn't and I believe him. The day of the murder, Randy arrived back in San

Antonio on a morning flight from Baltimore. He wasn't supposed to be back for another day or two but schedules got changed. He found out the night before the killing that he was free to return home until his next scheduled run which, if it matters, isn't until next week. Once he knew he would be coming home early, he called Julie but had to leave a message since there was no answer at home or on her cell. That wasn't all that unusual because she was often out at night with some of the other wives and was notorious for leaving her cell phone in the charger at home. He awoke at four in the morning our time to catch the early morning flight here, so he didn't call her until he arrived. That was about seven and again no answer. At that point he did start to worry. He had not gotten a message from her in response to the calls the night before."

"Randy drove straight to their house in the northeast suburbs, but when he discovered Julie was not there, he decided to check the condo they own not too far from the airport. En route to the condo he stopped to get some breakfast at a place close to the airport where both he and Julie loved going. I asked him why he stopped to eat if he was at all concerned about Julie. His answer here is admittedly weak. He claims that while he was concerned, his concern never reached the panic level. It was more like a 'What's going on?' worry. Additionally, he thought it was very possible Julie might be at the restaurant. Around noon, he left the restaurant to run up to the condo for a minute before heading back home to see if Julie had returned. Since they don't have a land line phone in the condo, he couldn't call first. He entered the building but in the elevator realized that he didn't have his door keys with him. He went to the condo anyway and rang the bell in the off chance Julie was there. No one answered, so he left and went straight home. He'd only been there about an hour when the police came."

Both Cynthia and Nita began firing questions at me and I did my best to answer them. A lot of the questions focused on areas which I had no answers. Specifically, was Julie fooling around? If so, with whom? Had she fooled around before, with me, etc., etc.?

"I can understand your interest in this line of questioning," I finally remarked. "But, you're approaching it from the wrong side. If we accept that Randy is innocent, then isn't it likely that Julie's past is only relevant in that it may lead us to her killer? Love and jealousy may not be the primary motives in this case."

Cynthia started to object but I cut her off.

"I know it may still be, but it may not be. Isn't that a possibility?"

They both acknowledged that it was.

"I'm sure the police will stick with the betrayed husband angle, so I don't plan on focusing my efforts there."

"Hold on for a second," Cynthia instructed. "What do you mean by your efforts? What do you think your role in all this is supposed to be?"

"Randy asked me to find out who killed his wife. I plan to give it my best shot."

"Are you a private investigator? Are you licensed in Texas?"

"No to both. I'm just a friend."

"Then why does Randy think you can help, and how do you plan to do anything here in San Antonio?" Cynthia still controlled the conversation. Nita quietly sat there listening.

"Randy knows I've got a lot of experience investigating crimes. I was hoping I could get a written letter from you or your firm simply stating that I am working as a consultant to your firm in this matter. That should be all I need to talk to the police and a few key witnesses."

They looked at each other. Cynthia again kept up their side of the conversation. "You know we already have a PI on retainer."

"I work for free. I'll keep you fully informed of everything I find out. Your firm can always pay your PI to repeat the same steps I take."

"We'll have to get the firm's approval first. What do you plan to do if we can't get it?"

"Talk to the next law firm Randy hires."

Both ladies got a little red in the face. I knew I had probably just pissed them off, so I decided to make it sound more like a compromise. After all, I liked these two.

"It's a win - win situation for both of us. You get some free help and I get some credibility in the eyes of the police. I won't get in your way or cause any embarrassment to your firm. If you need references I can give you a few, but I need to know right now whether or not this is agreeable to you two."

Again the pause, but I could tell from their expressions they were going to accept my offer.

"Assuming we accept your offer of assistance, what is your plan?" Nita piped up, probably to let Cynthia save face.

"Today I'd like to talk to the police. Find out what they have and what they don't -- at least to the extent that they'll talk to me. Then I'd like to talk to your private cop and find out what he or she has. Tonight I plan on calling a few old friends to get some background on Julie. Like I said, I haven't seen her in a while. Tomorrow I'll need to go through his house, his condo, their cars, etc. If the police didn't take their computers I'll look at them. Then I start talking to everyone else."

Cynthia resumed her role as head lawyer. "Okay," she said, "you'll want to contact Lt. Buzz Nosh. He's in homicide and his guys are working it. Tell him you're with us."

"Thanks." I tried to give them my most sincere look. "I mean it, thanks."

I doubt if either of them bought it.

"The firm may yet veto your involvement."

And lose a paying client? I didn't think so but kept my thoughts to myself. I offered to pay for the breakfast but Cynthia said they would get it. I didn't argue. Nita gave me the phone number I needed to reach Lt. Nosh and I stood up to leave.

"Before you go," Cynthia remarked, still wanting to reassert herself as the one in charge, "I'll need a daily verbal report."

"Sure."

"And, are you carrying a weapon, Jim?"

"No. I didn't bring one and don't plan on needing one."

"Good, thanks." I think that was what she wanted to hear. It would make my involvement more palatable to her bosses.

Chapter 5

My appointment with Lt Nosh was scheduled for two o'clock. Finding the grey and green tile building on West Nueva Street was easier than I thought it might be. I was there twenty minutes early. I had things to do and was hoping I could meet with the lieutenant earlier. Unfortunately, he wasn't even in the office until ten minutes past two, and then I had to wait another five before I got in to see him.

"What can I do for you, Mr. West?" And then, I guess to answer his own question, he went on talking. "I understand you're helping out Ms. Rich in her defense of Randy LaMoe. We really don't have any more information to pass on to her than what we've already provided her other investigator."

"Please call me Jim. I realize that you've been through this once already, but I'd appreciate having a few minutes of your time. Did you go to the crime scene yourself, or did a couple of your detectives handle it?"

"Well, Jim, I wasn't in town the day of the murder. I didn't get back until yesterday. Detective Frank Reynolds led the effort on this one for the department. From what I can see, it doesn't look very good for your client. There's motive and opportunity. By that I mean he was observed at the scene of the crime at the time of death and his wife was fooling around on him. She had sex with someone earlier that morning and your client acknowledges it wasn't him. DNA will likely verify that."

"Any sign that the sex may not have been voluntary?"

"Not at all. No sign of any struggle or of a break-in at the condo. No one saw anyone who didn't belong in the area either."

"But you still don't have the murder weapon?"

"True, but I imagine it will turn up."

I thought he was probably right about that. "Can I talk to this Detective Reynolds?"

"I don't see why not." He was probably happy to pass me on to someone else. "In fact, he should be your main point of contact while you're here."

He picked up his phone and buzzed Reynolds.

"He'll be right here," Lt. Nosh said as he stood up and offered me his hand. "Reynolds is a busy man. If you have any problems reaching him, feel free to give me a call."

"Thanks."

The door opened and Detective Reynolds poked his head in.

"Boss, you need me?"

After Nosh introduced me to Reynolds, I followed him out of the lieutenant's office and down the hall to his smaller, but still private, office. As I walked behind him, I couldn't help thinking that Frank Reynolds must have played college sports, probably football, in his younger days. He appeared to be in tremendous physical condition. I put him at six foot two, slightly taller than me, and imagined he weighed at least two hundred thirty pounds. I probably had more fat in my ass than he had in his whole body. And, in my opinion, I'm not in that bad of shape.

"I understand the lieutenant filled you in on what we have, Jim. I know it's not a rock solid case we have on your client, but I've seen many guys get convicted on less. We have no leads to encourage us to look in any other direction. You give us some and we'll pursue them. But until we have an ounce of suspicion leading us to look elsewhere, your man is it."

"I understand that and appreciate your candor. Do you know who Julie was seeing? Specifically, who may have been with her the morning she was killed."

"No, not yet. The DNA may help when it comes back, and we'll keep checking. We'd like to know who he was, too."

I stayed and talked with Reynolds for another twenty minutes. I did so mainly to build a rapport with him since I needed him as an ally. He was a likeable guy. Been with the police force for eight years and had just made detective a few months earlier. A graduate of one of the big universities in Texas, he had indeed played linebacker for its football team. He had a couple of nibbles from the pro scouts when he graduated but was deemed too small.

Frank told me that the crime scene was still under police control but that he would make sure I was allowed into it. They had already completed a thorough search of the condo but would keep control of it for a few more days. The police still had a team going through Randy's house, though that was not as high a priority, but he would get word to them about me, too. He instructed me not to remove anything from either residence. I promised I wouldn't.

After leaving the station, I drove north to Alamo Heights to meet up with Gary Grisshof, Caruzzo and Dilbert's retained private investigator. Alamo Heights is a small incorporated town long ago completely surrounded by an ever growing San Antonio. Grisshof's office was on the second floor of a Midway Bank building. It was a fairly nice location so I figured Grisshof was doing okay in the PI business.

I didn't have a specific appointment time. I had simply asked Cynthia to let Grisshof know that I would be coming over after I finished with the police. It was approaching four in the afternoon when I walked into his reception area. The place looked deserted. There was a receptionist's desk but no one was behind it and the top of the desk was spotless. The couch and two lounge chairs were empty. At least the lights were still on. Two doors led from the reception area but both were closed. I tested one and discovered it led into a storage closet. The other opened up into a short hallway that looked promising.

I could just make out a man's voice coming from the office at the end of the hall. The door to the office was open an inch or two. I walked toward the office, passing an entrance to a small conference room on my left and two closed doors on my right. At the end of the hall I rapped my knuckles against the door twice and stuck my head in.

The man inside was on the phone and looked up at me. My entrance seemed to have irritated him.

"Would you mind waiting in the outer room out there. I'll be with you in a few minutes. I'm on a private call."

I nodded, turned around, and did as I was told. He came down the hall about five minutes later.

"Sorry if I sounded rude, but most people don't barge in on me like that."

"That's all right. I thought you were expecting me, and there was no one out here when I arrived."

He looked at the empty desk. "I had to fire her. She talked too much to her friends about things that shouldn't have been talked about. Wasn't too smart either. My old partner used to tell me that I needed to hire them for what's in their heads, not for what's below their heads. Hate to do that, though."

I wasn't interested in his office personnel or lack of same. "Are you Gary Grisshof?"

"That's me. Who are you?" He didn't offer his hand.

"I'm Jim West. Cynthia Rich should have given you a call about me."

"Oh, yes she did." He looked at me for a minute to size me up. At six foot and just over two hundred pounds, I was considerably larger than he was. He sort of reminded me of the character who played the wizard in the old Wizard of Oz movie with Judy Garland. I didn't think he could intimidate anyone, but the way he talked it was obvious that he thought he could.

"What I don't understand is why you think you can come down here and do my job better than I can? She says you're not even a licensed dick in your own state."

We were still standing. "Gary, why don't we sit down and be a little more comfortable?"

I didn't wait for him to respond, instead seating myself in the nearest chair. He walked over and leaned against the desk. Not as comfortable, but it did finally give him the height advantage.

"I'm not here to do your job or to affect your relationship with Caruzzo and Dilbert in any way. I'm here to help a friend and that's all. I needed the cooperation of the law firm to give my involvement some credibility. They're not paying me a penny. When I'm done here, I'll go away. Nothing more to it."

Grisshof didn't say anything for about thirty seconds, no doubt weighing my comments against his suspicions.

"Well, you're wasting your time anyway. I'll bet you fifty dollars right now he did it."

I was tempted to take the bet just to accept the challenge but the last thing I wanted to do was give him any more of a reason not to help Randy.

"You may be right, but why are you so convinced?"

"Because, even though it's barely been forty-eight hours

since the murder, I've done my job." He stared again at me, but I kept my mouth shut. I needed to know what he knew, and if I had to let him brag about what a great job he'd already done, that was fine.

"Do you know that LaMoe's wife had been messing around with at least three other guys while he was away flying airplanes? And that's only in the past two years. And that's just at the condo. Who knows who she was shacking up with at her house while he was away?"

"Gary, how do you know this?"

"It's called detective work. It's what I am damn good at. A source of mine at the condo complex has watched different men spend the night in the condo with her while LaMoe's been gone. Other men have been seen popping in and out during the day, but we'll give her the benefit of the doubt on those." He rolled his eyes with this last comment.

"Okay, let's agree she was having an affair. Why do you think Randy killed her?"

"Because it's obvious. Whoever shot her had access to the condo. Whoever shot her was at the condo at or around noon. Whoever shot her needed a motive. Strike one, two, three: motive, opportunity and capability. Hell, if she was my wife I would have shot her. I sat down over a beer night before last with Detective Reynolds and then again over coffee yesterday afternoon with Lt. Nosh. They believe LaMoe killed his wife and feel a jury will too. No one else is even slightly implicated. I don't think the police are looking too hard elsewhere."

"Will you give me the name of your source at the condo complex so I can talk to him?"

"No."

"What are you planning to do next?"

"Nothing, unless Ms. Rich asks me to look into something.

I've got the feeling that as long as you're snooping around, I'll just be cooling my heels."

"If I need you to check something out for me, will you do it?"

"If Ms. Rich asks me to."

"Okay, that's fair." I looked around his office again. "How long have you been doing this?"

"Ten years this month. Used to be a city cop until I retired with my twenty-five."

"Congratulations. You look like you're doing well."

"I told you, I'm good at what I do."

"Since I do plan on trying to find another motive and another killer, any suggestions?"

"No. Like I said, you're wasting your time. If someone else killed her, it could be anyone in the city. The motive may even be harder to come up with. If you know the LaMoes, you know they have no money worries. They weren't involved in any criminal activity and have no enemies. If the police can identify who she was in the sack with, there may be something worth pursuing, but I doubt it. This was a cold-blooded hit. Someone got up close and fired one shot into her. I don't see someone who just had sex with her earlier in the morning turning right around and coldly shooting her in the heart. This was not a sudden passion killing. This was something planned out and executed."

"Where do you think the gun is?"

"In one of the lakes around here. That's where I'd toss it. Your best bet is to go visit your friend LaMoe and tell him to confess. Considering his wife's behavior, most juries would have a lot of sympathy. May only get ten years."

"You may be right." I didn't think he was, but I didn't want to totally alienate him.

"I'm a busy guy, so unless you have something else, I got things to do."

"No, that's all. Thanks for your time. I'll stay in touch."

He turned and walked back towards his office. No handshake, no good-bye. It took most of my patience to not kick his butt while he walked away.

Chapter 6

I got back to the hotel just as the rush hour traffic started to cause a grid lock on most of the outbound arteries. Luckily, I was heading into the city. It was a hot afternoon, like most of them are in San Antonio this time of the year. In need of a cold beer, I headed straight for the hotel bar.

The day had not been very productive. The steps taken were necessary but did little more than show me that the task ahead was not going to be easy. No one had the slightest interest in making much of an effort to find someone else to take the blame for Julie's murder. I would need to do some significant digging to come out with some other possibilities.

As I sat at the bar sipping on my Shiner, I saw Enrique report in for his shift. He saw me and nodded. Nice kid, I thought, but I was hoping the young lady behind the bar wasn't ready to go off shift. She was much nicer to look at. As if she could read my mind, she looked at me and smiled.

"Anything else before I take off?"

I ordered another beer and made some mental notes on the next steps I needed to take. It was obvious that Julie LaMoe had changed since I had known her, and that developing a better knowledge of her extra-marital activities was a must.

Randy had told me that Julie didn't work but had several hobbies and activities that kept her busy. She was a member of a ladies book group, a mahjong group, and a gourmet group. She also assisted with a few charities and had even helped out a couple of times building houses with Habitat for Humanity. Randy rarely got involved with her in any of these activities. But as we both acknowledged, how could any of them be a place where one would make enemies or inspire anyone to kill you?

Randy gave me a list of mutual friends. Two of the names I recognized from the past when we were in the Air Force together. I decided to start with one of those, Tim Davis, as Randy had given me his phone number.

The lounge was almost empty. There was no one at the counter with me, so I dialed Tim's number.

He answered on the second ring.

"Is this Tim Davis?"

"Yes, it is."

"Hey Tim, this is Jim West. Remember me from the old days at Ramstein?"

"Sure I do." He answered without pausing. "What are you up to these days?"

"Well actually, Tim, I'm here in San Antonio. Randy LaMoe asked me to come down to help him out."

"Jeez, I read about that. Sibyl and I feel terrible about what happened."

"How's Sibyl doing?"

"Fine, just fine. We both are. You know, Jim, Sibyl and Julie were fairly close. It was a tragic thing."

"Tim, can I get with you and Sibyl tomorrow and talk about this?"

"I'm leaving town tomorrow morning. I'll be back in a week, though. Is that too long?"

"Yeah, it really is. Can I ask you a few questions on the phone?"

"Sure, if it can help Randy. Shoot."

"The police believe she may have been having an affair. Did you or Sibyl ever have any reason to believe she might have been seeing someone else?"

There was a pause on our conversation. I started to ask if he was still there just as he spoke back up.

"Are you kidding me, Jim? You know as well as I do that Julie has been fooling around on Randy as long as we've known them."

Now the pause was at my end. "What are you talking about?"

"Are you serious? Sibyl and I have always thought you were one of her regulars."

"Sorry to disappoint you, Tim, but I never had a sexual relationship with Julie. And, maybe I was a bit naïve back then, but I never knew she was sleeping around on Randy. Are you sure she was, or did you just expect there were others like me?" I know I was being a little sarcastic, but I was also getting a bit irritated.

"No sweat, man. If you say you didn't sleep with Julie, then that's fine by me. But, I know a couple of the guys there did because they talked about scoring with her."

Tim rambled on for a while about who claimed to have done what with Julie back in Germany. I finally cut him off.

"Tim, I'm not really interested in what happened back then. Do you know anyone who may have been seeing her in the last year?"

"No. I haven't seen or talked to either of them in about a year. In fact, I haven't seen Julie in at least two years. You should talk to Sibyl. She has seen her more often and more recently than me."

"Is she there, Tim?"

"No, she's out playing bunko with some of the

neighborhood wives tonight. You know, Jim, we've been waiting for that marriage to break up for over a decade. Randy was either the most unobservant man in the world or simply didn't care that his wife slept around. Our guess was that he finally got wise to her and shot her. Is that what happened?"

"He says he didn't."

"And, that's why you're here?"

"Yes."

"Well, good luck, Jim. Sibyl and I always thought Randy was a nice guy."

We made some final small talk and then I hung up. I found it hard to believe that I could have been that close to Randy and Julie for a couple of years back then and never picked up on her extra-marital behavior. It made me think about my ex; not a topic I intended to dwell on.

"Another beer?"

I looked up and saw Enrique behind the bar.

"No, I'm good, but thanks."

"Where are your two lady friends tonight?"

"I don't know, but I should probably call them. Thanks for reminding me."

Instead of calling the lawyers, I dialed the number to the second name I knew from the list Randy had given me.

A man answered on the first ring.

"Is this Mark Johnson?"

"Yes, it is. Who's this?

"Mark, it's Jim West. How have you been doing since the old days in Germany?"

"Jimmy, my man, how the hell have you been?"

"Doing well, Mark, how about you?"

"If I was doing any better, my ex would want even more alimony."

"Which one?" I knew Mark had at least two former wives.

"Hell, both of them. What brings you to San Antonio, Jim? That is, I assume you're here in town."

"Nothing good. Have you heard about Julie LaMoe?"

"Sure, Randy and I have stayed in touch. The two of them, my current girl, and I do dinner every month or so. I can't believe he killed her. Are you here to help him?"

"Yes, I am. I'd like to meet with you tomorrow at your convenience and talk about it if you're available."

"Hell, I'm a financial advisor now. These days I have plenty of time. Do you want me to bring Bridget? We've been a couple for over a year, and she knew them pretty well, too."

"Absolutely, Mark." We talked a little longer about the old days and set a time to meet in the morning over coffee.

I looked around the lounge. For a nice hotel in a big city it was dead. Enrique was at the far end of the bar talking to three young women. Two middle aged men in business suits were drinking in the far corner. But other than that, nada – nothing, the place was depressing.

I decided to get out of there and find a place to grab a bite to eat. Finding a place was easy on the River Walk. Picking the place was the difficult part. Walking along the river after dark has always been a fascinating experience for me. I imagine it could get routine for those who live in San Antonio. But for me, the occasional visitor, walking the crowded mile up and down the river passing the multitude of night clubs and restaurants has always been a kick.

It was a nice night, so nearly all the restaurants had their riverside tables open. Many were taken, but, while I was on the return trip to my hotel, I finally squeezed into a vacant table at Casa Rio, a vintage Mexican Restaurant. I ordered the enchilada dinner and sat there watching the throngs pass by.

When my order arrived, I focused on finalizing my game plan for tomorrow and slowly cleaned my plate.

Who killed Julie and why was she killed? The "who" at this point could be anyone. The police, being content with their arrest of Randy, had not exactly spent a lot of time trying to identify another suspect. It was possible that someone else may have been seen around the condo, or that something in the family's correspondence may identify a possibility. However, with no information yet to work with, it was too early to spend too much time wondering who the killer was.

However, the "why piece" could be developed enough to help me plan my line of questions. She was shot once at fairly close range. She suffered no other violence or violation. None was needed, of course, but the type of killing told me something. Nothing was stolen and nothing was left behind. There was no passion in the killing. The shooter didn't keep pulling the trigger in a fit of rage. Simply put, it was a premeditated, precise execution. It wasn't any different from a professional hit.

Why, then, was Julie executed? Recalling my past experiences and studies, I knew organized criminal elements often killed someone because of a betrayal. However, individuals guilty of betrayal were often made an example of and therefore not usually killed with a single, well aimed shot. Opposition gang or "family" members might be assassinated with a single shot. But, I didn't think Julie was a member of any organized criminal element, so neither of these ideas seemed plausible.

The killer wasn't a crazy sniper killing people at random. The person had gained access to the condo and very likely knew Julie. I discarded the slim possibility the killer shot her thinking she was someone else. She was personally targeted.

In the world of crime, it wasn't uncommon for someone to be killed for knowing too much and perhaps blackmailing the wrong person. Now that was an angle I would have to look into. I guessed that she didn't even have to be blackmailing someone. Just knowing something she shouldn't could have put her at risk. I remembered an old case I worked long ago. In that situation, a naïve individual was talked into helping out in a narcotics smuggling operation, only to be shot and left for dead after his cooperation was no longer needed. When we finally had the shooter and his other accomplices safely behind bars, one of them referred to the attempted murder as "just tying up loose ends."

Was Julie just a loose end?

Chapter 7

It was nearly ten o'clock when I entered my hotel room. I decided it was too late to call either of the lawyers, so I undressed and headed to the shower. When I finished, I clicked on the local news to see if there was anything new breaking on the LaMoe murder investigation. I noticed there were two mints on my pillow casings and sat in a chair nibbling on the mints while I watched the news. Nothing was mentioned about the murder, probably old news by now, but the brunette anchorwoman was a knockout, so I deemed the effort worthwhile.

I went to pull the covers down on the bed and was impressed with how tightly tucked in everything was. It reminded me of my old Academy days. I loosened the sheets and crawled into the bed. I hadn't even had time to reach for the light switch when my right leg felt like a hot needle had jabbed it. I instinctively jerked to the left and another bolt of pain shot through my right leg. I threw the cover and sheets off me as I scrambled out of the bed, but before I could fully escape another needle hit me just above my right ankle.

"Damn!" I roared, as I finally made it off the bed. I looked down at my legs and saw nothing but the beginnings of some inflammation. My gaze went to the bed. I was stunned to see scorpions; seven I counted in my bed. One was crawling around in a circle, but the rest remained still.

I grabbed at the phone, furious at the hotel, and dialed the hotel operator. As a polite voice tried to speak to me, I cut it off.

"Put me through to whoever is running this place tonight!" The voice tried to inquire about my concerns, but I again cut it off. "Now!"

There was a click and then some music that did somehow calm me down a little. I noticed now that three of the scorpions had started to move.

"This is Lee Valentine, the night manager, Mr. West. May I be of some assistance?"

"You sure may, Ms. Valentine. I need you and your best exterminator crew up here in my room now."

"Can you tell me what...?"

I should have listened to the music longer.

"Ms. Valentine, I may need medical attention too, so if someone isn't here in two minutes I'm calling the press and then the paramedics." I hung up.

The scorpions were on the move, and I realized that I had better do something to preserve the evidence. I grabbed the hotel guide and quickly brushed all the scorpions back to the middle of the bed. I then pulled the sheets over them and tucked the sheets in tightly. I sat back down on the chair and looked around the room for more scorpions, spiders or anything else. The place looked clean.

I looked back down at my legs. The three whelps on my leg were already looking nasty. Seeing my bare legs made me realize that I had better put something more on than the boxers I had worn to bed. I had barely done so when there was a rap on the door.

I opened it and saw they had come in force. In front was a very attractive blond woman, dressed smartly in navy blue slacks, a white shirt, and a name tag that said Lee Valentine. To her left and right were two security personnel and behind her another male in maintenance garb.

"Mr. West, can we be of service?"

I had to smile at her. The scene brought me back to earth.

"Yes, sorry if I was a little agitated on the phone, but come in, all of you, and take a look at this."

I led them to the bed and then, with some minor theatrics, pulled back the sheets. As if on cue, all the scorpions started to move.

"My God!" proclaimed Ms. Valentine She stepped back bumping into one of the security guards.

I grabbed the brochure again and herded the little rambling demons back to the center of the bed.

"I'd rather not have them loose all over my room."

"Don't worry, Mr. West, you'll be getting another room." She turned to her maintenance troop and asked, "Harvey can you get rid of these?"

"Yes ma'am." Harvey opened his case and pulled out an empty plastic container. After unscrewing the lid, Harvey took the brochure from me and made quick work of flicking all of the scorpions into his container.

Ms. Valentine was giving Harvey more instructions about fumigating the room when I felt a tug on my left arm. I turned to look into the face of one of the security personnel, a rather burly red headed male. We stood eye to eye, but he had me by at least fifty pounds.

"Did you put those there yourself? Looking to sue the hotel or something? Because if this is some kind of stunt, mister, you're going to regret it."

The other security guy had moved in to show his support. Over his shoulder I could see Harvey departing with his catch in hand.

"If I was going to pull a stunt like this, which I didn't, do you think I would also be stupid enough to then crawl into bed with them?" I pointed down at my legs. The reactions to the three stings were each in its prime.

"You two can go now." Ms. Valentine instructed the guards.

Once they had left she looked back at me. "I apologize for their suspicions, Mr. West."

"Call me Jim, please."

"And I'm Lee. I've never seen anything like this, and I imagine neither of them has either. Sure we have the occasional spider or scorpion that freak out a guest, but I've never seen a bunch of them nest in a bed. I've never even heard of it."

"Maybe you have someone in housekeeping who likes to play pranks."

"I can't believe that, either, but I did ask Harvey to send up the person responsible for your room right away." She looked down at my leg wounds and then knelt down to get a closer look.

"You know the scorpions in this area have a nasty sting, but they are not deadly. I mean, you aren't allergic to bee stings or other insect bites, are you?"

"No, not that I know of."

"Do you need any kind of first aid or do you want me to call your doctor?"

She was getting to be quite a distraction kneeling like that right in front of me. Fortunately, I was saved from making what would likely have been a stupid reply to her question by another person knocking on my hotel room door.

"That must be housekeeping," Lee remarked as she stood up.

The door opened and a head popped in. "Ms. Valentine, did you need to see me?"

"Yes, come here."

A dark haired, smallish woman, maybe in her mid-fifties, entered the room.

Lee met her half way and took her by the elbow over to the far corner of the room. They huddled there and talked quietly. I could hear most of the conversation which took place in both English and Spanish. From what I could tell, the lady was feverishly pleading her innocence to her boss. To me, her body language supported her denial.

Lee turned to me and the housekeeper scurried out of the room.

"She didn't seem to me to be the type that would put a bunch of scorpions in someone's bed." I said in her defense, knowing full well I wouldn't know what such a person would, in fact, look like anyway.

"I agree, but her story of what happened tonight was strange and unbelievable, too. She claims that when she came to do her evening check of your room that someone else had already beaten her to it. She said the lamp had been turned on next to your bed. The breakfast room service menu was displayed on your bed, and two mints in a saucer had been placed on your pillow."

"That is how I found it."

"She assumed someone else had, for whatever reason, taken care of your room. She just looked around and left."

"Who else would have had access to my room?"

"Anyone in housekeeping, but access can be easily obtained by anyone working in the hotel. I don't know how those scorpions got into your bed, Jim, but I do intend to find out. I can't believe they were there by accident. One maybe, two unlikely, but seven or eight – no freakin' way."

Lee pulled her cell phone out of her pocket, pushed a button, and called the front desk. Her phone was one of those that also could act like a two way radio. "Kris, is anyone in the Tower Suite?"

"No, ma'am, it's free the next four nights." A voice promptly crackled out from the phone.

"Move Mr. Jim West in eight-eleven to it immediately, but keep his rate the same. Send someone up to help him move. Then block eight-eleven until further notice."

"Yes, ma'am."

Lee slid her phone back into her pocket.

"Lee, I appreciate it but it's not really necessary."

"Yes, it is, I need this room searched and fumigated by my pest control people. Besides this should have never happened, it's the least that we can do for you."

"Well, thank you. But I really won't need any help moving. I only have one bag."

"That's all right. The Tower Suite is on a floor that's controlled. It won't hurt to have someone show you the ropes. I don't think you'll be disturbed up there."

"Do you have security cameras in the hallways? They may have caught something."

"We have a lot of security in this hotel, Jim. I'm confident we'll find out who did this. My bosses will be just as interested as I am to get this resolved quickly and quietly."

I wasn't sure if her comment about "quietly" was targeted at me, but I responded to it anyway. "Don't worry, Lee, I don't plan on making what happened tonight a public issue, and I absolutely have no interest in filing any complaint against the hotel."

"Thank you, Jim. I really appreciate that. I work hard at this job and something like this could turn into a nightmare."

"Like I said, Lee, don't worry about me making this public, but I would also like to know who did this."

"I hope it was just a random act of some sick person. You don't think you were specifically targeted do you?"

"Very few people even know that I'm in town, so, no, I don't think I was targeted. But if I was, I would certainly like to know that, too."

"I don't blame you. I would too. From the hotel's perspective, I guess it would be better for us if you were picked because of a specific reason. The other possibility is we have an employee that did this at random, and that means if we don't catch him, or her, he will likely do it again. That is a possibility I can't tolerate."

"It appears we both have good reasons to get this matter resolved."

"You know, Jim, if someone had access to your room and wanted to cause you harm, I would think there would be a lot of things they could have done that would have been a lot simpler. They could have just injected something into the chocolate mints we leave at night on your bed."

I immediately wished she hadn't said that. It wasn't something I considered, and my stomach suddenly felt queasy. I was saved from dwelling longer on my gurgling gut by another person knocking on my door.

Lee reached over and opened it. A bell hop pushing a luggage carrier popped into view.

"Jim," Lee said from the doorway. "This is Richard. He'll escort you to the Tower Suite. I'm going to run now, but I promise I'll be in touch soon. Once again, I appreciate your patience with us."

"Hang in there, Lee."

With a smile she was gone and I was left with young Richard.

Chapter 8

My move to the Tower Suite was much more than your simple upgrade, and it was good that I had Richard along as my guide. I had to switch elevators on the eighteenth floor, and then use my new room key to access the private elevator that took me to the twentieth floor.

As we exited that elevator, I observed a manned concierge desk that guarded entry to the floor itself. Richard did all the talking, and we shot down the long hallway passing only a handful of doors as we did. Each door had a name on it rather than a number. I noticed the Alamo Suite, the Longhorn Suite, the Aggie Suite, the Lone Star Suite, and a few others. At the end of the hall, the facing wall consisted primarily of a double door and a placard identifying it as the entrance to the Tower Suite.

Richard opened the door and remarked that there was no actual tower. The name of the suite was in honor of a former U.S. Senator from Texas. Inside the suite, the foyer area was as big as my other hotel room. From the foyer one could go right to a small study, left to a small bathroom, or straight ahead into a large room that would have made a nice living room for most families. Once into the large room, I noticed a kitchenette/bar to my left and a bedroom to my right. I walked into the bedroom and tossed my gym bag on the king sized bed. The bedroom had its own connecting bathroom with a whirlpool bath and a two person shower.

"I'm impressed. All this suite needs are a couple of 'You Are Here' signs to help people find their way around."

"Anything else I can do for you, sir?" Richard asked while holding out my key card, oblivious to my attempt at humor.

I told him thanks, gave him a couple bucks along with my best million dollar smile, and sent him on his way.

Putting all the events of the day aside, I set out to explore my new digs. The bar in the kitchen was stocked and not with the little bottles you find in most mini-bars. I looked around for a price list and found none. One of the cabinets contained various small bags of pretzels, chips, and cans of nuts. The refrigerator contained water, soft drinks and beer.

I grabbed a Bud Light and proceeded to inspect the study and living room. Nothing of any interest could be found, so I proceeded to the bedroom. The bedroom closet disclosed an embroidered hotel logo bathrobe and slippers, half dozen pillows and blankets, and a fancy looking iron. None of which I planned to use. The bathroom sink displayed a tray of bubble baths, shampoos, lotions and fancy soaps. The sky blue towels felt twice as thick as the ones in my original room.

I went back to the bedroom and noticed there were two phones on the night stand next to the bed. One looked like a normal hotel phone, but the second had no buttons to push or dials to dial. I picked it up. There was no dial tone or ring.

"Mr. West, may I be of service?"

The phone was obviously hot-wired to the concierge in the hallway. I told him I was checking out the suite, and he told me if I needed anything to just let him know.

There wasn't anything I needed and, as it was closing in on midnight, I decided to call it a night. I noticed there were no mints on the bed but, more importantly, as I pulled the loose fitting sheets down to expose the entire mattress, I noticed there were also no scorpions in the bed.

Despite the comfort of the bed and the surroundings, I couldn't fall asleep. Rather, I laid there thinking about the scorpions and the possibility that, for some reason, I may have been targeted.

I didn't know anyone at the hotel. Only the lawyers and the police knew where I was staying, and it made no sense for either of them to be behind this prank. Only a few other people even knew I was in town. What motivation would they have?

Gary Grisshof came to mind. I didn't tell him where I was staying, but he may have already gotten it from the law firm. He might have a motive, too, if he thought I was cutting into his turf and affecting his source of income. He might also have the connections to get this done so quickly. The more I thought of it, the more it looked to me that Grisshof and I needed another face to face meeting.

As I fell into the early stages of sleep, I felt something on my leg. I was awake and out of the bed in less than a second. Turning on the light and pulling back the sheets I thoroughly inspected my leg and the bed. Nothing was there. It was just my imagination. I crawled back into bed thinking this was going to be a long night. As I tossed and turned, I did my best to get my mind off the bugs and back on Julie's murder.

Another possible motive for her killing came to me. What if it wasn't her jealous husband, as the police thought? What if it was a jealous spouse of one of her lovers? Although not the likeliest reaction by a wife who has discovered her husband has been cheating on her, it was not without precedent. To keep her husband, her family intact, her economic situation safe, eliminating the competition has been the chosen solution by more than just a few spouses in the past.

Sleep did finally come, and I was startled awake by the phone ringing next to my head.

"Morning Jim, this is Nita. How are you doing this sunny day?"

"Give me just a second." I stood up, stumbled to the sink in the bathroom, and splashed some cold water on my face before returning to sit on the bed. "Good morning to you. What's up?"

"Cynthia's a little pissed because you were supposed to call us last night. Don't you remember?"

"Tell her I had a rough night. Make that a strange night. I'll give you an update later today."

"Promise?" I could almost see her smiling through the phone and not in a sarcastic or deprecating manner. Rather, I got the distinct feeling that it hadn't bothered her that I didn't call, that it was just Cynthia who I riled. That she was, in fact, only making this call because Cynthia told her to do it. I imagined Cynthia simply wanted to remind me who was in charge.

"Yes, I'll call, unless I can talk you into taking my brief in person over dinner and a drink later this evening."

"That sounds nice, Jim, but tonight I'm involved with a charity event. I do have one question for you, though. When I dialed the extension to your room, a recording told me there was no one occupying it. What's your new extension and why did you move to a new hotel room?"

"That's the strange night part I was talking about."

Over the next several minutes I told Nita about the scorpions and the hotel's reaction. We agreed that it was probably not an accident, but we couldn't come up with an acceptable alternative. The most likely answer was that it was just a random act of viciousness by a hotel employee and I was the unfortunate recipient of the act.

"You know, half the lawyers here would die for a chance to assist you in suing the hotel and its parent company."

"No way, Nita. And that's a non-negotiable no. I don't need that distraction. Besides, something in the back of my mind tells me to ignore the event and just wait and see if something else happens."

"Do you think something else will?"

"Probably not, but if someone is trying to send me a message, I haven't gotten it yet."

We ended up talking about what I had done after leaving the two of them yesterday. After I briefed her on my phone calls, I voiced my suspicions regarding Grisshof and the scorpions. Nita told me she seriously doubted that Grisshof was involved in any way with the scorpions. She didn't think he knew where I was staying and that doing such a thing wouldn't have been his style.

I didn't know if I agreed with her, but my desire to confront Grisshof did fall a notch or two on my priority list.

After hanging up, I decided to shave. Once finished, I got dressed and headed down to find some breakfast.

Chapter 9

I walked into the restaurant and over to the section being used for breakfast, identified by a sign that read "Breakfast Nook". The place was crowded and I couldn't help but wonder why they weren't using more of the restaurant. I was directed to a small table for two in the near corner and promptly ordered coffee. I was studying the breakfast menu when a very pleasant voice said "Hello."

I looked up and saw Lee Valentine standing there before me. "I hope you don't mind. I asked the concierge on your floor to give me a heads up when you left your room. I was hoping to catch you. Did you know they have a free continental breakfast on your floor?"

"Don't mind at all, have a seat and join me. And, to answer your other question, I did not know there was breakfast available up there. But this is fine. Please, sit down."

"Thanks. I've been busy all night but I think we've made some real progress. Take a look at this."

She handed me a five by seven photo of a dark haired lady, probably Mexican ancestry, wearing the hotel's housekeeping attire. The photo looked like a still picture extracted from a security camera's video.

"Is this our culprit?"

"Yes, I believe so. Jim, do you recognize her?"

"No, sorry, but I don't."

"I didn't think you would. The interesting thing is that she is not a hotel employee."

"Are you sure?"

"Oh yeah."

"Then I guess you don't know her name?"

"That's right, but one of our security personnel is sharing this with the police right now. Hopefully they will be able to help us."

"I hope so, too. It's been a long night for you. Shouldn't you be off duty by now?"

"Yes, but I don't think I'll be going home today anyway. There is always a lot to do and with this it can be overwhelming. I can bunk here and get some sleep before tonight's shift starts up again."

"I hope you don't make that a habit. Can't be much fun."

"I have no life but this job, so I really don't mind."

The waitress brought me my coffee and then poured one for Lee. I ordered a cinnamon role and Lee declined the waitress' offer to get her something.

"You should really try one of our breakfast tacos."

"Tomorrow."

"From the security video, it appears that the lady in the photo there," she nodded towards the picture in front of me, "was specifically looking for your room. She was checking the room numbers as she went down the hall and then selected yours to enter. She also closed your door behind her once she was in your room. A definite no-no for someone in housekeeping."

So it appeared I wasn't just a random target. Interesting, I thought.

"Jim, there is one question my boss wanted me to ask you. Why do you think someone would do this to you? And, I guess there is a second part to it. Should we expect another attempt to harass you while you are a guest in our hotel?"

"I have no idea why that lady put the scorpions in my bed. And, I have no reason to expect anything else will happen to me while I am here at the hotel."

"That's good because we don't want anything else to happen either."

We sat quietly for a minute or two and then I had to ask. "Why did you say you have no life outside the hotel?"

"Because it's true. It hasn't always been that way but it has been for the last few years. Are you married, Jim?"

"Once, not anymore."

"Same here. Got married young, had one child and stayed married for nearly twenty four years. When my daughter married an Army Lieutenant, and they moved off to Italy, my husband said he needed to get away for a while, too. I thought he meant a week or two. He left three years ago, almost to this day, and has never returned."

"Have you heard from him?"

"Every couple of weeks at first. He's up in Montana somewhere still living with a bunch of hippies, I suppose. He divorced me two years ago, and I haven't heard from him since the divorce was finalized. I shouldn't complain. I got the house, the car, everything, including the bills."

"How'd your daughter take it?"

"Shocked, just like me. Everybody said he must be having a mid-life crisis, but what could I do?"

"Not much I guess."

"By the way, Jim, here is my card with my cell phone and my office number. Although I'm only the night manager, the general manager has asked me to be your point of contact while you are here. If you think of anything that might help us in resolving this matter please give me a call. Likewise, while no one expects anything more to happen, if something does, call me direct, twenty four hours a day. Deal?"

"Deal. What if I just get bored and need someone to eat dinner with me?"

"Then give me a call." She had a sexy smile.

She stayed and we talked for another ten minutes. Before she left, she reassured me the hotel had ramped up its security in response to the incident.

I headed to the hotel parking garage and found my Mustang just where I had parked it. I walked around the car appeasing my paranoia. Everything looked in order. I drove it out of the garage taking a right on Market Street. There was less traffic than I would have expected, but almost immediately after exiting the garage I noticed a large dump truck of some sort pulling up close behind me. I sped up to put some distance between us but got caught by a red light a short distance down the road. I stopped at the light and noticed the truck behind me seemed to be making no attempt to slow down.

I looked back up at the light and verified it was still red. Traffic shot across in front of me, and the truck was within seconds of rear-ending my car. At the last second, I turned my steering wheel hard to the right and floored the gas pedal. The Mustang responded with a squeal of rubber, and I managed to pull between two thoroughly angered drivers by my action. The driver of the Mercedes I cut in front of gave me a long honk and a wave of his hand out his window that I didn't think was a Texas howdy–do sign.

The miraculous thing was the truck shot right through the red light and the intersection without hitting anyone or getting hit itself. I could hear the screech of brakes but neither heard nor saw any sign of impact.

I pulled off to the right at the next intersection and planned on doing two more rights to somehow get behind the truck. Unfortunately, the next intersection was a one way street moving to my left, and I was stopped at that street by another red light. My adrenalin had kicked in, and I realized my hands were starting to shake. I took a deep breath and decided chasing the truck down was not practical. Once the light changed, I continued back onto my original route to meet Mark Johnson and his current lady friend Bridget.

Although I had intended to use the drive to the Johnson's suburb, which was just northeast of San Antonio, to go through the questions I needed Mark and Bridget to answer, my mind wouldn't stay focused. I wanted to believe that the truck driver had just fallen asleep or was texting someone on his cell phone, but I couldn't shake my conviction that the truck driver meant to hit me. I saw his eyes in my rear view mirror. He knew what he was doing.

It made no sense. What had I done to piss off San Antonio? Heck, I was even somewhat of a Spurs fan. Nobody really knew me down here, and, for sure, no one knew enough about my whereabouts or my schedule to harass me with such effectiveness. How would anyone know what car I was driving, or where I was staying, or when I would be leaving the parking garage?

Like I said, it made no sense. Thinking about it, however, brought back a memory of what a sage old Colonel, who was my boss early in my career, told me. "What once seems illogical, and even unbelievable, normally falls into perfect place once you know who did it and why. It's that lack of knowledge of what's in between the question and the solution that contributes to our own bewilderment."

Although I hadn't been paying close attention, I hadn't noticed anyone following me to San Antonio or since I arrived.

That is until this morning's incident with the truck. It was on my tail shortly after I pulled out of the garage. I hadn't noticed if it was sitting on the street waiting for me, but it could have been.

Once I accepted the likelihood that someone was trying to harass me, if not something more serious like crush me with a dump truck, I tried to think who might want to do so. There were a few people in my past who would probably love to get their hands around my neck, but I couldn't imagine that any of them had any idea I was in San Antonio. However, considering the incident with the scorpions and now with the dump truck, it only seemed logical that someone wasn't happy with my being here.

As I neared the selected meeting location, a small restaurant named Abel's Diner just off I-35, I forced myself to stop worrying why someone was out to get me. If it happened again, I just needed to be on my toes and do my best to be ready for it. Meanwhile I had to focus on the task at hand.

Chapter 10

The parking lot of the small restaurant was nearly full when I pulled in, so I had to park at the far end of the lot. I didn't like it because I wouldn't be able to keep an eye on my car while inside. Becoming paranoid, I just hoped it would be there when I came out.

There was a line of people waiting to get in, but I eased through them to see if Mark was already there. He was and waved at me from a window booth as I walked into the restaurant. He looked the same to me, sandy brown hair, five foot maybe ten inches, and still not an ounce of extra weight.

"Hey, Mark, you look great. Are you still running?"

"Not as much as I used to but still about ten miles a week. Good to see you, too, Jim."

We shook hands and he gave me a "man hug", something I've never gotten used to.

"This young lady is Bridget, the love of my life."

Bridget stood up grinning and extended her hand. "Nice to meet you, Jim. Was Mark this full of BS when you knew him in the old days?"

"Afraid so, Bridget. We all knew to keep our hands on our wallets when we were around Mark back then."

"Well, he obviously hasn't changed a bit."

The three of us sat down.

"This place must be pretty popular."

"It is. Good food and good prices, it's a local favorite."

Just then I saw a waitress go by with a cinnamon roll the size of a dictionary. Too bad I had already eaten. I just ordered a coffee. They both ordered breakfast tacos.

Mark and I went through the obligatory catching up for about five minutes or so. I noticed that Bridget appeared interested in our small talk but kept to herself. She seemed like a nice lady, probably five or ten years younger than Mark. She was attractive and her build certainly gave me the opinion that she was a runner like Mark.

"Fire away with any questions you have for us Jim." Mark said, once he felt we had visited enough. "As I told you on the phone yesterday, we both want to help Randy. We don't believe he killed Julie."

"Why do you think he's innocent?"

"Don't you?" Mark asked surprised by my question.

"Yes, I do. But why do you feel that way?"

"I know him." He looked at Bridget. "We both know him. He doesn't have… no, let me say it differently. His personality and behavior are such that, even if he found out that Julie was having an affair, he wouldn't kill her. He wouldn't do anything violent at all. Randy would be more likely to move all the family money out of their joint accounts without her knowing it, change where all his pay goes, and then just leave. He would want to make a point, but he would not want to physically hurt her."

Bridget finally joined in. "Jim, I have only known them for the past year but I agree that Randy doesn't seem like the violent type. I really don't know if Julie has had any affairs, but I believe she has. I only say that because of a few things she has said and done in my presence. On the other hand, I don't believe Randy has any interest in other women. He is friendly and nice, but I never got the impression that he was looking."

"Do either of you have any suspicions as to who else Julie may have been seeing? She was apparently with someone the morning that she was killed. The police believe Randy went there after the individual left and shot her, but there is always the possibility that whoever was there simply shot her before he left. So far no one knows who that other someone is."

They looked at each other and Mark answered. "I don't know who she may have been seeing. I know the stories that have followed her around, and I imagine some of them are true. But, she never hit on me, and I never had a relationship with her. I liked them both. When we were with them, they seemed to get along better than most couples I have known."

The memories of my past marriage started to fill my mind but I shoved them back into the abyss where they belonged.

"I guess I always gave her the benefit of the doubt; figuring if he liked her, why should I mess with their relationship."

"Did you ever talk to him about your suspicions?"

"No way, man."

Bridget leaned forward. "I kind of asked Julie what she was up to one time when we were alone shopping down town. I mean, I didn't accuse her of anything, I didn't know her that well. I just asked her if everything was all right between her and Randy."

"What did she say?"

"She said that Randy was a great guy and that she really loved him. Julie then said that she sometimes thought something was wrong with her. She didn't elaborate but said that she never wanted to hurt Randy, so she was extremely careful. Those weren't her exact words. I don't remember specifically what she said, but, in essence, I felt she was confessing that despite her love for Randy she had done things of which she wasn't proud, and, for whatever reason, she couldn't stop doing them."

"Bridget and I have discussed this in the past. We think Julie must have had some mental disorder. We never knew what to do about it, so we both decided to just try to support them by being their friends."

I stayed and talked with Mark and Bridget some more but nothing much came out of the rest of our meeting until just before I left.

"Who else are you talking to here?" Mark asked me.

"A few people I don't know, and last night I got to chat with Tim Davis a little on the phone. He didn't really know anything either."

"You may want to talk to Sibyl, Jim. I don't want to talk out of school, but there may have been more there between Tim and Julie."

"Thanks, I will." I had already decided to talk to Sibyl once Tim left town, and now I had a solid reason to do so.

I left the restaurant after committing to calling them again before I left town. I hadn't planned on having to stay very long, but now it seemed my visit to San Antonio might turn into a lengthy one. Unless I got a break and identified Julie's most recent lover in the next day or two, I would have to return to Clovis, get a more complete set of clothes and supplies, and come back.

Once I was back out on a side street, I pulled over and called Sibyl. I got lucky, and she answered on the first ring. She agreed to meet me at a coffee shop that was close both to her house and to where I was at the moment. She lived in Schertz, a small suburb that hugged I-35 northeast of San Antonio. Our meeting place was called Java Junction. As the name implied, it was a very nice, small coffee house. She was already there when I arrived.

Even though I hadn't seen her in years, I recognized her right away. Her hair was as red as ever and, like Mark, she hadn't gained a pound. We used to call her Red. The name would still fit.

After the initial hugs and small talk, we ordered coffees. She had something with at least four words in its name, and I had a cappuccino.

Sibyl surprised me by her direct jump right into the heart of what I wanted to discuss.

"Jim, Tim told me you are here to help Randy. I don't think Randy killed Julie, but he would have had a good justification to do so. I think long ago he decided to ignore all the smoke and simply not accept that there could be a fire there. Do you follow me?"

"Yes, I do."

"Julie was slick. She was a pro at what she was doing. I don't know how else to describe it. We've known her for years, and, in a way, I guess until the day she died she was still my friend. But about three years ago, I could have killed her. Tim was the realtor who helped Julie find and purchase the condo. You know the condo in which she was murdered."

I nodded that I knew.

"But in the process he was out of the office and late coming home way more than normal. Knowing Julie, maybe I was just paranoid. But then I saw an email from her thanking him for all his help and for going, if I may quote, 'all the way with her.' I confronted Tim and asked him what the hell she meant. He denied anything happened, but I could see it in his eyes that he was lying to me. It almost broke up our marriage, and, as you know, we've been married a long time."

"Did you confront Julie?"

"Yes, of course. She simply denied anything happened. She

looked me straight in the eyes and denied it. She was very good at lying, or I was overreacting."

"Do you think you were?"

"No. I have my sources at the office Tim runs. One of the women there is a close friend of mine. I had lunch with her just after I confronted Tim. He didn't know about it, still doesn't. She told me that Tim and Julie had a habit of going to bars for Happy Hour after they had spent the day looking at condos. Most of the time, the two of them went alone. My friend told Tim that it didn't look proper, but he just told her not to worry about it. After Julie closed on the condo by herself, as Randy was out of town, Tim took a bottle of champagne to Julie at her new condo. He didn't come back to the office that day. My friend said she didn't know what to do. She wanted to tell me but she had no proof anything happened."

"Perhaps nothing did," I said, fully believing something had.

Sibyl looked at me with an expression that implied if I believed that, then I was dumber than dirt.

"I told Tim, at the time, that if I ever heard he spent another minute alone with her, I would castrate him in his sleep. I meant it. I don't think he has seen her alone since then."

I wouldn't have either, I thought.

"How did you both remain friends?"

"Not because of me, that's for sure. It's just that we share a lot of the same interests, besides Tim. I run into her a lot. She never allowed my aloofness to interfere with our relationship. I finally came to believe she accepted my aloofness as her punishment to endure. In time our relationship got more relaxed like it had been before. She had never been a best friend and would certainly never be one after her fling with Tim, but I guess I'd have to say she was a friend."

"Do you have any idea who she might have been seeing lately?"

"Not really, but she made a few jokes about how happy she was that the condo had a pool boy, and how she always wanted a pool boy. The kind of comments a lot of women may say in jest, but with Julie I always wondered. You may want to talk to him."

By the time we said our goodbyes, I was feeling as though some progress had been made. The good old pool boy conspiracy, I chuckled to myself. It was time to visit the crime scene anyway, so I pointed the Mustang in that direction and drove off.

The condo was just off the inner loop near the airport. It was an attractive, fairly new complex that took up a good portion of the block. There was plenty of visitor's parking, so I took a spot close to the main entrance. The front doors could only be opened by an electronic key card. I had to push on the buzzer for someone to let me in. Within seconds I heard the tell-tale click and was able to open the door and enter. A middle aged man wearing glasses was sitting behind the reception counter as I entered. Through a doorway behind the counter area, I could see the profile of a second gentleman sitting in the office in what appeared to be a security uniform.

"May I help you?" offered the man at the counter. He was small in stature, with thin reddish brown hair, and a smattering of freckles that had faded with age. The pair of glasses he wore looked too wide for his face.

"Yes, you may. I'm Jim West and I'm helping the law firm of Caruzzo and Dilbert with their defense of Randy LaMoe."

"Oh yes, a terrible thing, just terrible. I was here that day, an awful day. So was Steve." He nodded to the man in the office. "Steve actually saw the body. He accompanied the police and let them into the unit. It was just terrible. I didn't see her. I didn't want to. But I saw the stretcher when they took her out. I'm also the one that placed Mr. LaMoe here at the scene of the crime. Oh, don't misunderstand me. I can't say if he was the murderer. I just told the police he was here. He was, you know."

He certainly didn't need any encouragement to start talking.

"I mean, they asked me so I had to tell them the truth. I only answered their questions. What else could I do? I even told them that he was only in the building for a minute or two. He came in with old Mrs. Golding. She has one of those Scooters, like they advertise for old people who have trouble walking. Almost every day she goes to the grocery store down the street a couple of blocks. She says it's the only life she has outside of her two cats. I know because Mr. LaMoe helped her with her grocery bag as they came in and to the elevator."

Steve, the man from the office, walked out to the counter but kept quiet.

"Mr. LaMoe has never caused us any trouble. I told the police that, too. He always says hello. You know, a lot of people don't."

"Did he appear any different that day?"

"No, not at all. He was talking to Mrs. Golding about something and they both seemed chatty. She always is. Sometimes she'll stop by here and just talk. I think she must get lonely."

"Did he use his key to get in, or did they use Mrs. Golding's?"

"Oh, I don't know."

"Is the key that lets you in here the same one that works on the individual condo units?"

"No, for security we have different keys. Isn't that right Steve?"

Steve just nodded.

"By the way, I didn't get your name."

"Hank, Hank Stills, but no, I'm not part of that band." He grinned as though I was supposed to immediately understand his joke. Luckily I knew the band he was referring to and could smile back.

"Too bad, Hank, but that's life. Before that day, Hank, had you ever witnessed any type of altercation between the LaMoe's?"

"No, never and I told the police that, too. They got along real fine. Although, I know it's none of my business, but on a few occasions while Mr. LaMoe was out of town, you knew he was one of them airline pilots, didn't you?"

I nodded.

"Well, as I was saying, on a few occasions while he was out of town, she would have some male friends spend the night. I guess they had what we used to call an open marriage, if you know what I mean?"

"Did you tell the police that too?"

"Well, yes, cause they asked me a lot of questions. They wanted to know who the boy friends were but I didn't know their names. Never asked. Not any of my business. I told them she wasn't the only person here that had late night visitors. You'd be surprised to know what goes on here when a husband or wife is out of town. Heck, people don't behave like they did in the old days. The management here don't tolerate drugs or loud parties, but they've told us not to pay attention to who has what guests as long as everybody's peaceful. Ain't that right Steve?"

Again Steve just nodded as though he was bored with our conversation, but something told me that he hadn't walked out here, closer to us, just to be bored.

"Thanks Hank. I really appreciate your talking to me. I know the firm will appreciate it."

"Come to think of it," Hank mentioned scratching his thinning hair, "I already talked to someone from the law firm."

"Shorter guy with dark hair?"

"Yeah, he looked kind of squirrely."

"The head lawyer asked me to double check everything he has done. They think he didn't pay very good attention to detail, if you know what I mean. But don't tell him I said so, if you see him again."

"I understand. He was kind of shifty looking. I didn't like him much. He talked down to me."

"Well, I appreciate your assistance Hank. I would like to take a look at the crime scene. Do you think it would be all right for Steve to take me to it?"

Steve answered for himself saying that he would be happy to do so. Once in the elevator, Steve pushed the floor button and turned and looked at me as though he was studying me.

"I already knew you might be coming Mr. West. That's why I came out to listen to your conversation with Hank. Detective Reynolds said you might show up. He told me, if a patrolman wasn't guarding the room, to make sure you could get in."

"You know Reynolds very well?"

"Not too well. I actually know Lt. Nosh a lot better. We went to the police academy together and we've stayed in touch. There was a murder right in front of the complex about three years ago. Nothing to do with us, but I saw a lot of what went down. The Lieutenant was in charge of that case. We spent a lot of time together working it and getting caught up on old times. He stops by, now and then."

When we arrived at the condo, Steve moved the police tape and opened the door for me. He took a couple steps inside, I guess to make sure everything looked okay.

"If you don't mind, I'll just leave you here. Just don't take anything. Lock the door when you leave and please stop by the front desk to let us know you're done."

"Will do. But before you run, Steve, do you have any idea who may have been with Julie before she was killed."

"No, I sure don't. I know the police claimed there was someone with her but no one in the complex saw anybody that morning or the night before. I can tell you, if you don't let on whom you heard it from, that she used to have a fairly regular visitor up until a few months ago. He was a tall guy, maybe six and half feet tall with a thick mustache. I have no idea who he was and haven't seen him around the place for at least two to three months."

"Did you tell the police that?"

"Yes, but they weren't interested."

"Is there another way into the complex besides the front door?"

"Well there are a few emergency exits but you can't enter through them. You can come in through the garage but you would need the same key card to enter the building as you need at the front door."

"Do you have security cameras?"

"Yes, at the front door and in the garage. The police have already taken the media from them for analysis. I don't think they showed anything. At least that's the feedback I got from the Lieutenant."

"Thanks, Steve. Do I need a key to lock up?"

"No, just pull the door shut behind you."

"I'll let you know when I'm finished."

After he left, I slowly walked from room to room to get a feel for the place. It was not very big. In fact, I didn't think it was as big as the suite I was in at the hotel. The condo had a nice but small kitchen, a fair sized room that was partially utilized as a dining area and the remainder as a living room, two bedrooms, two bathrooms and a small balcony that overlooked the street. The kitchen and bathrooms were tiled in large dark grey tile, and the rest of the place was carpeted in a neutral beige. The furniture looked fine but not extravagant.

I did the easy rooms first. The bathrooms yielded nothing. I found toothpaste, toothbrushes, and a bottle of aspirin, but no prescription medications. The guest room was sterile. If someone had ever stayed there, you couldn't tell. The dining room and living room area held nothing of interest either. Next, I went to the kitchen and found some top-shelf booze, a couple cans of Bud Light, soft drinks, bottled water, assorted nuts, chips, and bread. I noticed sandwich fixings, eggs, butter and a few other typical things in the refrigerator. Nothing with which to make a real meal, but I guessed they ate out while they were here.

I ended my search in the master bedroom, the scene of the crime. The bed had been stripped. I assumed the police had taken all the linens for evidence. The nightstands against the wall on both sides of the bed revealed a variety of books, magazines, crossword puzzles and other items equally worthless to me. I looked under the bed, in their dresser, and inside the large closet. The clothing in the closet was mostly informal and casual wear. A few sweatshirts had sayings on them: "There's no I in team", "The last word in Awesome is Me", and, finally, my favorite, "If a Man speaks in the middle of the ocean, and there's no Woman there to hear him, is he still Wrong?" I went through pockets and shook out shoes.

After about an hour, I was tired and hungry. I had not discovered a single item of interest to the investigation. I was anxious to get to the two leads worth pursuing: the pool boy and the tall guy with the mustache. However, I didn't want anyone at the condo complex to know of my interest in talking to the pool boy.

Additionally, I still needed to look through the LaMoe's house in the suburbs, and I had a few more names that Randy had given me to contact.

I stopped at the front desk on the way out to again thank Hank and Steve for their help. While there, I reassured them I had not taken anything and had locked the condo up when I left.

I left my car at the complex and walked over to the restaurant where Randy said he had eaten at the morning of the murder. I didn't have any real expectations but thought retracing his steps couldn't hurt. Besides, it was a short walk, and I needed some fresh air.

The sign at the entrance said please seat yourself, so I grabbed a small booth against the window that gave me a nice view back towards the condo complex. I looked out and saw a man walking quickly toward the restaurant from the direction of the condo. He was within ten yards of the entrance when he suddenly stopped, looked around, and then crossed the street. Once there, he stopped and began leaning against the wall of a building where he could keep a good watch on the restaurant I was in. He was trying to act nonchalant, but it was obvious to me that he was watching the entrance to the restaurant.

I looked around inside the restaurant and saw four other tables occupied by groups of three or four people. There were no other singles, and all of the patrons had already been served their food. I was the only person in the restaurant who had recently arrived. Therefore, I deduced, I must be the person whom the guy on the street was following.

If it hadn't been for the truck this morning and the

scorpions, I wouldn't have thought much about the guy, but my paranoia was in full bloom. I ordered three crispy beef tacos and a diet coke and sat back observing my pursuer. I didn't think he could see in through the darkly tinted window, but I still tried to keep my observation of him covert.

For the twenty five minutes it took my food to arrive and be eaten, the man never left his post. While I was there, I asked a couple of the wait staff if they remembered Randy eating there the day of the killing. They looked at me as though I was from Mars and said they knew nothing. I didn't know if they were serious or just didn't want to get involved. I would have thought that the police had already covered the same questions with them.

Two of the groups had finished their meals and had left. I could see the guy scrutinize those leaving, but he held his ground. I had planned on going back to my car when I finished but I needed to find out if he was really trailing me. If he was, then why, and who was he?

There was one of those large, national-chain sports stores a block further down the road away from the condo, so I headed in its direction when I left the restaurant. The street that separated us was busy with traffic which would normally make his following someone less obvious. In this case, however, it helped to conceal my observation of him.

He stayed with me all the way to the store. I tried hard but unsuccessfully to determine if anyone else was helping him in his surveillance. My guess was that he was alone.

I entered the sports store simply to kill a few minutes and to see if he would follow me into the store. He walked past the entrance without entering. After about five minutes I walked back out and headed back to my car. He was still there, leaning against the building. I was able to see him with my peripheral vision, so I still didn't think he knew I was on to him.

About half way back to my car, I turned to my left, entered an alley, and waited for him. I needed to find out what was going on, and he offered me my first good opportunity to do so. I saw his shadow before I saw him and was ready when he walked by, looking for me down the alley.

I grabbed his arm, pulled him into the alley, and then let go of him.

"Hey!" He shouted in surprise.

I had him by four inches in height and maybe fifty pounds in weight.

"Why are you following me?" I asked forcefully, but I wasn't yelling. I thought between our size differences and my handling the situation with minimal aggression, he might be a little more responsive than otherwise. I was wrong.

He didn't say anything. His response came fast and furious. In a split second his hand arched toward my chest. At the end of it was a nasty looking switch blade. It ripped across the front of my shirt. I grabbed at his knife hand with both hands and caught it only after it had caused its damage. I had a good grip and twisted his hand and arm violently. Simultaneously, I pulled it down and toward me. As I did this, I turned my whole body away from him, dragging his arm with me, and forcing him to follow it.

He dropped the knife and tried desperately to get ahead of my turn. I threw him into the wall of a building, kicked the knife away, and then backed away a few steps myself.

"Why are you following me?"

He looked at me for two to three seconds and then bolted towards the street. I lunged after him grabbing the back of his shirt. It was his turn to turn and twist, almost breaking my fingers in the process. I had to let go. Once free, he continued his sprint away from me and, unfortunately, directly into the path of a Ford F-250 pickup that had a metal grate fastened to the front bumper.

The Ford had no time to stop. The impact was violent, and I instinctively recoiled and looked away. When I looked back it was all over. Both my follower and the pickup were a good twenty yards down the road.

"Crap!" I mumbled to myself. I used my handkerchief to pick up the knife, closed it, gently wrapped it in the handkerchief, and stuck it in my pocket. Only then did I realize the blood all over my shirt. I hadn't even noticed any blood on the knife. Pulling out the collar of my polo shirt I saw the long gash across my chest. I didn't think it was very deep, but it was bleeding freely.

I had no doubt that the man who had been following me was now dead. Losing the chance to find out what was going on was much more aggravating than my wound. I walked out to the street and down to the location of the Ford pickup and the body. A crowd was already forming around them, and traffic on the busy street had come to a standstill. Horns were going off further up and down the road where drivers couldn't see what had happened but were now stuck in the traffic jam.

I saw Steve, the condo security guy, approaching the scene from the other side, and waved at him to catch his attention. He saw me and diverted his approach to meet up with me.

"Jesus! What happened out here? Were you hit, too?"

"No, but can you call your friend the Lieutenant? See if he or the detective can come out here. I think this, well not the actual accident, but that guy had something to do with Julie's death." I pointed at the body on the ground.

I could already hear sirens approaching, but I knew the first responders would not be familiar with the LaMoe murder.

"Sure," Steve responded and pulled his cell phone off the clip on his belt. He walked away from all the noise and talked on the phone for a few minutes before coming back, returning at the same time the first police cruiser pulled up.

"Nosh said he would get word to the responding units that he wanted to be kept apprised as to the condition and future whereabouts of the accident victim. He said he can't come out right now, but for you to call him or Detective Reynolds to let him know why you think there's a connection. I told him if he could see you now, he might understand. He asked me what I meant, but I told him you better explain it. You know when the ambulances show up they better take a look at you. You're losing some blood."

"I'll be all right."

"Mister, are you okay?" I turned and saw a teenager staring at me. Behind him I realized there were quite a few people looking at me now.

"Yes, I'll be fine." I lied, as I was starting to feel a little light headed.

Another police vehicle was pulling up at the scene and right behind it was an ambulance. I saw a couple of bystanders point me out to the police and then to the ambulance crew. One of the cops broke away and came over to me.

"Are you okay sir?"

"A couple bandages and a clean shirt, and I'll be fine officer."

"Were you involved in all this?"

"Indirectly, yes. It's a long story officer, but to summarize – that man over there, the man who was struck by the pickup, attacked me with his knife in that alley over there. I managed to get the knife away from him. But when I did, he fled by running straight out into the street. The truck had no opportunity to stop. Neither the man nor the truck saw each other until it was way too late."

"We'll need to get a statement from you. First, though, I need your name and your contact information. Second, you need to have your wound tended. And then, third, we can get your statement."

I gave him the info he wanted and said that I would be happy to give them a statement. He left, saying that he would send someone from the ambulance over since the accident victim was already dead.

Steve came up closer to me and spoke in a hushed, conspiratorial tone. "Why do you think he was involved in the murder?"

"I've been followed off and on since I arrived in San Antonio. My only purpose here is to help solve Julie's murder. I noticed him following me after I left you this morning. I walked around in circles enough to verify that he was indeed following me. When I confronted him, he pulled his knife and attacked me. I know it doesn't make much sense, Steve, but the fact is someone wants to keep track of me while I'm here or wants me to go home. The only plausible reason is that they don't want me digging into the case."

"Jesus! So you think someone else did kill Mrs. LaMoe?"

I felt like just saying "Duh??" But I simply said, "What would you think if you were in my shoes?"

He thought for a while. "I see what you mean."

I was saved from further discussion with Steve by a young, dark haired paramedic. She looked too young and perky, barely out of high school I thought.

"Sir, could I get you to come with me to the ambulance so I can take a look at that wound of yours?"

"Sure, lead the way."

We walked over and into the back of the ambulance.

"Sit right over there and remove your shirt please." She instructed as she pulled a screen to block the view from the street. The police had gotten most people off the street, and the traffic was moving slowly, but there were still a lot of gawkers.

I pulled off my shirt and would have tossed it into a trash can if one had been available.

"That looks like a nice clean cut. What did it, a razor blade?"

"A knife."

"Must have been a sharp one. This may hurt a little," she remarked as she started cleaning the cut with gauze she had moistened with what I assumed was an antiseptic.

It did sting, and I involuntarily sucked in some air. She smiled.

"Tough guy, I see you've been through this before." She studied the small variety of scars that covered parts of my chest, stomach and shoulders. She looked back into my face, studying it for other old wounds.

"Were you in the war?"

"No, I was in the military, but never served in direct combat. No, these scars are nowhere near as honorable as theirs."

She got back to the business of patching me up. She used seven butterfly bandages to hold the wound shut. "I think that will do it. But don't do anything strenuous for the next week or so. Have you had a tetanus shot lately?"

"Yes, ma'am."

"You may want your doctor to look at it in a few days to make sure there is no infection. Other than that, you're good to go."

"Thanks, you're quite good at this. How long have you been with the Emergency Services?" She looked too young to be this skilled.

"Not long, only a few months, but I just got off active duty with the military where I was a med tech for a few years."

"Well, thanks and take care." I hopped out of the ambulance carrying my shirt and ignored the stares as I walked over to my car. I unlocked it and was just getting into it when I heard my name being called. I looked up and saw one of San Antonio's finest jogging towards me.

"I haven't forgotten about you. I was just going to get a new shirt and then check in down at the station."

"That's okay," the patrolman replied. "Lieutenant Nosh wants you to come see him when you can this afternoon. He said you know who he is and how to get in touch. He'll get the info from you and share it with us. Does that make sense to you?"

"Yes, it does. Thanks."

He nodded, turned around, and returned to the accident scene. The ambulance with the body was already driving off.

I started my car and was just beginning to back up when I saw Steve walking from the condo complex toward me waving a black tee shirt.

"Here, this should fit you." He shouted as he approached. "Might be a little loose on you but its clean."

"I don't want to take one of your shirts."

"Don't be silly. You can always bring it back. Not that I care if you don't."

I took the shirt and thanked him. It would save me from having to go back to the hotel. I wanted to get out to the LaMoe's house before I went to see the lieutenant, and the day was already moving along.

I drove up Broadway, getting on the inner loop and taking it east to I-35. From there I went northeast almost to the town of New Braunfels, nearly thirty miles from the center of San

Antonio. The LaMoe residence was in a small development just outside San Antonio city limits and just before New Braunfels. It was a nice neighborhood with all the residences sitting on large, treed lots. The houses looked like they ranged from five to ten years old. They still had that new look, but the yards had had enough time to get established.

Randy had told me that they liked the house and neighborhood. They purchased the condo primarily for an investment. Bad timing, he admitted, as the real estate market had flattened just after they made the purchase. But it was convenient to the airport, close to downtown, and fun to get away to now and then. However, with Julie's murder occurring at the condo, Randy said he would put it on the market as soon as possible. He never wanted to set foot in it again.

I saw the police cars before I knew exactly which house was his. There were two of them parked in the street in front of the house. I expected them to be finished by now, but I guessed they were going through everything in search of the gun, ammunition, or anything else that might link Randy to the murder. That meant a thorough scrub of the garage, attic and yard as well as the inside of the house.

The front door was open but police tape ran across it. I shouted to get someone's attention before I tried to enter. An officer looked out at me from around the corner of the room immediately inside and to the right.

"What can I do for you?"

"Hello, I'm Jim West. I'm assisting Caruzzo and Dilbert, the law firm that is representing Mr. LaMoe. The lieutenant said I could look around inside."

"Which lieutenant?"

I couldn't help but think that he already knew. He was just playing by the book.

"Nosh."

He looked at me for a moment. "Okay, come on in, but don't move or take anything."

"Can I touch?"

"Yes, you can touch, just don't take."

I ducked in under the police tape. The officer went back to his inspection of the room. I looked in and noticed he had every light switch and electrical socket cover off the walls. I almost commented that a gun would never fit in those places but bit my lip. Let them look.

I strolled through the two story house to get a feel for it. Three more police officers were inside. They gave me some suspicious stares, but no one questioned my presence.

I knew they would not be interested in what I was looking for, and vice versa. I needed to find any and all info that linked Julie to other people and any data involving Julie's business activities of any sort. Was she a closet addict who had pissed off her supplier? Did she have a gambling problem? Was she a blackmailer? None of these seemed plausible but anything along these lines would give me something to pursue. I was also looking for anything that linked her to other men.

I was looking for photos, newspaper articles that had been saved, correspondence, financial records, etc. What had she done to cause someone else to kill her? There was no sign of a struggle, so she must have known the killer. He either had a key to the place, or she let him in and then got back into bed naked. She clearly was not expecting any violence. There was no indication she was trying to flee. Not a very nice surprise, but a surprise just the same.

I started with the kitchen since it looked like it had already been thoroughly searched. My search went quickly as there was absolutely nothing of any interest to be found, with the exception of a calendar on the black granite countertop. The calendar had dozens of abbreviated notations on various dates in the current month. I turned back a page and saw the same plethora of abbreviations throughout the previous month. I studied the pages but could not be sure what the notations meant. Some of the dates were colored yellow. I would need Randy's help on this.

I wanted to take the calendar but left it there on the counter for the time being. Next, I headed to their study. I saw a computer and a printer. I took a close look at the printer and verified that it was also a copier. I went back to the kitchen and returned with the calendar. I was still alone. I could hear someone out back shouting to someone else.

The printer was still plugged in and turned on, so I quickly copied the four pages that made up the last two months. I folded the pages and put them in my pocket. I returned the calendar to the kitchen. That was easy I thought.

Once back in the den I started going through the desk and filing cabinets. I found their financial records right away. While the records may not have been inclusive of all their accounts, those that were there indicated that Randy and Julie were financially comfortable. They were not rich but closer to it than most. I even found their checkbook and copies of their credit card accounts. Nothing stood out as unusual. There were no unusual deposits or withdrawals indicating possible blackmail in either direction.

Then I found what I was looking for. It was even flagged in its own way for me. A file folder, among the dozens of others, that was labeled Julie's. I grabbed it, peeked in, and set it aside. I continued through the cabinets without further success.

I sat down at the desk and started analyzing the contents of the folder. There was no way I could sneak the whole folder out and it would take me a while to copy the entire contents. The folder itself was subdivided into four pockets. The first section contained separate sheets of paper listing the members of the various activities she participated in or belonged to. The page titled "Gourmet Group" had a list of thirteen names. The officers of the group were identified, and everyone's phone numbers and email addresses were included.

I found sheets of paper with lists of members for both the mahjong group and the book club. The officers were identified, and member's phone numbers and email addresses were annotated similar to the gourmet group list.

I set these lists aside. The rules to playing mahjong, the by-laws for the gourmet group, and the lists of books to read for the book club I returned to the folder.

The next pocket or section of the file folder contained twenty two pages cut out or taken from different issues of the San Antonio Express newspaper or the San Antonio Magazine. Each page had at least one photo on it depicting a scene at a charity event or fundraiser. Julie LaMoe was depicted in a number of the photos but not all. Most of the individuals in the various photos were identified by the newspaper or magazine. In many cases where they weren't, some names were written in, probably by Julie.

The photos went back six years. That was about the time they moved here, I thought, and Randy got his job with the airlines. Randy was only in one of the pictures, standing next to Julie. Next to them were Tim and Sibyl Davis. Julie had her arm through Tim's arm, not Randy's. I looked for the date on the photo but didn't see one. I noticed that none of the pages had dates on them, neither hand written or as part of the article. I got the impression Julie didn't want any dates on them.

Other than Julie, I didn't recognize anyone in the other

pictures. However, in one of the pictures I noticed Julie standing next to a very tall man sporting a mustache. Coincidence? I didn't think so. The paper identified him as Jack Wilson. I set all the pictures aside.

The next pocket in the file contained assorted pages of personal contacts that Julie had accumulated since arriving in San Antonio. She had stapled a business card to many of the pages with contact information that she wanted to remember. Some of the pages were blank bond paper with a few written notes and some were company flyers. She obviously wanted to have a name for reference in case she ever needed to call a business. Bluebonnet Ford had cards for both a sales rep and a service rep. The pages for Frost and Broadway banks had cards for vice presidents stapled to them. She was a classic networker.

Jack Wilson's card was not among the one's she had. Neither was one from Tim Davis or a pool boy. Did their absence mean anything?

I thought about copying all the cards but decided not to. I could always come back. I got the impression from the contents of this section that they were exactly what they seemed, business contacts she could use to cut through the red tape.

The last pocket in the folder contained names of all her relatives, including nieces and nephews, along with their birthdays, addresses, etc. Julie appeared to have been a very organized individual.

I was still alone, so I copied the pages I had set aside. When folded, the copies fit snugly in my back pocket. I put the originals back into the folder and filed the folder where I found it.

I looked through the unused bedrooms in the house. One was used as an exercise room and the other as a guest bedroom.

Neither contained anything of interest to me in them. I entered the master bedroom to find two police detectives dismantling just about everything they could. They looked at me.

"Sorry to disturb you guys." I decided I had enough to work on. I could always return. Plus, Lt. Nosh was waiting for me at the station.

I walked out of the house, under the police tape, and to my car without seeing or talking to anyone else. Looking back at the house, however, I saw one of the policemen staring out of the upstairs bedroom at me. I waved and got into my car.

Driving back downtown, I thought about what the two searches added to my existing knowledge of Julie. She was definitely organized and I already knew she was intelligent. I found no indication that she was on any prescription medication or other drugs. I had discovered nothing that might indicate her involvement in any illegal behavior. She was a voluntary participant in all her activities. She was not an officer, manager, or someone responsible for financial accounts in any of them.

The key had to be with one of her relationships. Was Jack Wilson married? Maybe the wife wanted the relationship over, once and for all. Did the pool boy try to blackmail her? If she responded by taunting him for trying, could her taunts have put him far enough over the edge to shoot her? Was there someone new, a Mr. X, who was more dangerous than Julie ever realized? Did Mr. X decide the relationship had to end, and this is how he ended it? If I was to follow that lead, were there other similar murders still unsolved in the greater San Antonio area?

Traffic was light on the way back into San Antonio. I was still analyzing the possibilities when I arrived at the main police station. I was ushered right in to see the lieutenant. He offered me a chair and got right to the point.

"I thought you weren't going to show, Jim, but I'm glad you did. Now what's this about our John Doe being involved in the murder of Julie LaMoe?"

"By John Doe, I assume you mean the individual who was killed trying to run through a fairly large pickup truck today?"

"Unless you were referring to someone else in the message that was relayed to me earlier today."

"No, we're talking about the same person. Do you not know who he is, or are you calling him John Doe for some other reason?"

Nosh looked at me, probably trying to decide whether the answer was even any of my business. "We have no idea who he is. He had no identification on him. We're running prints right now. Do you have any idea who he is, Jim?"

"No, I don't. Let me start at the beginning, Lieutenant. It may make more sense to you if I do." I filled him in on my run-in with the scorpions, and the results of the hotel's security cameras that implied I was specifically targeted by someone who was not an employee of the hotel. I told him about the dump truck almost squashing my car with me in it. I finished with the story about being followed after I left LaMoe's condo by the man he referred to as John Doe.

"I walked a simple dry cleaning route before I confronted him. There was no way he wasn't following me. I confronted the guy adjacent to where the accident took place, but he wasn't a talker. His first attempt at communication was to try to cut me in half with his knife. I got the knife out of his hands and he fled into the street. Not a very smart choice."

"What happened to the knife?"

I reached into my pocket and pulled out the knife still wrapped in my handkerchief. "Here it is. His finger prints and my blood should still be on it. It's a switch blade, so be careful handling it."

Nosh placed the wrapped knife on his desk and buzzed someone on his intercom asking them to come into his office. We sat there for about ten seconds before there was a knock on the door and a head appeared.

"Bailey, take this into evidence. Log it in as being received from Mr. West." He looked at me, "Jim, you don't mind signing a release on the knife do you?" I told him I didn't, and he addressed his comments back at Bailey. "Log it in on the file we have on the John Doe who got hit by the pickup this morning. I also want the lab to tell me all it can about the knife."

Bailey seemed to know who Nosh was talking about and took the evidence with just a "Yes, sir," for a reply.

When he left, Nosh leaned back in his chair and folded his hands behind his head. "Have you ever lived in this area before?"

"No."

"Do you have any reason to believe you have any enemies here?"

"No."

"Well, I don't know what to tell you, Jim. I guess it's one of two possibilities. The first is that someone obviously wants to mess with you or, at a minimum, doesn't want you here. But you just arrived a day or two ago. Who the hell even knows you are here?"

"Almost nobody."

"That's my point. The second possibility is that you are just a bit paranoid. We have car accidents in San Antonio all the time. There are a lot of bad drivers here. The fact that a truck almost hits you is routine in this city. The guy following you on foot, if that is really what he was doing, could just have been targeting you to rob. A word of advice – don't be confronting the men here in San Antonio. Getting stabbed or worse is a normal result, especially in some of the neighborhoods here in town. And the scorpions, someone was probably having fun at your expense. I don't mean to be rude West, but it seems like you may have gotten yourself in over your head. Things are starting to get to you."

"I don't think I'm overreacting. I think there is a connection to this case. Someone does want me out of town."

"I doubt that, Jim. But if you think that's the case, then maybe you'd better leave. It would be safer for you, and I'm sure LaMoe would understand. We can work the case without you."

I was getting pissed at his condescending manner and did my best to control my emotions. "Lieutenant, I know your office is fully capable of investigating this case. I don't plan on doing anything to interfere with your efforts. I'm just looking at a few different angles and will certainly keep you informed of anything I uncover."

"Jim, I think a lot of this is just in your mind. However, if someone is out to cause you harm, I'd rather that it not happen in my town. Why don't you go home?"

"In a few days, in a few days."

He continued on about my leaving, and I just stopped listening. This was going nowhere. I wondered how hard they had tried or would ever try to come up with another suspect. Not hard, probably. I began to doubt that they would even spend much of an effort to identify John Doe. If the prints didn't come up with something, he would likely remain a John Doe.

"If you identify our John Doe, will you let me know who he was?" I asked when Nosh stopped talking.

"You haven't been listening, have you? I said I would, but I think you're just wasting your time."

"Sorry, I was distracted for a second. I appreciate your time Lieutenant."

I left the station and made a mental note to direct all my future coordination with the police to Detective Reynolds. Clearly, Nosh was tired of me and wished me gone. I didn't want to overstay my welcome any more than I had to.

Traffic was getting heavy in the late afternoon as I made my way to Broadway and headed back towards the condo. I wanted to talk to the pool boy to see if he could shed any light on the murder and Julie's other affairs.

Steve and Hank greeted me like we were old friends when I arrived at the complex. I thanked Steve again for the shirt and reassured him that I would return it.

"Guys, do you mind if I just walk around the complex? I'm trying to get a better feel for how the murder may have occurred, if in fact Randy is innocent. You know, it will help me better understand the big picture." I really didn't care about the 'big picture' but didn't want to reveal my actual interest in being there.

"You want one of us to go with you?" Hank inquired.

"No, I would prefer to go alone, if that would be all right. I'll be able to think better."

"Okay," Steve responded, "but will you stop by on your way out?"

"No problem."

I left them standing there appearing a little disappointed they couldn't tag along, but I needed my next interview to be done in private. A map of the complex was posted on the wall in the entry foyer. I had studied it on my previous visit, so a quick glance was all I needed to get started in the right direction.

Once I arrived at the elaborate pool area, I was faced with an immediate dilemma. There were two men working on what I assumed was the filter tank. They had the cover off and tools lying across a nearby table. I approached them and they both looked up at me.

"You can still swim. We'll have this fixed within the hour," announced the one closest to me.

"Do you both normally work the pool area?"

"Yes," they both answered in unison.

Not making my job any easier, I thought. I hated to go with guesses, but the one closest to me was by far the one I would choose to hang around with if I were Julie. His blue work shirt had the name Al written on it.

"I take it your name is Al, is that right?" I asked him.

He looked down at his shirt. "That's what it says."

"Could I please get you both to take a one minute break, so I can talk to you Al, in private? It's quite important."

"They looked at each other. "Go ahead," said his partner.

Al and I walked about ten paces away.

"I'm Jim West, Al. I'm here in San Antonio working with Randy LaMoe's defense team. It has come to my attention that you may have been fairly close to his wife, Julie."

I stopped talking and let my bluff sink in. I knew if he was the murderer I was playing with fire, but I didn't think he was. If there was a relationship here, then I was betting on the stereotypical one, just a fun romp in the hay now and then for both.

"What are you getting at?"

Good, I thought, no denial just a little irritability. He was in pretty good shape and about my size, so I didn't want to irritate him too much.

"Al, I'm not here to cause you any trouble with your job, and

I don't believe you were involved with her murder. But, I need to talk to you. I believe you may have some information that can help me." He started to deny something, but I cut him off. "You may not even realize that you know something that's important. What time do you get off work? I'd like to buy you a beer and ask you a few questions."

"I should be off now, but Bill and I needed to fix the leak."

"I noticed just down the block there's a bar. I think it's called McClanahan's. Do you know it?"

"Mister, I don't think I have anything to talk to you about. I'm sorry."

"It's either me, or the police, or Steve in security here. I imagine the management may want your relationship with the victim fully explored."

He only paused for a few seconds. "Okay, I can meet you there in about forty five minutes."

"I'll be there. Thanks."

I shook his hand and left him. I walked over to the same entrance leading back into the condo that I had come through a few minutes before and noticed it was locked. It apparently required the same type key card as the front door to gain entry. I looked back at Al and he pointed me toward the poolside locker room. Once inside the fancy locker room I found shower stalls, a toilet and sink area, a wall of lockers, and a door that opened into a residential hallway. The outer locker room door that I used to enter had a sign that said the door was locked when no pool personnel were on duty. There was no sign on the inner door leading out of the locker room into the condo complex. While it looked as though the door could be locked with a regular key, it wasn't.

I made my way back to the central reception area where I met up with Hank and Steve.

"This is a nice place. I like your pool area. I noticed there is a metal fence securing the area from the outside world. Is there a gate on the fence?"

"Yes, but it's kept locked," Hank explained. "We only have a gate there because it's city code. No one uses it."

Except maybe the murderer, I thought. "Do you have security cameras out there?"

"Not of the actual pool area. There is an issue of privacy, and you know this is almost exclusively an adults' only complex." Hank was becoming defensive.

"We do have cameras, Jim, focusing in toward the entrance to the building itself from the pool area," Steve elaborated, "just none facing out towards the pool and beyond."

Not much help I thought. "Well thanks guys. By the way, I'll get this shirt back to you tomorrow."

I left through the main entrance and proceeded to walk around the complex. I wanted to check out the lock on the gate by the pool area and to see if there were other ways to get into the structure. The outside of the complex was well manicured with lantanas, sage bushes and mountain laurels. Inside the brick and wrought iron fence stood the occasional live oak and another species of a smaller tree I didn't recognize.

It just took me a few minutes to find the gate to the pool area. There were actually two gates adjacent to each other. The first was a pedestrian gate that had a fairly new looking pad lock on it and the second was a larger vehicle gate that had an older padlock on it. It looked like the vehicle gate had not been opened in a long time. The grass around and under it looked well groomed and displayed no indication of recent tire tracks.

The pedestrian gate at first glance also looked unused. I knelt down close to the ground and, in the late afternoon shade, could see the track recently left by the gate being opened and shut. It didn't prove anything, but it did support the possibility that the killer could have avoided the security cameras by coming in through here. The locker room entrance wasn't very far from the gate. If no one was in the pool area, it would only be a fifteen second walk and you could be inside. I checked the lock; it was secured. It would be a pain to jump the fence, but it could be done.

Al and his partner were still engrossed in their work and didn't look my way. No one else was in the pool area. I continued walking around the complex and ran into another entrance that led into the garage. The door was locked and looked like it needed an actual old fashioned key to be opened. There were no other exterior doors until I arrived back at the main entrance.

I continued on until I got to McClanahan's. I picked a small wooden table in the corner near the window. The place wasn't crowded, but there were enough people there that I wanted some privacy. The spot I selected would give us enough separation from the rest of the guests to talk without being overheard. I was a few minutes early, but I had nowhere else to go. I also wanted to think about my conversation with Lieutenant Nosh. It had pretty much been a waste of time. He didn't appear to accept my impression that someone was targeting me and seemed to just want me out of the way. He was a busy guy, so I guess I couldn't blame him for dismissing me, but it was still frustrating. Next time I needed to talk to the police, I would stick with Detective Reynolds.

Al must have gotten the pump fixed quicker than expected. I saw him crossing the street and coming my way. In his jeans, boots and work shirt I could see how he could be attractive to women. Tall and in good shape, he looked like he could be in a TV commercial or even a soap opera. His long strides brought him quickly across the street. He entered the bar, saw me, and came over.

As he approached the table, I motioned for a waitress to do the same. The waitress was slightly overweight which made the short tight plaid skirt and the tight green blouse look less attractive than it could have. She should have gone up a size. It would have looked nicer on her and let her breathe a little easier.

"What would you like?" I asked Al as he sat down.

"Miller Lite."

I turned to the waitress, "One Bud Light and one Miller Lite please, and some chips and salsa."

She nodded and hustled off towards the bar.

"Okay, Jim, what do you want from me?" I could tell Al was doing his best to keep the underlying hostility out of his voice.

"Like I told you at the pool, Al, I have no desire to cause you any problems. I just need to know everything you can tell me about Julie LaMoe. Everything Al, even about her relationship with you."

"If I have anything to say, what happens to the information I pass to you?"

"It stays with me. I don't think you had anything to do with her death, but you may have information that could help me find out who did." I knew there was always a remote chance he was the killer, but I needed him to talk.

Al sat there for a second looking me straight in the eyes. I maintained his gaze.

"I didn't kill her, and I don't know who did. Everyone says her husband did it."

"Okay, but what about Julie and you? How did it get started?"

Again, the pause and the stare. Finally, he started talking and looked down at his hands and the table.

"It just did. I don't remember the actual day, sometime last summer or early fall. Randy was away, flying somewhere, and wasn't expected back for a couple of days. She often came down to the pool, mostly to sunbathe. She liked to get her sun. On this one occasion, as she got up to go back to her condo, she yelled over to me and asked me if I liked wine. She was always pleasant to me and to everyone. I walked over to her. We were the only ones in the pool area. I told her I preferred beer. She said she had that, too, and, if I was interested, to come up to her room. She said Randy was out of town and she hated drinking alone. With that she walked off."

"Did you follow her to the condo?"

"Not for a few minutes. I thought about it. I'm single and was then, but I knew she was married, and I knew management doesn't want us to mess with the owners. I wasn't dumb. I didn't believe she just wanted me to have a beer with her. But the longer I sat there, the sillier it seemed not to follow her. Hell, I'm almost thirty, never been married, and this older women is hitting on me. Don't get me wrong, I have plenty of dates who I can go out with, but I wasn't serious about any of them. Most of them I go out with just for the sex."

"Al, I'm not judging you, I'd probably do the same thing."

"Well, I went to her condo. She answered the door wearing a bath robe. She seemed genuinely pleased that I showed up. We sat there, drank, and talked for a long time. She wanted to know all about me. She seemed sincerely interested. We also talked about her. She said she was happily married that she wasn't looking for someone to replace her husband."

"Did you believe her?"

"Yes, and, for a while, I thought I had misread all the signs.

Then she got up off the couch and walked over to me. I was on the Lazy Boy next to the couch. She reached out and took my hand."

Al paused for a second. I imagined he was visualizing the scene.

"As she did, her bathrobe opened up. She was wearing nothing underneath it, nothing at all. Needless to say I stayed the night."

"Was that it or did the relationship last a while?"

"It lasted until she was murdered."

I didn't expect that. I felt my theory of another man taking a big hit. But then, as if Al sensed that something was bothering me, he continued with his story.

"You need to understand something, Jim. While we would occasionally get together, our relationship wasn't what you might expect. Julie was a unique woman. I've never met anyone like her. I never once doubted that she really loves, I mean loved, Randy. She was extremely nice to everyone. She did a lot for a couple of the charities in town."

"Did you two get together each time Randy was out of town?"

"No, you don't understand. That's what I mean about her. In the last year or so since our relationship started, we've had sex maybe five times. More often she would just sit down by the pool with me and we would just talk. She looked at her relationships with her friends, and that's what she called me, different than the rest of us do. In that way, I came to believe she was more mature than the rest of us."

"What do you mean?"

"I realized right from the start that I was her friend. There was no chance that I was going to replace Randy. Not that I ever wanted to, but she was good at making sure I understood that from day one. And, she was also good at controlling the sex in the relationship. More than once I tried to initiate it, and Julie, in her very nice but firm way, made sure I understood that she would let me know when we could have sex. I know this must sound odd, and I guess it was, but with Julie it all seemed normal."

"What if you weren't available when she wanted you?"

"No problem at all. She was always encouraging me to find some girl I could become serious about. We often talked about my girlfriends. Julie wasn't domineering or demanding. It may sound silly, but I thought when it came to her relationships with other people, she operated on a level that was a hundred years ahead of the rest of us. She didn't seem to worry about the petty jealousies and envy that the rest of us suffer from on a daily basis."

"Was there anyone else that Julie was seeing besides you?" I saw a sudden reaction in his eyes. I knew I hit something in there somewhere.

"I don't know. I wondered about that."

I sensed he wasn't telling the truth. I also sensed that he probably knew, or at least suspected, that she was seeing someone else, and that he didn't like it. She might be above the fray, but I didn't think Al was. I pulled the picture of the tall, mustached banker out of my pocket and showed it to Al.

"Could this have been one?"

He didn't have to answer. I could see it in his eyes and feel it in his breathing. I left the picture on the table in between us.

"I think so. But I couldn't swear to it. I saw him around the place a few times last winter."

"How did you feel about that? Randy aside, she was your gal."

"No, that's what you don't understand, she was not my girl.

I understood that. We were good friends."

"It didn't bother you? You didn't even talk to Julie about it."

He sat there quietly. The waitress walked by. There were more people in the bar, and she was being kept busy. I ordered two more beers and noticed a droplet of sweat on her brow.

"Did you confront Julie?" I asked quietly, trying not to make the conversation a confrontation, but I wanted a reaction.

"No, not really." Again the pause, "Listen, I was a little pissed. I was. At the same time I knew I had no business to be. One day early this spring at the pool, something I said must have made her realize I was mad. She came out straight and confronted me. I didn't confront her. She said I was her special friend. If she was cheating on anyone it was Randy, not me. She was sorry if I felt hurt but that I shouldn't. She said she needed me to be her friend. It was okay if I never wanted to be with her again, but she valued our friendship. We talked a long time about my feelings. You need to know that she never admitted that she even had a relationship with the guy in the picture and never mentioned his name."

"Did you ever confront the guy?"

"I never saw him again after the day Julie and I talked."

I wondered what that meant. Did Julie break off the relationship to appease Al?

"Was there anyone else after this guy?" I motioned toward the picture on the table.

Again the hesitation in his eyes. "No, I don't think so."

I felt he was lying or at least denying something to himself. I didn't push it. I could always talk to him again. We sat there and finished our beers. I reassured him that I would keep the information confidential, and he assured me that he would call me if he thought of anything else. I'm not sure if either one of us fully believed the other. We said our goodbyes in the bar.

I waited until he was gone before I paid the bill and left.

The sun was setting as I walked out of McClanahan's and headed for my car. The day was still hot, and the two beers had just made me hungry. I was debating where to head for dinner when I caught sight of Al up ahead across the street. He had stopped and was looking around to see if he could see someone, probably me, I thought. I started to shout at him and get his attention, but, at that moment, my route away from the bar had taken me behind a van. I happened to see him by looking through an open side window and front windshield. Just before I stepped in front of the van, he turned away and raised his cell phone to his ear. Something about the furtiveness of his actions caused me to stop and just watch him. He was too far away for me to hear him. Suddenly, he became animated while talking, undoubtedly trying to make a point to whomever he was talking to. He talked less than a minute and then looked around again. I slid back behind the van.

I wondered what that was about. It could have been nothing more than a call to a girl friend, but the way he looked around, as though he didn't want to be seen making the call, caused the little seeds of suspicion in my mind to begin growing.

We were both heading toward the condo complex. I decided to follow him for a while. He was walking toward the complex parking garage. It made sense that the employees had dedicated parking in the garage. When he disappeared inside, I hustled over to my car in the visitor lot. I got in and started the Mustang. Its three hundred horsepower engine growled to life. I backed out of the slot and tried to find a spot in the lot that gave me the best angle to observe vehicles coming out of the garage.

I barely got situated when a black motorcycle shot out of the garage and turned left passing right in front of me heading uptown. There was a small American flag attached to the back of the seat waving furiously in the wind as it went by. Despite the full protective helmet he was now wearing, the boots, jeans and work shirt gave Al away. I turned the Mustang to my own exit but was blocked from entering the road by the oncoming traffic. A steady flow of vehicles shot by me, while the motorcycle raced away. When I finally had an opening, I pulled out and followed the bike's route. The motorcycle was no longer in sight. There were too many cars in front of me, and I had no idea if or where he may have turned off.

I drove for a few minutes hoping to catch a glimpse of the bike but soon figured my pursuit was quickly becoming a waste of time. I decided to head back to the hotel to regroup.

I had mixed feelings about the day so far. I felt like I had made some progress in identifying some of the other men in Julie's life but, at the same time, wasn't any closer to coming up with a motive or a suspect. For the moment my gut was telling me that Al wasn't the killer. But, he was holding back something, and I needed to find out what that was.

I needed to meet with Julie's tall mustached friend, Jack Wilson. I also needed to try to identify other potential lovers from the documents I picked up at Randy's house. One of those men might be the man I was looking for. I also wanted to talk to Detective Reynolds. My conversation with Nosh had pretty much been a waste of time, and there was a bunch of questions I needed answered. It would also be a good idea to call Nita at the law office and bring her up to speed. They may be able to trace Wilson for me. Finally, I needed to talk to Randy again.

I pulled into the hotel's parking garage and caught sight of a man leaning against the wall by the entrance. My paranoia was in high gear, so I slowed down once inside the garage and stared into my rearview mirror. No sign of him. I pulled into a vacant slot and got out of my car.

I could see the entrance. No one appeared to be peering in, but I decided to walk down and see if he was still there. I wasn't sure what I could do even if he was still standing there, but I was curious. When I arrived at the entrance, I walked out of the garage and towards where I had seen the man standing. He was gone.

I was in the process of telling myself to quit being so paranoid when I saw him across the street and about a half a block away. He was walking fairly rapidly. Odd, I thought. Then he made his mistake. He turned around and saw me looking at him. His reaction was like many of the rookies I had taught surveillance techniques to in the past, when they got burned in their surveillance exercises. His eyes widened and a sudden look of apprehension crossed his face. He looked like the kid who just got caught with his hand in the proverbial cookie jar. Too hastily, he turned away and quickened his pace. At the corner he turned right and out of sight.

The man had on old jeans and a tee shirt that had the face of whom I thought was Che Guevara on the front and something written on the back. I thought he would be easy to follow from a distance. I didn't want to confront him. I was just interested in where he went and with whom he might meet.

I strolled after him. It was early in the evening, and the shadows from the downtown buildings were already blocking out the sun. By the time I got to the intersection where he left my sight, he was nowhere to be seen. I proceeded down the block to see if I could catch a glimpse of him on the side street. Sure enough, as I got to the next corner, I could see him nearly two blocks away. He must have run for a while to be so far ahead but had now slowed to a normal pace.

I crossed the road diagonally to fall in directly behind him. I was far enough back, and there were enough other people on the sidewalk, that it would be difficult for him to spot me. He turned right at the end of the block, and I again lost sight of him.

When I arrived at the point where he turned, I realized he had entered La Villita. This was an old part of downtown San Antonio filled with art galleries, boutiques, restaurants, and had access to the River Walk via a small open air amphitheater. He was nowhere to be seen, but I continued straight down the steps of the amphitheater. I caught sight of him again. He was heading to the right along the River Walk.

I slowed some to let him get a little further ahead. This part of the River Walk was usually not very crowded. Soon, though, I knew he would be entering an extremely crowded part of the River Walk, and I would have to close the gap to keep sight of him.

I saw him pass Dirty Nellie's and glance backwards. There was no indication he saw me. I made sure he continued straight and didn't turn right towards the River City Mall or cross the walkway bridge to the restaurants on the other side. He had to slow down some on the narrow, crowded sidewalk simply to avoid being bumped into the river. There were no railings to keep someone from falling into the water.

He continued on past the Hilton and Mad Dog's. I moved in as close as I dared. It was darker here, as the early evening light was blocked by the buildings that hung tight and close to the river, but I still wanted to keep as much distance as I could between us. He took the next walkway bridge and crossed to the other side of the river. I waited until he was well away. He was still heading up river toward The County Line, Hard Rock Café, and other heavily populated restaurants that overflowed onto the sidewalk.

This was one of the many parts of the River Walk where the pedestrians walked between and around tables of patrons eating and drinking their way into the evening. He wasn't looking around anymore, not interested in the tourists, and no longer worried about being tailed.

Suddenly he veered left and entered Jaime's, a small bar that advertised a "light menu." I didn't think there was such a thing in San Antonio. I hung around outside for a few minutes feeling impotent. I didn't want or need another altercation, but I didn't follow him this far just to sit outside.

I entered Jaime's and looked around. There were a few small groups of people at tables or around the bar. Three men and three women dressed in shorts and tee shirts, huddled around a table for four, were talking and laughing in voices loud enough to be heard throughout the place. Tourists, most likely, who already had too much to drink. Two men in jeans and button up shirts were standing at the bar watching the loud group of six. They had all the signs of being ranchers, probably in for a good time on the town. The other small groups could have been locals just off work and having a drink before they went home or met someone for dinner elsewhere. Jaime's didn't appear to be the type of place to draw a dinner crowd.

However, there was no sign of the guy I was following. He didn't leave by the front door and I didn't see a side door. He could have gone through the kitchen but he would have to know the people here to do so. If he left by a back door, then I had already lost him. I wondered if he could be an employee, so I ordered a draft from the bar and grabbed a table close to the entrance to wait and see.

No one seemed to have any interest in me, and in the fifteen minutes I sipped my beer I saw no trace of him. During that time, two men in white aprons who apparently worked in the kitchen came out briefly to get a coke from the bar. I didn't recognize either one. I decided to call it quits.

Outside the sky was already dark as I headed back to the hotel. What a waste of time, I thought. Mark it off as exercise and it wouldn't be a total loss. The smell of the grill at Boudro's almost sucked me in as I walked by, but I wanted to see if I could find someone to join me for dinner.

I was back at the hotel in ten minutes. There was a crowd at the reception desk. It looked like a group of tourists from Japan or Korea had just arrived and was checking in. I scooted around them, headed towards the elevator and pressed eight. It was only when the elevator door opened that I remembered I had moved to the Tower Suite. I reworked the numbers in the elevator.

I nodded at the concierge when I finally made it to the right floor.

"Hope you're having a pleasant evening," he greeted me. "Anything I can do for you this evening?"

I mumbled a "no thanks," and walked down the long hallway to my room. As I opened my door I glanced back at the concierge. He was just hanging up the phone. Reporting on me, I wondered.

"I am getting paranoid," I told the empty room as I closed the door behind me.

Chapter 11

Once in my room, I pulled off my borrowed shirt and tossed it on a chair. I took the wad of papers out of my back pocket and placed them on the table and then grabbed a Corona out of the refrigerator.

I sat down at the table, took out my cell phone and called Nita. Might as well report in, I thought. A voice in the phone said that Nita was not available so I left a message that I would call Cynthia. I preferred to talk to Nita but Cynthia would have to do.

She was available but sounded preoccupied. As a result our conversation was perfunctory. I filled her in with the fact that I had been to the crime scene and to LaMoe's house. I also told her I had been able to identify a couple of the men with whom Julie had recent relationships. I didn't tell her about my altercation. I couldn't tell if Cynthia was disappointed or bored with my call.

I spread the papers I had brought from Randy's house out on the table. The newspaper photo of Julie and her tall banker friend was on top of the stack of photos. I was thinking about how to get to a computer to do an internet search on him when I heard what sounded like a door bell. A hotel room with a door bell, what will they think of next?

"Ooohh! What happened to you, Jim?" Lee Valentine was my visitor. I answered the door forgetting that I wasn't wearing a shirt and that I had a recent slash across my chest.

"Come on in. Let me get a shirt on." I thought about grabbing the black tee shirt but walked past it to the bedroom. When I came back out, Lee was sitting on one of the stuffed chairs.

"What happened, Jim? That wound looks fresh."

"It's a long story, what brings you up here? Not that I'm not happy you're here."

Actually it was nice to see her. Dressed for work like she was the night before, I couldn't help but think that she still looked a little different. Maybe I was just finding her more attractive.

"I asked the concierge to call me when you returned to your room. I hope you don't mind."

"That's fine. It's nice to see you again."

"I just wanted to update you on what we have found out about the lady we think put the scorpions in your room. I also wanted to make sure that everything was going well with your stay since the incident."

"I haven't had any problems since moving up here. You and the hotel have been super. I appreciate all you've done."

"Good. Unfortunately all that we have been able to find out about the lady is that she walked in through the back door wearing shorts and a sleeveless tee shirt. She was carrying a large bag. She went to the ladies room by one of the conference rooms and exited a few minutes later wearing our hotel's housekeeping attire. She knew where to get a housekeeping cart, and, once she had one, she proceeded directly to your floor and to your room. She simply reversed her steps and left the hotel through the same exit."

"Did she change back into her civilian clothes?"

"Yes, in the same ladies room."

"She obviously was well acquainted with the hotel."

"That she was. We think she had to have an inside accomplice."

"Still no idea who she was?"

"No. We have coordinated with the police, but they haven't been much help."

I wondered who they had coordinated with but decided not to ask. "Guess you can't blame them. They likely have more pressing cases to deal with than the harassment of a hotel guest."

"What are you working on?" Lee nodded towards the papers scattered on the table.

"Just a puzzle I'm trying to solve." I didn't want to discuss it, and, probably sensing my evasion, she didn't pursue it.

"Have you eaten yet?"

"Just finished. I'm on duty but if you grab a bite here in the hotel, I'd be glad to have a glass of tea and keep you company."

"I don't feel like a formal dinner in the dining room. If you don't mind meeting me in the lounge in about twenty minutes, I'll be glad for your company."

"It's a date," Lee said with a smile. She stood up, and I walked her to the door.

After showering, feeling refreshed, I studied the slash across my chest in the bathroom mirror. It looked all right, and I thought it would heal fairly quickly. The young medic had done a good job patching me up. There had been minimal bleeding from it through the afternoon. I noticed my other, older scars and thought that I needed to start taking better care of myself. Getting hurt wasn't supposed to be part of the job description these days.

The lounge was more active than the past two nights. I took the only available table and studied the crowd. A good portion of the room was taken up by one large group spread out across four tables. They seemed to be having a good time laughing and harassing each other.

Closer to me, two tables were pushed together and occupied by what I guessed were eight individuals from the Asian tour group I had seen earlier. They were also having a good time but doing so much more quietly than the larger group. Every now and then one of them would glance over at the larger group and say something laughingly to his group. He probably had the best grasp of the English language and was keeping his friends apprised of what was going on with the larger group.

The rest of the tables and most of the counter were occupied by smaller groups or individuals. I didn't recognize anyone.

"Hey, Mr. West, what can I get you tonight?"

I looked up and saw Enrique standing there smiling at me.

"Don't they ever give you a night off?"

"Tomorrow, but I try to work whenever I can. I need the money."

"Well, let's see. How about a Corona with a lime?"

"Can do, I'll be right back."

"And, Enrique, a ginger ale for me, please." Lee had approached us from behind and took the seat opposite me and in front of where Enrique was standing.

"Yes, ma'am, coming right up." Enrique gave me raised eyebrow as he walked away.

"No tea?" I asked.

"I remembered the tea in here never seems very fresh. We've been working on fixing that."

"Sorry about the small table but everything else was taken."

She looked around. "Nice crowd. With all the local competition we rarely get many people to stay in our lounge."

"I imagine a place this size really keeps you busy."

"It does, even when things are routine. But then there are

crises like yours. That's when things really get hectic. I don't mind, though, I like staying busy."

There was a loud roar of laughter from the rowdy group across the room. Lee looked at them.

"Looks like someone is having fun," she commented and rolled her eyes at me. "As long as they stay peaceful, we don't mind. Officially, that is. I personally get tired of the loud, obnoxious ones. Especially those who think that everyone in the whole hotel wants to hear them whenever they talk."

"Do you ever have any real trouble with your guests?"

"Not here, yet, but we haven't been open that long. I've seen it all though at prior hotels I've worked: a knifing, a shooting, women stripping, even live sex acts. We call the police immediately for violent criminal acts. For drunken behavior, we just use our internal security and get them to their rooms or, if they aren't hotel guests, out of the building as quickly as possible."

"Must be interesting," I commented.

"Ninety percent of the time it's just busy and not very interesting. But, we do get our surprises. Your scorpion attack was the first I ever heard of in the hotel business."

Enrique brought our drinks and I ordered a club sandwich for my dinner.

"Good choice," Lee remarked. "If I may brag a little, we do make a good club sandwich here."

"How long have you been working in the industry?"

"Many years," she grinned as though telling me would give her age away. She didn't need to worry. She was younger than I was, and, from my vantage point, she looked pretty damn good for her age, whatever it was.

"What brings you to San Antonio, Jim?"

"A friend called and asked me to come down and help him

out with a problem he's having."

"How long will that keep you here?"

"I'm not sure, a few more days at least. If you need to move me out of the suite, that's fine with me. It's a little nicer than I'm used to anyway."

"That's not why I asked. I was just curious." She stared at me for a moment. "What kind of work do you do?"

"Well, what I normally do and what I'm doing at the moment here in San Antonio are different altogether. I retired from the Air Force a few years back and now do the occasional professional lecture at a college or to a civic group. It's just me and my dog at home. As I receive a pension from the military, I don't need much other income. I'm just trying to take things easy these days, maybe even lower my golf handicap."

"Can you tell me what kind of problem your friend has?"

"Not really, it's a legal issue and I'm working on it with his law firm." My involvement in the LaMoe murder case wasn't a secret, but I didn't want to get into it with her.

I was able to get the subject back on tourism and San Antonio, and for the next thirty minutes, while I ate my sandwich, we had a nice conversation. I was just finishing when Lee stood up and said she should get back to work before someone realized she was goofing off.

"See you around," I said as she turned to leave.

"Oh yeah," Lee replied, grinning sexily.

"Your ex must be an idiot." I mumbled to myself once she was out of range.

I walked up to the bar to order another beer and to pay my bill. Enrique, who had been pulling duty both behind the bar and as a table server, came over to me.

"Another Corona, Mr. West?"

I told him yes and glanced around the lounge again as he

went to fetch it. Most of the crowd had departed and things were quieting down.

Enrique delivered my beer and leaned clandestinely towards me.

"Mr. West, I heard about the incident with the scorpions. That was true, no?"

"Yes, it unfortunately was. What do you know about it?"

"Nothing specific, just what I was told by Kris, she works the front desk. But I'm worried for you Mr. West. That scorpion stuff is a Mexican Mafia thing. They do that to warn people. You mess with them and if they don't kill you first, they give you a warning, like with the scorpions or something else. Maybe they throw a dead cat into your car or shoot out the windows to your house."

"I get the idea, but why would the Mexican Mafia be mad at me?"

"I don't know. Maybe they aren't. It's just that the scorpion thing is like their calling card. I wanted to warn you."

"Well thanks, Enrique I appreciate it." I did, too. Another piece of the puzzle, I wondered?

The bar was fairly empty so I moved down close to the television that had been turned on behind the bar. A football game was ending, and the nightly news was next.

The news started with a breaking story about another homicide being discovered in the city. I took a big swig of beer and imagined that television news channels prioritized their "breaking news" around murders, abductions, fires and floods. I could see the editor yelling at his staff, "just find me some bad news quick!"

I was only half listening. Another shooting, a young man found dead with a single bullet to the heart. Then something caught my eye. The camera scanned across the crime scene.

The body was covered, the police were standing around, the trees and bushes were swaying gently in the night breeze, and then the camera focused in on a motorcycle parked at the scene. Attached to the back of the seat was a small American flag waving softly in the wind.

There was no doubt about it. The bike was the one I saw Al riding that afternoon. The hairs on the back of my neck started a little dance and I rubbed them, still fixated with the television.

"The victim, an unidentified white male in his late twenties or early thirties, has not yet been identified. The police believe he was a victim of a robbery since his wallet is missing. The area where the victim was found is just off a dirt road that is rarely used by anyone. Why he would be here is a question the police may need to first answer if they want to solve this mystery. A police spokesman told me the victim was discovered by a fortunate circumstance, barely an hour or so ago, when a patrol car missed a turn off the main road and pulled into this dirt road to make a u-turn. Once they saw the reflection of the tail light of the motorcycle in the distance, they pulled on in to check it out." The television reporter went on to identify herself and her station.

I grabbed my cell phone and dialed the number Detective Reynolds had given me. He answered on the second ring. He was obviously waiting for a call from someone and was somewhat short with me when he finally realized who I was.

"Look, Jim, I'm tied up right now. Call me tomorrow."

"If you are out at the shooting of the guy on the motorcycle, I think I know who he is. I'd like to talk to you about him."

There was a pause at the other end of the line. "How do you know about the shooting?"

"It's on the news, Detective. I saw the motorcycle. I think I recognize it as belonging to a guy I was talking to today. A male, maybe thirty years old, white, good build maybe 6 foot one or two."

"Jim, would you recognize him if you saw him again?"

"Yes."

"Would you mind taking a drive out here? We could have someone swing by and pick you up. He'll be here for another half hour or so."

I told him I would come, and he gave me the directions. He said it should only take me about fifteen minutes this time of the night. Not knowing the area very well, I wasn't as optimistic, but the drive out of town on I-37 to the south was fast. I made it to the crime scene in thirteen minutes. A patrolman on the outer perimeter stopped me, but when I identified myself and said I was there per the request of Detective Reynolds, he let me through, instructing me to park this side of the police vehicles already at the scene.

As I climbed out of the Mustang, I saw Reynolds walking towards me. He looked like he had already had a rough day.

"Jim, thanks for coming out. The body is over here."

He guided me up to the body. As we approached, a camera flashed off to the side.

"Enough of that, Peggy, or we won't let you back in at the next scene." Reynolds snarled.

I glanced over and saw four individuals huddled together off to the side. The local press I assumed.

"Don't get too close, Jim. We're pretty much done with the crime scene, but the forensic team hasn't released the body yet."

I stood still about six feet from where he was lying. It was Al, no doubt about it. His faced stared wide eyed at the bright moon above us. There was no remnant of any emotion on his face. I felt sorry for him. He wasn't a bad guy.

"His name is Al. He works at the condo complex where

Julie LaMoe was murdered. He was having an affair with her. You should check his DNA with the evidence on that case. I just talked to him this afternoon. Did you find his cell phone?"

"No, there was no cell phone here, no wallet either. Why do you ask?"

"After he left me, probably just before six, he called someone from his cell phone. A few minutes later he drove off on his bike. I thought there might have been a connection between the call and where he went on his bike."

"Jim, do you think he might have murdered Julie LaMoe?"

"No, I don't. But I do think he knew something he didn't tell me."

"Detective," a female officer in uniform approached us. "Sorry to interrupt, but they are ready to remove the body and motorcycle, unless you want to keep them here longer."

"No we're done here for now, I suppose. We'll keep the area sealed off till daylight and take another look around." He looked back at me. "Let's go somewhere and talk." He started walking toward the cars.

I didn't know if he meant over by the cars or somewhere away from the crime scene but I followed him. I could tell he had a lot on his mind.

"Johnny," Reynolds shouted across to another guy in civilian attire. "Your turn to do the initial reports."

"I know," Johnny responded. "See you tomorrow."

"Your car?" Reynolds asked me.

I pointed to my Mustang and we both climbed in.

"Where to?"

"Back the way you came, there's a place where we can stop on the way." He sat quietly for a few minutes. "Thanks Jim, for giving me a lift. It's been a long day. I needed to get away from everyone. Sorry you're stuck with me."

"That's all right. I didn't have anything else to do tonight. Plus, I needed to talk to you."

His phone rang and he spoke to someone for a couple minutes. The call had to do with some other case involving the death of a minor. He pointed to a Jim's Restaurant just off the highway, so I pulled off and maneuvered into a slot near the front door. Despite the hour, the restaurant was fairly busy. I had been to a Jim's before, there must be about a dozen in the area, and knew they served good basic meals twenty four hours a day.

I got out of the car and stood by it, waiting for Reynolds to finish his call. It was a calm, pleasant night, and traffic was busy on the interstate coming into and out of San Antonio. When he did climb out of the car, he stretched his arms up high and behind his shoulders.

"This place okay with you?"

"Sure," I hadn't planned on eating much, so it really didn't matter.

He walked in and I followed. Once inside he slid into an empty booth up front that bordered the window looking out into the parking lot and the highway beyond. A waitress was at our table by the time I sat down.

"Evening gentlemen, do you need a menu?"

I was going to say yes, but Reynolds beat me to the answer.

"Not me, let me have your Rustler's Roundup breakfast with a cup of coffee."

They both looked at me.

"Can I get a cinnamon roll and a cup of coffee?"

"Yes, you can. Anything else?"

I told her no, and she shuffled off towards the kitchen.

"Detective,.."

"Call me Frank."

"Frank, did you get a chance to check out the people Julie may have called from her cell phone the day or two before she was murdered?"

"We never found her cell phone, but we should be getting her phone records soon."

"That's odd. Two lovers killed within days of each other, both with one shot to the heart, and both their cell phones are missing."

"Think someone is killing them for their cell phones?" Frank said with a grin.

"No, but it is peculiar."

"I don't think this guy was shot with a 9mm like Julie was. It looked to me to be a much larger caliber, maybe a 45."

"But both shots to the heart?" I was still drawn to the similarities. "And what was Al doing at that location? It's in the middle of nowhere. You weren't supposed to find the body this fast. I think Al was drawn there to meet someone, and the robbery angle was just added to hopefully hide the real motive."

"You sound like a cop."

"I spent a lot of time doing this kind of stuff."

"You have some good points. I will most definitely follow up on the DNA comparison. The relationship angle makes the coincidence of the two killings interesting. But it's still hard for me to believe LaMoe didn't kill his wife. He had motive, access and opportunity. What I don't understand, though, is why you aren't trying to blame this victim with killing LaMoe's wife? If we have a DNA match, a good defense attorney could say that he, too, had motive, access and opportunity. Sure would muddy up the circumstantial case."

"I imagine Randy's lawyers would try to do just that. But my gut tells me Al didn't kill her either. He really liked her, and I just don't see him as the killer type."

Frank grinned again. "Is your gut ever wrong?"

"Sure, but not that often."

The waitress delivered our meals. Frank's meal was more like a feast. Three eggs, a small mountain of bacon, a thick slice of ham, two sausage links, a mound of hash browns, and four pieces of toast were piled on a large plate.

Over the next twenty minutes we ate, or I should say that Frank ate, and we discussed sports and life in San Antonio. Frank was friendly and chatty, and my earlier perceptions of him were reinforced. He seemed like an all around good guy.

As we got back into my car and headed into the city, Frank stretched and remarked that he could sure use a night's sleep.

"Where's the lieutenant tonight?" I asked.

"Luxury of being the boss, he had to leave to go to something going on at his kid's school. Left just after the call came in and the rest of us were heading out. Luckily, I don't have a family to worry about."

"Frank, don't you think it's a bit odd that both cell phones are missing?"

"What, you mean the LaMoe woman's and this guy's?"

"Yes."

"Not really. They get pawned all the time. It slows down our getting our hands around who they've been calling. We can still get to the records, but it's not like punching it up on the phone."

"Are cell phones stolen in most of your homicides?"

"No, but I've heard of it happening before."

"How about one shot to the heart murders?"

"What do you mean?"

"Do you see many of them?"

"No. But you can't read too much into that either. One shot, ten shots, heart, head, stabbings, beatings, you name it, we see all types. I haven't seen a stat chart. I told you the perp didn't use the same weapon in this one. That would be more common. Most killers have a single weapon they like using. It would be real rare for him to mix up his guns just to throw us off."

"I guess you're right about that, Frank. But you know we may be dealing with a pretty smart guy here. There is a definite connection between the two murders. I'd bet you another one of your big breakfasts on it."

He looked at me and grinned. "You're on, although something tells me that I shouldn't be taking this bet."

I dropped Frank off at the station and headed back to my hotel. I had mixed emotions and because of that I felt a little odd. Al had seemed like an okay guy. His death was unfortunate, but I felt like the momentum in the investigation was starting to swing my way. I couldn't buy that his killing was just a weird coincidence. There had to be a connection and I wondered if I had caused it.

Chapter 12

The next morning I took advantage of the small dining room set up for breakfast just past the concierge desk on my floor. It was a buffet that offered a fairly wide selection of items. The buffet was manned by two attendants. There were no other people in the room. The food was hot and fresh, but by my take the whole operation was a waste of time and food. My guess was that a few powerful people liked to have their own private area to eat, so the hotel kept it available.

I skipped my morning walk and headed straight to the law offices of Caruzzo and Dilbert. A meeting with Randy's defense team was due, whether they knew it or not. I called before I left my hotel and was told that the lawyers were not yet in but should all be in by nine. My arrival would be a little early, but I didn't care. I had things to do, and they needed to know what I knew and what I suspected.

It was a nice morning, so I had the top down on my car. In addition to enjoying the drive, by its being down, I also had much better visibility. I needed to stay more alert than I had been. Someone was playing awfully rough, and I was convinced that in getting involved in the LaMoe murder investigation, I had entered his playground.

The law office was in its own building, a rock and brick single story building situated between a small shopping strip and another professional building that appeared to house a financial services outfit along with an accountant. The area looked upscale, and even the shopping strip looked kept up with its Starbucks, a small Italian restaurant and a few other specialty stores.

The front door to the law firm was locked and I didn't see a door bell or buzzer. It was close enough to nine that I decided to go ahead and knock on the door. No one came so I knocked again, a little bit louder.

The door was opened by a lady who looked to be in her thirties, with curly hair, wearing dark slacks, a yellow wind breaker, and a purple and black scarf. I couldn't tell if she was of Mexican descent or racially mixed, but she was very attractive.

"Sorry, sir, but we're not open yet. Could you come back in a few minutes?"

"I'd rather come in and wait. I'm working on a matter with Ms. Rich, and it's extremely important that I speak to her when she first arrives. It should only take five minutes. I would like to speak to her before she gets involved with something else."

I treated her to one of my best, I'm-really-a-nice-guy smiles.

"Okay, you can sit with me in the reception area until she comes in." She held the door open for me, and I entered. "She is expecting you, I assume?"

"I hope so." It was the only truthful answer I could come up with.

She went and sat behind a nice desk that was located in the center of the room. A name plate on the desk said Terry Shelf. Behind her were bookshelves and two doors that led to the back area of the building. On both sides were doors that led to the opposite wings of the building. They were all shut. I sat on an expensive looking lounge chair and left the couch for any larger groups that might show up.

Despite the warmth of the day outside, I realized as soon as I walked in why Terry was wearing a coat. It was outright cold in the building. The air conditioning must have been set on freeze.

"Somebody storing fish in the building?"

She sniffed the air before she realized what I was implying.

"Oh, you mean the temperature." She leaned towards me and whispered. "I hate it. They keep this reception area too cold in the summer and too warm in the winter. I don't think it's healthy, but they think the clients like it for the short time they spend out here."

Just then Nita Ybarra opened one of the side doors and took two steps towards one of the doors leading to the back of the building. She noticed me and stopped.

"Well, good morning, Jim. What brings our pro bono sleuth here so early?"

"Another murder and the chance to see you again." I grinned, wondering if she believed either part of my reply.

"Seriously?"

"Yes. I was hoping you or Cynthia had a few minutes you could spare."

"Sure, come on back." She reversed direction and led me back through the door she had just come through.

The temperature was instantly warmer in the hallway and then even warmer in her small office. She closed the door behind us once we were inside her office.

"Cynthia has a dental appointment today, so she'll be late. What's going on?"

"Did you watch the news last night?"

"No, I was tied up late. When I finally got home, I took a bath and went right to sleep."

I went on to tell her of Al's murder, his involvement with Julie LaMoe and the fact that he was killed within an hour or two of his talking to me.

"I told Detective Reynolds that there was a good chance his DNA will match that found at the crime scene."

"Then, you think he killed Julie?" She jumped to the obvious conclusion.

"Unfortunately, no, I don't. I think he really liked Julie and accepted the relationship for what it was. I don't see him as the killer, but, if his DNA does match up, I think the possibility that he could have been the killer would substantially weaken the prosecutor's case."

She didn't say anything right away. I could almost feel her "little grey cells" digesting the information and formulating theories for the defense.

"So, what do you think Jim?"

"I think both Julie and Al were shot by the same person. Different weapons but each died from one shot to the heart at fairly close range. Julie and Al knew each other very well. They both probably knew the killer. They both had their cell phones taken."

"Cell phones taken? Is that a big thing?"

"I think so. Why would the killer take the time to locate and steal his victim's cell phones? We know Julie's killing was no robbery, and, despite the fact that Al's wallet was also missing, I don't think his killing was either. The phones were taken to preclude, or at least delay, the police from seeing what was on them. Either a phone number, a call placed, a text message, someone listed as a favorite, something that might link the killer to the victim. Something that the actual phone records may not show."

She didn't argue with my theory. That raised Nita a notch on my short list of women I'd like to spend the rest of my life with, but never will.

"Even if this Al of yours was having an affair with Julie, what makes you think that Al may have been the last man with her before she was killed? You said he didn't admit to it, right?"

"That's right. Admittedly it's the weakest link in my theory, but it is also irrelevant to everything but Randy's defense. As I said, I don't believe he killed her. But, he worked at the condo complex, and he may have had an idea who Julie was seeing. He was aware of Jack Wilson."

"Who?"

"Jack Wilson, a tall, mustached banker Julie was also seeing on occasion. By the way, is there someone here who can check him out and let me know how to find him?"

Nita picked up the phone and buzzed someone. "Can you do me a favor? See if you find an address, work place, or a phone number for a Jack Wilson. He works at one of the banks in town. Thanks." She hung up the phone. "Should only be a minute or two."

"Thanks."

"You looked through her things at the house and condo. Didn't you find something to identify Wilson there?"

"That's another interesting angle to all this. Julie had quite the database of business cards and names. She appears to be a classic networker. She had a newspaper clipping with Wilson's picture on it. While the newspaper identified him, there was nothing in any of Julie's other files that mentioned him."

"Do you think Wilson could have killed Julie and then killed Al?"

"Depending on his alibi, you could make as good of a case for it, as the one the prosecutor will do on Randy."

"Especially if the phone records show that Al called Wilson after he talked to you."

"See, now you're thinking like me."

Nita returned my grin and was about to say something when the phone rang. She answered it, listened for a while and then hung up.

"Your Jack Wilson is a vice president at South Texas Bank & Trust."

"That was easy."

"He is quite involved with city events. He is also married with three children. If you're going to approach him, I'd walk softly."

"Don't worry about me. I'll be on my tip-toes."

We talked for a few more minutes, and, after Nita gave me Wilson's work address and phone number, I made my exit.

Chapter 13

Wilson worked at the main offices for the South Texas Bank & Trust. The address was on Nacogdoches Street, just outside the inner loop or 410 as it was known numerically.

"Just past the Der Weinerschnitzel restaurant," Nita had said, "you can't miss it."

I almost pulled in for a mustard dog but passed the fast food restaurant by, turning into the parking lot to the bank building instead.

A branch of the bank occupied the first floor and, after asking for Wilson, I was directed to the elevators and told to go to the third floor. The elevators opened to a large foyer which was furnished with two desks, a number of chairs and coffee tables. Open corridors led to the right, left and straight ahead. Two women occupied the two desks in the foyer. Their primary duty, it seemed, was to serve as gatekeepers.

"May we help you?" The brunette on the right asked. They were both staring at me as though no one had come through those elevators in years.

"A lady downstairs told me I could find Jack Wilson up here."

"Do you have an appointment?" The grey haired lady to my left asked.

"No, I don't. I'm Jim West. If you could please tell Mr. Wilson that I would like to speak to him. Let him know it's very important that I talk to him."

"Mr. Wilson is an extremely busy man, Mr. West. I'll be happy to leave him a message. I'm sure he'll contact you as soon as he can."

I looked for a nameplate on grey hair's desk and saw one that said Penny something or other.

"Penny, how about this? I write a very short personal note for Mr. Wilson, and you hand deliver it to him? If he doesn't want to see me, then we'll play it your way."

She stared at me for a second not wanting to give in. I stood up walked over to her desk, tore a blank sheet off her memo pad, and wrote a short note on the page. Then I folded the page in half and stapled it together. I figured the extra little melodrama was needed. Besides, I enjoyed doing it.

I held the paper in my hand and shifted my gaze back and forth between the women.

Finally, grey haired Penny stood up. "Oh, all right, give me that. I'll take it to him."

She grabbed the paper, turned around, and walked down the hallway that was directly in front of the elevators. She knocked on the third or fourth door on the left side of the hallway and after a brief moment entered the room.

I sat down in a chair that continued to give me a view of the hallway and the door she entered. She was in the room for less than a minute. She returned to her desk and without looking at me said, "Mr. Wilson will see you in a few minutes."

The younger brunette looked at me with what I thought wasn't love in her eyes.

I was fairly sure Wilson would see me. My note had simply said, "I need to talk to you about Julie. Me or the police?"

About five minutes after the note had been delivered, I saw a tall man come out of the office I was sure Penny had entered, not look in my direction, and walk quickly towards the rear of the building. I thought I heard the faint ringing of an elevator's bell coming from down the hallway.

"Is there a back exit and elevator to this building?" I asked.

"Of course," answered Penny. I was still getting the evil eye from the brunette.

"Damn," I muttered to myself. I jumped out of my chair and was past the two women before they knew what was happening. I half jogged to Wilson's office door, opened it, and saw that he had gone. I went on down the hall to check for a restroom. I ignored the two ladies yelling at me from behind. I found it and went inside. It too was empty.

When I emerged, three men had now joined the ladies in the hall. All of them were staring at me wide-eyed like I was some crazy person.

"Sorry," I said in my humblest of voices. Holding my stomach, "that was an emergency. I wouldn't go in there right away."

I walked past them and punched the down button to the elevator that I used earlier. Luckily the elevator opened immediately, and I left the gang behind, still quietly watching me.

At the ground floor I walked hurriedly out of the building and around to the parking lot. As I got to the edge of the building, a black Mercedes sedan shot by me. I just got a glimpse of the driver, but I saw enough to know it was Wilson. He had such a jump on me I thought I wouldn't have any chance to follow him. At the parking lots entrance to the street, however, Wilson had to stop as the light down the road had just changed, and the traffic was heavy going by him.

I contemplated running down to his car but decided he could just drive away and not let me in. Instead I sprinted to the Mustang, jumped in and drove after him. He was pulling away from the parking lot as I quickly backed my car out of its slot. I raced to the road but had to slam on my brakes, narrowly avoiding an old Volkswagon van that crept by.

I shot out around the van, barely beating a new horde of cars coming from the stop light. I could clearly see the Mercedes as it headed north about two blocks ahead of me. He was heading straight up Nacogdoches away from downtown. Unfortunately, he cleared the first light we came to, and I didn't.

Again I thought he would get away, only to watch him get stopped by a light further down the road. When my light changed, I picked up the pursuit once more. We continued to hit and miss lights for the next several miles. I never really closed the gap by more than the initial two blocks we had between us. At times he would get nearly half a mile ahead of me only to get caught by a light that would allow me to close in once again. Traffic was heavy on the street, and I couldn't help but think there was a quicker way to get out of town.

Wilson didn't seem to be in any real hurry. I doubted if he noticed me following him despite my being in the only jet black, convertible mustang on the road that day. All of the sudden, though, we seemed to be leaving the city and starting to get out into the country. Traffic suddenly thinned out and Nacogdoches changed from a four lane road to a two lane one.

There was still one car between us and I was at least two hundred yards behind him. The road became narrow and lost all pretense of going in a straight line. Finally, the car providing my only interference pulled off at a quarry. Another stop sign slowed me down again. I knew Wilson was still ahead of me but had now lost sight of him. I picked up my speed. Live oaks and cedars lined the roadside and when I could see the adjacent land, it looked like farm or ranch land. I went by a picnic area set up on a private field to my right. There was no sign of Wilson.

I had only passed a couple of small, dirt road turnoffs since I last saw his car and didn't think he took one of those, so I pressed on. A small creek now paralleled the road to my left. I had the car up to sixty despite the forty five mile per hour speed limit, but still it didn't seem like I was gaining any ground. In an overreaction, I glanced in my rearview mirror. No, not there either.

I slowed to cross some railroad tracks, and my suspension rattled as I hit the uneven pavement. This was beginning to get irritating. Some clouds had started to move in and turned the bright shiny day into a cloudy, more ominous one. The winds were beginning to pick up. I wondered if there were some storms heading our way.

I rounded a bend in the road and saw his Mercedes parked off the road on the left hand side. There was no shoulder; he had just pulled over on the dirt. I slowed and passed his car. No one was inside. I looked down behind the car and saw a small cemetery and thought I saw movement. I drove another quarter of a mile before I found a spot where I could turn around and drove back to his car. I parked off the road facing his car.

The small cemetery was situated in some trees about a hundred yards from the road. There wasn't a building in sight in any direction. I could see someone, probably Wilson with his back to me, sitting on a concrete bench in the cemetery. I leaned against the Mustang and considered giving him a few minutes. Small gravesites like this were common around San Antonio. Rarely used anymore, many were maintained by volunteers.

The wind was blowing in cooler air, so I put the top up on the car. I got back out, and decided I had given Wilson enough time.

As I approached him, I called out his name. "Wilson, I need to ask you a few questions."

No response and no movement. I walked around to his side. He was staring at the gravestone immediately in front of him. I looked at it and read its inscription – Jack Wilson, December 1, 1908 – February 3, 1995, J.W. – We'll always remember you.

"Your father?" I asked. He still had not shown any response to my being there.

"My grandfather, but he raised me like a father." Still no eye contact.

I looked back at the gravestone.

"You shouldn't have followed me."

I looked back at Wilson and saw that he now held a large handgun in his right hand. It looked like an old Colt .38 caliber revolver. He wasn't looking at me, and the gun wasn't pointed at me, but it still looked nasty. He had both hands squeezed between his legs close to his knees when I had approached him. The gun must have been hidden by his legs.

"I brought this gun to use on myself. Now I wonder if I shouldn't just shoot you."

"I don't understand. What's going on?" I tried to sound my most innocent. Of course I understood right away. I had walked into his life and let him know that I knew about Julie. No doubt, that was a part of his life he wasn't prepared to face, if it became public.

"J.W. was a great man. He was a rancher, but he could have done or become anything. He was the smartest person I ever knew. He could reassemble an engine in the dark, shoot a flying dove at fifty yards with this gun, and resolve any problem you brought to him. People across the county used to come ask his advice on things. He would always help out. We didn't go to church much, but he knew the Bible by heart. He was always being urged to run for this or that public office. He always said no thanks. He said that if he got into politics, he'd probably just end up shooting someone. He couldn't abide pompous, crooked people. That's what he would always tell me. How can people live with themselves when they live a lie?"

Wilson still hadn't made eye contact.

"He must have been a good man. Were you named after him?"

He nodded his head but didn't say anything.

"Why don't we go back into town, Jack? Let me buy you some coffee and we can talk. I'm not here to blackmail you. I just need to know a few things?"

He finally turned his head and looked at me. I looked into his eyes and saw nothing. If he had killed Julie, my odds of getting out of there alive were not good. It had not been very smart of me to follow him out here alone. Now, all I could hope was that I could talk him out of shooting me, first, and himself, second.

He shifted the gun from his right hand to his left. I didn't know if that was good or bad. He pointed the gun at me.

"Sit over there." He pointed with his right hand at a low flat tombstone about four feet to my right.

I did what I was told.

"There is no reason to shoot me or, for that matter, yourself. Like I said Jack, I'm not here to cause you any problems."

"What the hell!" He stood up when he shouted this. "You come prancing into my office giving me a note that says you know about Julie and threatening me with the police, and now you say you're not here to cause me any problems. You dumb ass, you couldn't have caused me a bigger problem if you tried. And," his voice calmed down, and he sat back down, "you shouldn't have followed me out here."

He stared back at J.W.'s tombstone. "I've tried to lead a good life. I've worked hard and have been fair with other people. I have a wonderful wife and three great children. We attend church regularly. I do a lot of charity work. I help out coaching with my kids' sports teams. I'm even a big volunteer with the annual Fiesta events in the city."

Wilson looked back at me. "Sounds like I'm almost a saint, doesn't it?"

I didn't answer him.

"Then I met Mrs. Julie LaMoe. It was like I was drugged when I was around her. I'm not even sure how it got started. I couldn't get enough of her. I can't really explain it. I had a lot of girlfriends before I got married, but until Julie I had stayed loyal to Emily."

"Don't blame yourself, Jack. She apparently had that affect on men."

He didn't seem to realize that I had said something.

"At the end, she broke it off with me. She told me that she never meant for me to get so serious in our relationship. She said she was sorry. She said I had a good wife and children who needed me, and that our relationship had to end. I told her I couldn't live without her; that I didn't want the relationship to end. Despite my pleas, she refused to see me. I wrote her letters. I suppose you have them, begging her to let me see her again, but she refused. I even went to her condo once, but she wouldn't let me in. She told me to go home. Go home, she said."

"When was that?" I asked, hoping he wasn't going to say the day I shot her. It might help get Randy off the hook, but at the moment I was worried more about me.

"About six months ago."

From my angle I could see a white Sherriff's sedan pull up

and stop by our cars. Two deputies in black and khaki uniforms came out and started walking in our direction. Wilson hadn't noticed them.

"Jack, did you kill Julie?"

"No, I could never have killed her. I'm still in love with her. That's the sad part. My wife suspected something at the end and confronted me. I lied to her. I said there were no other women. I looked her in the eye and lied to her. I guess I have some of J.W. in me because I can't live with this lie."

"Mr.Wilson," one of the deputies called to him. "Is everything all right?"

Wilson turned and saw the two men for the first time. He stood up and held the gun up aimed somewhere between me and the deputies. I could see the panic in the deputies' eyes as they both reached for their guns. Wilson aimed his weapon back at me. However, something in his eyes and in his expression indicated to me that he had no intention to shoot anyone.

I started to raise my hand to the deputies and tell them everything was okay. But it wasn't. Wilson swung his gun towards the deputies, and, in response, they fired. I heard three shots from their Glock 22, .40 caliber pistols, as I reached out grabbing Wilson's shoulder and pulled him to the ground.

"Quit shooting!" I shouted.

"What the hell, Mister, back away!" One of them yelled back at me.

I showed them both of my hands and moved back. Wilson was lying flat on the ground, his eyes shut. I couldn't tell if he was breathing. Blood seemed to be pouring out of his chest onto his shirt. His head was slightly inclined against his grandfather's tombstone.

One of the deputies was already on his radio calling in the

shooting and requesting an ambulance. The other deputy looked menacingly at me. I kept my hands where he could see them.

"He was going to shoot us! We had no choice!"

I could see the deputy was losing it. He had to wipe the spittle off his lips. The other deputy noticed him, too.

"Joey, cool down man. See if the guy is still alive."

Joey promptly knelt down and looked for a pulse.

"Yeah, he's got one but it's faint. Is the ambulance coming? It better hurry."

I figured it was time for me to speak up. "We'd better do what we can to stop the bleeding. I don't think he was going to shoot anyone but himself. Your arrival made it easier on him."

They both looked at me without understanding what I was saying, but they did respond to his injuries. Joey seemed to have gotten himself together and was already applying pressure to two of the bullet wounds. I leaned over and pressed on his shirt where the other seemed to be.

"I'll get the kit," the other deputy said, while he sprinted towards their vehicle. He came back carrying a sophisticated first aid kit. As soon as he arrived, I stepped aside and let the two of them work together. They were efficient as a team, and I could sense their urgency in their attempt to keep Wilson alive.

No one could blame them for shooting Wilson. What were they supposed to do when he swung that nasty looking revolver towards them? At the same time, my comment about him wanting to die had to affect both of them deep down inside.

I could hear an ambulance in the distance. I hoped it was coming here. Assuming Wilson was still alive, it meant the heart or a major artery wasn't hit. As long as one lung was still operating, and they could stem the loss of blood, Wilson would have a chance.

I noticed that the second deputy had turned on the patrol car's flashers when he retrieved the first aid kit. Good move, I thought. It will ensure the ambulance wouldn't accidentally drive past us.

A second and even a third siren could now be heard. Reinforcements were rapidly approaching. I looked back at Wilson. The deputies had fastened an oxygen mask to his face. His eyes were still shut, and there was no sign of any movement. The deputy named Joey was now talking to someone on the radio as they both continued with their efforts.

The first responding vehicle, another one of the sheriff's Ford Crown Victoria cruisers, slid in behind the three cars parked along the road. The ambulance arrived shortly after the cruiser and pulled halfway down the embankment.

I stepped further away from the scene, as it was now surrounded by nearly a dozen people. One of the recent arrivals, also decked out in a sheriff's black and khaki deputy uniform, started taking photos. At one point, I noticed he turned his camera toward me.

The medics made quick work of Wilson. He was placed on a stretcher and was on his way to the ambulance within minutes. A good sign I hoped.

As Wilson was being taken away, the two deputies involved in the shooting were walked off to the side by a third deputy that looked about my age. They huddled together, and I imagined the senior deputy was getting a quick explanation regarding what went down. For the moment, no one was paying any attention to me.

Once the ambulance drove off, most of the remaining people who responded to the scene started to depart the immediate area. Most got into their vehicles and drove off, but a couple were content to just sit in their vehicles. The deputy, who had the role of the photographer, was no longer taking pictures and had moved over to another concrete bench about ten yards away from the one Wilson had occupied a few moments earlier. He must have arrived with the senior deputy, who was still huddled with Joey and his partner.

I contemplated leaving since no one had made any attempt to talk to me, but I knew the senior deputy would most likely want a word with me once he finished up with the two shooters. Suddenly, the sound of thunder rumbled out of the clouds. The thunder helped to break up the conversation across the cemetery. All three deputies stepped back from each other and looked up. The senior deputy looked at me, said something to the other two, and then started walking in my direction.

As he approached me, the deputy, who had been taking all the pictures, stood up and joined him. The older deputy had a small notebook in his hands and did all the questioning.

"What's your name sir?"

"Jim West."

He looked around, then back at me. "What happened out here?"

"The guy, who was shot, is Jack Wilson. He came out here intending to shoot himself. That's his grandfather's grave right there. I followed him out here to talk to him, not knowing his intentions. When I arrived, he was sitting right there on the bench facing his grandfather's tombstone. I didn't know he had the gun until I was talking to him. He was having some marital issues and implied that he didn't want to face them. I was trying to reason with him when the deputies pulled up. They knew who he was as they called him by name. I think the idea came to Wilson at that time. All he had to do was point the gun at the deputies, and they would do the shooting for him. I don't think he had any intention of shooting me or the deputies, but he gave them no choice."

He was taking a few notes. I was hoping he wasn't going to make me go into detail about why I followed Wilson and what the problems were.

"West, I'll need you to follow us back to our office. Think you can do that?" I wasn't sure if that was really a question.

"Yes sir. But I do have an appointment for lunch," I lied, "will it take long?"

"No, we just need you to document what you have told me here and maybe answer a few more questions." I figured he wasn't telling me the whole truth either.

They let me drive my car. I followed them into New Braunfels to their offices. If they hadn't done it already, I had no doubt they were tracing my license tags and getting all the information they could on me prior to my arrival at their office.

The Sheriff's offices filled a large beige concrete building on old San Antonio Road. Once there, the deputy taking the notes immediately escorted me to a small interview room and left me there. The room was equipped with the obligatory one way mirror and small table with three chairs. This one also had a video camera mounted on the ceiling angled to monitor me or whoever might be sitting in the seat I now occupied.

There was nothing I could do but wait and think, so I tried to piece together what had happened that morning. There had to be more troubling Wilson than just the affair with Julie. Why or how did the responding deputies know who Wilson was? Why did they show up when they did? How the hell was I supposed to get anywhere in this case if my key witnesses keep getting shot and killed?

I didn't come up with any answers. Soon the door opened and the note-taking deputy walked in. He was accompanied by a heavy set female deputy rather than the one with the camera.

This time the female deputy had the notebook.

"West, if I didn't introduce myself earlier, my name is Duffy Smith, and this is Deputy Alspaugh. She's going to work with you to get your statement transcribed. Since she wasn't out there, you may have to get into a little more detail than you did with me."

I told him that was fine and Smith left the room. Over the next hour, Deputy Alspaugh picked through my brain and plucked out every little detail that was in any way relevant to the shooting incident. I was impressed with her thoroughness, despite not actually wanting to divulge Wilson's involvement with Julie and my own involvement with Randy's defense efforts.

As it turned out, it was good that I was open with her. Just before I left, she confided in me that the Sheriff's office had received a call from Wilson's office to look for him at the cemetery. Wilson had left a suicide note in his office for his wife, so everyone was out looking for him. One of the secretaries at the office had talked to Wilson's wife and discovered that Wilson would often come to the cemetery to talk to his grandfather when he was under a lot of stress.

She also let me know that Wilson was in critical condition but still alive.

I left the Sheriff's office a little more optimistic than when I arrived. I hoped Wilson could hang in there. It seemed so stupid that he wanted to throw his life away.

It also irritated me that he used two officers of the law to do his dirty work for him. If Wilson died, the shootings could torment the two for the rest of their lives.

In my statement when asked why I believed Wilson had not intended to shoot me or the deputies, I told them it was very simple. Wilson had all his fingers wrapped around the grip.

He never put a finger near the trigger. I could have also told them that when I looked into his eyes, as he raised his gun toward me, they were almost ghost like. There was no emotion. I could have told them that, but I didn't. They would have simply written my comments off as my imagination.

I swung the Mustang onto I-35 and headed south toward San Antonio. Large raindrops sparingly collided with my windshield. I knew they needed the rain down here. They always did, but this year it had been drier than normal.

Traffic was light during this lunch hour and I made good time getting back into the city center. The rain never did develop. I was in a hurry, but to do what, I hadn't decided. I needed to learn more about Wilson and his involvement with Julie. As with Al, my gut told me he wasn't her killer. But did he know who did shoot her or why? There had to be more to his desire to commit suicide than just the affair.

I needed to get back with Randy to get a better understanding of Julie's files and activities. Did he know Wilson or Al? I also needed to talk to Detective Reynolds to bring him up to speed. Could there be a DNA match with Wilson? I wanted to talk to the two guys at the condo again. Finally, I needed to bring the law firm up to date.

No one was going to be happy with my involvement in Wilson's shooting. It would be easy to point a finger at me for causing it all to happen. Unfortunately, despite all my efforts, I wasn't even getting any closer to proving someone else, besides Randy, was the shooter. From the standpoint of Randy's legal defense, I was certainly throwing a lot of crap into the tidy case the prosecutor may have thought he had against Randy. But, nobody was going to like the smell of that crap.

As I turned off the highway onto Commerce Street, my phone buzzed. I thought about ignoring it, but since it had a

210 area code, I knew it had to be related to Randy's case.

It turned out my decision regarding my next step was made for me. Detective Reynolds was on the phone.

"West, where are you?"

"Heading to your office," I lied.

"Don't come here. The lieutenant is fit to be tied. Do you know where the County Line restaurant is on the River Walk?"

"Yes, I walked by there the other day."

"Let's meet there in twenty minutes."

"I'll be there."

I had barely hung up the phone when it rang again. This time it was Cynthia Rich.

"Jim, what the hell is going on?"

"What do you mean?" One more lie today and my nose would probably start growing.

"My boss just got a call from Lieutenant Nosh. Needless to say Nosh was pissed, and now my boss is too. Nosh wants you off the case and out of town. My boss wants you in the office now."

"No way I can get to your office in the next hour, but I can get there around three. How's that?"

"Not good, but it may give him time to calm down. What is going on? Nosh told my boss that you have already gotten two people killed."

"Damn, did Wilson die?"

"I don't know who has died, Jim. I just know I wouldn't want to be in your shoes."

"Thanks. See you at three." I hung up.

I should have told Cynthia four instead of three o'clock. I needed some time to get this figured out. Too bad about Wilson, I was hoping he would pull through.

I parked back at the hotel. It was only a couple minutes

walk from the hotel, and I wasn't sure if I could find the County Line by driving to it. The river wound around so much, it would be tough to find the correct small road that went to that restaurant.

It was nearly one o'clock, but it seemed much later than that. A lot had gone on already, and the clouds made the day darker than it would normally be at this hour.

I crossed the road right in front of the hotel rather than walking down to the cross walk. To my left and slightly behind me, I noticed a tall thin man start crossing in the same direction. I was getting paranoid but decided to keep an eye on him anyway. I turned right once across the street and walked towards the River Walk. I didn't look back. I knew there was a place ahead where I could see if I was being followed. Plus, if he was following me, I didn't want to lose him or spook him. I had an idea.

I didn't get a good look at him, but he was tall and had on a dark base ball hat. As I went down the steps to the river walk, I ducked into a gift shop. Like all the others along the river, this shop was full of tee-shirts, hats, sun tan lotion and everything else a tourist might need. I walked over to a counter that displayed dozens of ball caps all adorned in different ways with the Spurs logo. The counter gave me a perfect view of anyone passing by outside.

I saw him just seconds after I found my place behind the counter. He was looking frantically around. I picked up one of the hats and went to a cashier to purchase it. I had them put the hat in a bag, and I walked out trying to look as nonchalant as I could. I didn't know if he saw me in the shop or spotted me after I came out and resumed my trek, but I sensed him behind me again shortly after I left the store.

Without further delay, I strode on to the County Line. I

looked around inside and, after not seeing Detective Reynolds, took a table adjacent to a window that allowed me to look out at the pedestrian traffic on the River Walk. The restaurant smelled of smoked brisket and ribs. I was hungry immediately.

It took me only a few minutes to find my follower. He was perched on a bench almost directly across the river. Although he was trying to look like he was just taking a break from the daily grind, every few seconds his eyes would look back at the entrance to the restaurant.

Reynolds walked in and looked around. His big frame was easy to see. I waved at him to let him know where I was. He sauntered over taking in the rest of the room as he did.

"Afternoon, Detective," I stood to shake his hand.

"I'm glad you didn't say good. You've stirred up a hornet's nest this morning."

"Not on purpose, I assure you."

"I believe you, but, like I told you, the lieutenant is fit to be tied." It was the second time he had said that, so I wasn't going to argue. "Jim, I know you are here to help a friend, but it might be best if you headed back home ASAP."

I started to protest, but a waiter came up with menus and took our drink orders. Once he left, I had to ask. "What specifically is it that I have done that has everyone mad at me?"

"Jim, I don't even know where to start. This morning I was updating the lieutenant on last night's murder. When I told him you had just talked to the victim yesterday afternoon, he said he knew. He said the vic had given him a call shortly after talking to you. The vic said you were trying to pin the killing on him."

"On whom?" I assumed the vic referred to Al, but who was 'him?'

"On the victim, this Al guy. He was acquainted with the

lieutenant because of another murder near the condo a couple of years ago. Anyway, that irritated the lieutenant. He already had some people check out what you were doing yesterday evening."

"That shouldn't have been hard. I was eating dinner at the hotel."

"Then this morning, we get a call from the Comal County Sheriff's Office checking up on you. Shortly after that, someone from the bank talked to someone at headquarters, who passed on to the lieutenant, that you were trying to blackmail this guy Wilson and may have been the reason for his shooting. Finally, the lieutenant thinks you are obstructing our investigation into the LaMoe murder because of a note you gave to Wilson asking him if he would rather talk to you or the police. To make a long story short, I think he's about to throw the book at you."

"I was trying to develop information. I didn't have any information that I was withholding. I tried to make it plain last night to you Frank. Anything I get, you get. I'll also share it with the lawyers, that is, if they're still speaking to me."

"I know, Jim. That's why I wanted to meet with you and talk. I know the lieutenant is off base here. I don't know why. He's usually a pretty easy going guy, but you must have hit a nerve. Maybe he liked this guy Al, I don't know."

"Frank, I don't blame him. It seems like everyone I talk to gets killed. Why would anyone want me around? One more person dies and that young mayor of yours will probably have me run out of town."

"Don't be too hard on yourself. I understand Wilson has a good chance to pull through."

That was a surprise. "That's great. Someone mentioned earlier that he had died. At least that's what I thought I heard." At the moment I couldn't remember who had told me.

"Why did you want to talk to Wilson?"

"I had pretty good information that he, like Al, had an affair with Julie. This affair might have stopped a few months ago, but I still thought it would be worthwhile to talk to him."

"Do you think he was involved with her killing?"

"No, and I don't think he was with her earlier that day."

"Then why the interest in talking to him, Jim?"

"Before I talked to him, I had no idea if he was involved in her killing or had any information that could help me out. It was only after I talked to him, that I came to the belief that Wilson wasn't involved in her killing. I don't think he has even seen her in months. He claims to still love her, but she stopped seeing him. She told him to go back to his wife. I think he was getting too serious with her, and that was a no-no."

"Doing a DNA comparison with him will at least let us know if he was or wasn't the guy who slept with her just before she was killed."

"I'll be amazed if you get a match. Unfortunately, I think there are a couple more men out there who Julie may have slept with in the past year. But, as of right now, I have no idea who they are."

"Still not buying the possibility that we already have the murderer in jail?"

"No. There are a couple things besides an eye witness that I don't think you have. Things that you would need to really prove your case, Frank. For example, no weapon to link Randy to the crime and no gunpowder residue on his hands. No one has told me you don't have the residue evidence, but if you had it, it would probably clinch your case."

"The residue could have been washed off. You know that Jim."

"If he knew to do so and knew to be very thorough about it.

It's not that he couldn't have washed it off, Frank, it's simply that not discovering any on him weakens your circumstantial case."

"So, Jim, what are you going to do next? I need some specifics so I can tell the lieutenant, if not the chief, that I have you under control."

"I'd like to talk some more to Wilson, but I'm not sure if he'll talk to me, or if he even has any more to say. Do you know which hospital he was taken to?"

"No, and I wouldn't recommend you go anywhere near him, if I did. You don't need to complicate your situation any more than it already is."

I wasn't sure how complicated my situation was, but I knew if I didn't keep digging, I might as well go home. I changed the topic.

"I guess I'll talk to some of Julie's acquaintances to see where that will lead me. Maybe she confided in one of them."

"Promise me one thing, Jim."

"What's that?"

"No more notes threatening anyone to talk to you or you're going to sic the police on them."

"That wasn't a threat, just an option." I smiled as I said it. I knew Detective Reynolds would know I was just quibbling.

The waiter returned with our drinks, and we both ordered the rib special. It turned out to be a good choice. Frank and I discussed possible motives for someone other than Randy being the killer. We went through all the ones that I had already considered. By the time we had finished lunch, none of the other motivations seemed any stronger or weaker than they had before.

As we stood up to leave, and after I promised to stay in touch and be an obedient citizen, I pointed out my tail still sitting across the river.

"See that guy over there?" I made sure he was seeing the right guy. "He followed me here from the hotel. I walked. The other night someone was following me around and, as you know, the guy who got hit by the truck was also following me. I'd love to know who he is, and why they are keeping an eye on me. They aren't with you, are they?"

"No. Are you sure you are being followed?"

"Yes. I have a suggestion. Let me leave first, and you watch and see what he does. If he's following me, will you stop him and find out who he is and maybe why he's following me? It has to be related to this case, but I can't imagine why."

"Okay, deal. But, if he doesn't follow you, I'm heading back to the office, so stay in touch."

"He'll follow me." I walked out of the restaurant and headed back towards my hotel. I walked fast and then stopped, pretending I was interested in something in a store window or a restaurant menu. I resisted the urge to look back for about two minutes into my hike. When I did, I saw Reynolds closing in on my tail. I looked up in the sky so as not to spook the guy and looked back again when I estimated Reynolds had enough time to get to him. He was there, but the guy tailing me broke into a run. Bad mistake. Reynolds was fast on his feet and caught the guy half way across a pedestrian overpass above the river. I imagined he had sacked a number of Big 12 quarterbacks scrambling to get away in just the same manner.

I trotted back to the bridge where a crowd was already developing to watch what was unfolding on an otherwise peaceful afternoon.

"Excuse me," I said to the gaggle of onlookers. "Let me through, I'm with the police officer."

The crowd parted reluctantly. By the time I made it to the

scene, Reynolds had the individual handcuffed and had finished patting him down.

"This the guy?"

"That's him, Frank. Why did he try to run?"

"Don't know. He says he doesn't speak English." Reynolds looked at the guy. "I don't believe him, but what can I do. I'll simply have to take him to jail. It would be a lot easier for him if he would just talk to us for a minute. Hell, if he would only tell us why he was watching you, we could probably let him go."

The guy looked at Reynolds and then me. He may have understood what Reynolds had said, but he didn't say anything.

"Any ID on him?" I asked.

"No, didn't even have a wallet."

"Curious, I would think most people would carry some form of ID."

I saw a couple of bicycle cops working their way through the crowd towards us. The gaggle was breaking up now as they realized there wasn't going to be anything exciting to watch.

"Your backup?"

"Yes, I called them as soon as I realized the jerk was following you. Hopefully, one of them can speak Spanish."

"You want me to stick around?"

"Yeah, just don't say anything unless asked."

"No problem." I didn't blame him. He was already putting himself out on a limb working with me instead of just trying to get rid of me. The lower my profile, the better it would be for both of us. I moved back a few steps and leaned against the pedestrian bridge's railing.

Both of the approaching police officers were tall and thin. I imagined riding around town on the bikes probably kept them in good shape.

"What's up?"

"This guy has been surreptitiously following that gentleman around. I wanted to know why, but when I approached him and identified myself, he started running. I tried to ask him what he was doing, but he won't say anything. Claims to not speak English."

One of the bicycle cops walked up close to my follower. "Que pasa, hombre?"

No response. The cop looked back at Reynolds. "Maybe he doesn't speak Spanish either."

His partner laughed. "You know damn well he can speak Spanish and probably fairly good English. He just doesn't want to talk to us. Detective, you want us to take him downtown? Maybe he'll talk to someone down there."

"Might as well. I would like to know who he is and why he was following this guy around. He probably won't tell us anything, but maybe his prints are on file."

As they walked off with their prisoner, I turned to Reynolds, "How are they going to get him downtown?"

"Not on their bikes, if that is what you mean. There's a patrol car out on the street. They'll walk him there and then come back and get their bikes."

"Can you hold him for following me around?"

"No, but refusing to identify himself to me gives me justification to have him taken down and fingerprinted. He'll be back on the streets by dinner if he's not identified as someone with an outstanding warrant. My guess is that he knows that already."

"Too bad, I sure would like to know why I'm being followed."

Reynolds grinned and shook his head.

"I'd better head back to the office and check on our friend

there. I'll give you a call if we get a name or an answer to your question."

"Thanks," I did appreciate his help. "And I'll keep you posted if I develop anything."

He left in one direction, and I took the other. There was no doubt in my mind that my being followed had to be related to Julie's murder. But why the surveillance? And why the sole use of Mexican Americans? Certainly Julie wasn't involved with the Mexican Mafia. I hadn't forgotten about Enrique's warning to me, but I never gave it much credence.

I had done a couple of things in my past to piss off the Mexican Mafia, but it didn't make sense that those incidents could be related to this one. There was no reference to any dealings with anything Mexican in any of her notes. But then, there was no mention of Al or Wilson in her files. They were just in the photos. The photos, I had better take another look at them. It could be that she kept pictures cut out of the newspaper or magazines to remind herself of her lovers but nothing else. That seemed a little odd to me too, but this whole case was already oozing into the weird category.

I headed back to the hotel. There were a lot of things I wanted to do, but first I would take another look at the items I brought back from the LaMoe's house.

I was back in my room at the hotel in less than ten minutes. I grabbed a Diet Coke from the refrigerator and put all the documents back on the table. I went to the pictures first. I set aside the photos of Wilson, Al and Tim Davis.

There were still nineteen different photos with multiple people in most of them. There was no way Julie was having affairs with all these people. In most cases, only one or two of the people in the pictures were identified. I was getting frustrated until the third from the last newspaper clipping had a picture of a Mr. Eduardo Royale receiving a plaque from San Antonio's Chief of Police. Standing next to Royale and snuggled in close was Julie. In the background were a number of policemen all decked out in their formal uniforms. Lieutenant Nosh was easy to see standing close by and looking at the camera. I thought I could make out Reynolds in the far corner.

The newspaper stated that Mr. Royale was receiving the plaque on behalf of his company, Royale Construction, which had made a large donation to a charity that supported policemen's widows and orphans.

Was this my connection? It would almost be too easy I thought. It made sense if I wanted to settle for stereotyping and profiling. A Mexican American owned construction company in south Texas, how could it not have bribery and corruption written all over it? Of course, I did know better. There was just as much chance that the company and Royale were clean. Even if they were clean, Royale, assuming he had an affair with Julie, and wanted to know where I was snooping and where I wasn't, could easily employ other Mexican Americans to keep an eye on me.

I looked at the final three pictures. No other Latinos, so I set them aside. I picked up the large Yellow Pages that was at the end of the kitchen counter and promptly found Royale Construction. Its headquarters was listed as being on North Alamo Street. From the lower street number, I figured it wasn't far from downtown.

It was already three o'clock, so I either needed to get to the law firm quickly or call and tell them I would have to come in later. I thought about just blowing them off completely but then decided it would not be wise to further alienate them. I called Nita's number and told her I was on my way.

When I arrived, the cute receptionist ushered me immediately back to one of the partner's offices. I expected it to be a Dilbert or a Carruzo, but it ended up being neither. As soon as I was in the large office the receptionist disappeared, closing the door behind me. Only Nita stood up.

"Jim, this is Austin A. Travis. He is one of the partners here at the firm."

I wondered if the A stood for Alamo. With a name like that, I would have expected a big guy. Travis wasn't. He also looked too young to be a partner. The large desk separating us made it difficult to shake hands. Travis never stood up, so I decided just to nod and took the one empty chair in the office.

"Jim, I received a disturbing call from the San Antonio police earlier today. They told me you are a loose cannon, and if we didn't rein you in, they were going to let you cool your heels for a few days downtown. I was going to tell them that they could have you, but Ms. Rich, here, said that she thought we should give you a second chance."

I looked at Cynthia. I never thought I had her in my camp. Either Nita had talked her into supporting me, or I had misread her. Both were possible, as I had made misreading the opposite sex a lifetime pastime. Nothing in her eyes gave me the answer.

"I appreciate that Austin. I think I'm making some progress."

"And getting a few people killed in the process?" A smart ass question like that needed no answer, so I simply ignored it.

"I've identified two men who have had recent affairs with Julie. I have suspicions on a couple more. All of them or their spouses could have motives. All would seem to have access. I think, with what I have, you'll have more than enough to discredit the prosecution's case."

"But are all these men dead now?" Travis almost sneered

when he asked this.

"No, only a guy named Al is." I was hoping Wilson was still hanging in there.

"Well, Jim, I know you have briefed these ladies on what transpired since you have arrived in town, but since I now have the police looking at me for answers, I suggest you tell me everything that you have been doing in the last twenty four or so hours."

Over the hour, I filled Travis in on my activities, and the four of us discussed what conclusions we could come up with for what was happening. We then focused on possible leads to pursue. By the time I left, I still thought Travis was a nerdy jerk, but I had to acknowledge that he wasn't stupid. All three impressed me with their questions and conclusions to my briefing.

None of them knew Eduardo Royale, but all three had heard of him. In addition to being a near billionaire, he was once an active community leader in San Antonio. He had sponsored numerous activities supporting the non-Caucasian majority in San Antonio and was reported to be very close with the Roman Catholic leadership in the city. He came from and had a large family. As a result, we all assumed he was well connected.

They asked me how I was going to approach Royale. I told them I wasn't sure. Actually, I knew I was going to wing it by using a lot of bluff and appealing to his Christian side. I just didn't need their advice or second guessing.

I left their law office and headed to Royale Construction. Luckily, the company's main office was in an office building easily assessable to all. If it had been out on a site somewhere, it would have made my job a lot harder. I didn't want to meet with him in his office, so I needed to find his parking spot. Once he left, I could follow him to his residence where I hoped to ultimately make contact with him.

The first part went easily enough. All the parking was out back and the reserved spots for the corporate senior leadership were clearly marked. Although a lot of the spots were empty, a large navy blue Cadillac sat in the spot reserved for the CEO.

I parked as far away from his car as possible without losing sight of it. After about an hour of sitting there, trying to stay awake, I saw a short, stocky, dark haired man walk out to the car and start it up. He was followed after a few minutes by two men who both walked to the rear of the Cadillac and climbed in. The car sped out of the lot, and I settled in about fifty yards behind him for the ride I hoped would take him straight home.

The Cadillac merged onto the inner loop, or 410, and headed west. I followed at a safe distance. After a few minutes it turned onto I-10 and headed northwest. We stayed on the highway for about fifteen minutes leaving most of the city behind us. There was a lot of traffic on the interstate, so I felt invisible. Finally, the car exited the highway and continued on the frontage road for about two miles before turning into an upscale residential development.

There was a nice looking country club off to my left and a golf course on my right. A sign announced we were entering The Dominion. Entering was not really an accurate statement as we rounded a bend and had to immediately stop at a manned security checkpoint. I was starting to think that there was no way I was getting into the neighborhood, when I noticed two men climbing out of a black Lincoln that had been parked off to the side by the gate shack.

I realized the car ahead of me was not moving and the security guard was watching me. So much for my invisibility. There was nothing for me to do but play the hand out. I rolled down my window as the two men approached. When they came near the car they separated, one going to my passenger side and one to my window.

"Why are you following Mr. Royale?" the one who came to my window asked. He did not sound threatening, but I knew he expected an answer. He was about five eight and looked like he was in good shape. The wind breaker was not needed for warmth, so I figured he was armed. Were these guys Royale's private security, or was this just an added perk for living out here?

"My name is Jim West, and I have an extremely urgent matter to discuss with Mr. Royale. I mean him no harm. It really is a matter of life or death, but not mine or his. I don't think I can discuss the matter in any more detail with anyone else without first getting Mr. Royale's consent."

"Why don't you call his office and make an appointment?"

"Because I knew that without divulging the details of my reason for wanting to talk to Mr. Royale, I wouldn't get past his staff."

He looked at me for a few seconds and then walked up to Royale's car. He talked to someone inside the car, probably Royale, for about fifteen seconds, and then returned to my window.

"Mr. Royale says you are to follow his car." The security guy nodded toward his partner on the other side of my car. "But, he goes along with you as your passenger. We don't want you to get lost."

"Fine with me," I said.

The guy turned and started walking back to his car.

"Hey!" I shouted, and he turned around. "Thanks."

I unlocked the car, and my passenger climbed in.

The Cadillac started moving again, and I hurriedly moved the Mustang up close to it. I glanced over at my passenger.

Blond hair cut close, not as tall as me but he had the build of a weight lifter. He also looked a little familiar. He was looking at the military sticker on my windshield.

We slowed for a second security checkpoint and then moved on through.

"You in the military before?" So my passenger could talk.

"Yes, I served in the Air Force."

"What did you do?"

"Spent twenty years with the Office of Special Investigations."

"Damn! I thought you looked familiar. I spent six years in OSI myself. I'm Bert Falls." The name, like the face, seemed familiar, but I never really knew him. Bert had a big smile on his face. He looked like he had just found an old friend.

"I'm Jim West. How did you end up doing this?"

"I was assigned to the Anti-terrorism Specialty Team when this job offer came. It was too good to turn down, plus my fiancé's family was from here. It's pretty easy work, and Mr. Royale's a great guy. What were you doing following him?"

"It's like I said, I just need to talk to him. I'm temporarily working on a matter with a law firm in town. How did you all get on to me?"

"You know they trained us well. Two of us from OSI started working for Royale at the same time and have helped with the training here. A video surveillance of the parking lot had you coming in and just sitting there. No big deal by itself, but when you pulled out just behind Mr. Royale, we got suspicious. We passed it on to the driver who started watching for you. When he saw you get onto I-10, he knew there was trouble. Mr. Royale has had some issues with some bad people, especially with his company's operations south of the border. But you'll like Mr. Royale."

"That's good to hear because I'm not too sure he'll like what I'm going to bring up. Don't get me wrong. I'm just looking for information, but it may not be a topic he will want to be made public."

"Well, whatever it is, I think you'll find him okay. Just stay away from his son, Fernando. He's a nasty one. The old man doesn't know what to do with him. He's got four other kids, all moved out and doing well, but Fernando hasn't grown up. Still lives at home and, if it wasn't for his old man's influence, would have been in jail long ago."

"Hopefully, I'll just need five minutes of the old man's time, and then I'll be on my way."

We pulled onto a driveway that circled in front of a beautiful two story mansion. Bert jumped out and escorted me into the house close behind Royale's entourage. The large foyer area of the house was impressive. The expensive looking marble flooring was brightened by a huge crystal chandelier hanging high above it. There was a heavy, dark wood, narrow table lined against the wall to my left. I figured the foyer itself would sell for more than my house back in Clovis.

Bert led me to a small office just inside and to the right of the foyer, so I didn't get to see the rest of the house.

"Have a seat, Jim, and here's my card. Let me know if I can ever do anything for you. I mean it, I miss the old days."

I thanked him for his help and told him I would. I grinned as he left, thinking that he was probably in his early thirties and his "old days" probably weren't that old yet.

I walked over to a large book shelf and was looking at the titles when my perusal was interrupted by a female voice behind me.

"Mr. West, Mr. Royale will see you now. Please follow me. And Mr. West, his dinner is being brought up from the kitchen now, so please limit your time to five minutes."

"Sure." I hoped five minutes would be enough time, but I considered myself lucky to get this far so I had no complaint.

My escort was a serious looking woman with reddish brown hair pulled back tightly into a bun on the back of her head. She was a thin five foot five and was decked out in black slacks and a dark green blouse. I wondered what else she did here.

She led me a short distance further down the same hall I had already seen to another larger room that was also set up as an office or study. Royale was seated behind his desk, talking to a young man who, based on the similarities in their appearances, I took for a son.

"Oh, excuse me, sir. They said you were ready…"

Royale cut her off. "That's okay, Cindy, bring Mr. West in. Fernando was just leaving."

Fernando looked at me and then back at his Dad. He didn't look very happy, but he left without saying anything to me or to Cindy.

"Do you want me to stay, sir?"

"No, I don't think I'll need you, Cindy. Besides, I have it on good authority that Mr. West poses no threat to me." He smiled at me when he said this and put out his hand to shake.

I stepped forward and accepted it, introducing myself. I sat in the chair offered me, directly across the large desk from Royale.

"Bert has passed on word to me that you are an okay guy. So, Jim, what is it that's so important you have to meet with me in this way?"

"I was asked to come to San Antonio by Randy LaMoe." I closely watched Royale's face for any reaction as I spoke. "As you may have heard, he has been charged with his wife's murder. I don't think he is guilty and have been working on the theory that there may have been other men in his wife's life who may also have had a motive to kill her."

His eyes narrowed and his forehead creased a little.

"Continue, please."

"I have come up with some documents that have implicated a few men who may have had an intimate relationship with Mrs. LaMoe."

"West, if you have come here to try to blackmail me, then you are a fool, and Bert is a very bad judge of character."

"I am not here to blackmail you. I'm here looking for information. I need to know what you know about Julie LaMoe. How well did you know her? When did you last see her? What theories do you have on her death? That is all I came here for, not to blackmail you."

He paused for a minute before speaking.

"What do you intend to do with any information that I might be able to provide to you, Jim?" Back to Jim from West. A good sign, I hoped.

"Use it to prove Randy didn't murder his wife."

"Listen closely then, Jim, and don't expect me to put this in writing or ever discuss it with anyone again. I liked Julie. She was refreshing, smart and to me, sexy. I worked with her a lot on two different charities I support. She was a hard worker, and she was fun to work with. On one occasion, two years ago, we both had too much to drink and spent the night together in the Sheraton downtown. Never since. I haven't seen or talked to her in at least a month. I was saddened by her death. I would very much like to see her killer brought to justice. If you say her husband was not the killer, and I too have my doubts that he was, then let me pass on another theory."

Royale sat back in his chair, tilted his head upwards and closed his eyes.

"My theory, Jim, is more than a theory, although I have no proof. I have many friends in the city and elsewhere. I hear a lot of things. I pay people to let me know things. I think it is possible that Julie was killed because she saw something. Something she was not supposed to see. I would expect that this thing she observed was when she was with another man. I do not want to say who this other man may be, but I would guess if you have documents, I think that was your word, then you may have information implicating him. I also think you may be putting yourself in grave danger by pursuing this matter, Jim. Very grave danger, do you realize this?"

I told him I did. I briefly related the story about the scorpions, the trash truck and being followed. He grinned at the story about the scorpions.

"I tell you what, Jim. I might be able to keep some of these nuisance things from happening again, but that is not where the true danger comes from. You need to understand that."

I started to respond, but he cut me off.

"That is all the time I have, Jim. I've already said too much. Remember, I will not repeat these words to anyone again. Good luck and do be careful."

With that he stood up and the door opened behind me. Cindy was standing there.

"Cindy will escort you to your car, Jim."

"This way, Mr. West," Cindy instructed and started walking without checking to see if I was following. I walked behind her while my mind tried to analyze the conversation I had with Royale.

What "things" had Royale heard? It was believable that he had sources throughout the city, but so did the police. Why would he develop any information that would be any different than what the police could develop? Perhaps, I thought, because the police weren't looking for any new information.

And why did he call the scorpions and the people following me nuisance things? Hell of a nuisance, all right. But according to Royale this wasn't from where the real danger would come. Why not and how could he know this?

I was outside, approaching my car. Behind me, I could hear Cindy tell me to have a good night. I just waved over my shoulder and then heard the door shut. My mind was absorbed in thought, and I didn't hear the sound of an approaching person until it was too late.

I looked over my shoulder and was roughly shoved into the side of my car.

"Stay still and nothing will happen to you." The English was good, but the voice had a Mexican accent. A hand quickly frisked me. I was spun around. In addition to the man close to me, four young men were standing about fifteen feet away. One of the four had his hand inside a plastic shopping bag with something pointed at me. Hopefully, it was just a bottle of Jack Daniels, but I doubted it.

"What do you want?" I asked Royale's son who stood in the middle of the group.

"I need to talk to you but not here. Let's go for a ride."

I motioned to my car, but he shook his head and pointed to a Cadillac Escalade parked about twenty yards away.

"Give your keys to Juan. I don't want you coming back here. He'll follow us in your car."

I quickly debated the situation. I could shout out and maybe draw someone's attention from inside, but that would probably just delay this 'discussion' that Fernando wanted. I didn't think he would take me from the house and then do something stupid to me. Certainly going through the checkpoints, if not leaving the grounds, someone would see us leave together.

"Okay," I tossed my keys to the guy who had frisked me and walked towards the Escalade.

"In the back with me," Fernando instructed.

I hopped in, and the four of us drove off. I looked behind to make sure my Mustang was following. It was.

"What were you doing? Trying to shake down my old man?"

"No. If you heard anything, then you know I wasn't."

"I heard enough, mister. My old man is a good guy, but he's soft. He don't need some stranger coming to his house trying to shake him down."

"As I said, I didn't try to shake him down. I have no reason to cause trouble for him or anyone in your family."

We drove out of the neighborhood and took a side road that headed away from the city. We were soon out of sight of other houses and in an area that looked like civilization hadn't yet made use of it.

"Where are we going?"

"I just want to show you something."

We rode along in silence for about ten minutes. The driver pulled the Escalade off the paved road onto a dirt one. I didn't like the looks of what was happening but the guy riding shotgun had turned to keep an eye on me. He was the same guy that had the plastic bag earlier.

I figured the best course of action was to try to stay cool. We hit a couple of rough spots, and I hoped the Mustang didn't bottom out on some of the ruts in the road. The headlights were still behind us.

Suddenly we came to a dead end. The driver pulled the car to a stop under a huge live oak tree.

"Come with me."

I followed Fernando out of the car and into the underbrush.

I was surrounded by four men with flashlights, so picking my way along the partially overgrown trail we were on wasn't hard.

"I used to come here as a kid and play. It's a neat place. This whole area belongs to a friend of the family. What I want to show you is just up ahead."

No one else said anything.

We rounded a particularly thick patch of sage and mesquite trees, and the ground dropped off in front of us.

"See those?" Fernando pointed at five small wooden crosses that stood along the ledge about ten yards away. "They represent five people who got in my way. Each went over at that point. The drop over there will kill you. Over here where you are it's a lot safer. If you cause me or my family any more problems, mister, there'll be six crosses standing there. Understand?"

"Yes." What else was I going to say?

Suddenly, I was grabbed from behind. I twisted and jerked my body downward to throw my attacker off balance. I succeeded in tossing him over my shoulder only to be grabbed by the other three men. Despite my struggles, I was flung backwards and over the precipice behind me. The initial fall was only a few feet, but the slope was such that I tumbled and bounced off rocks for about thirty more feet. Despite the darkness, I could see the rocks and small bushes in my way as I bounded down to the creek bed. I did my best, while bouncing and rolling down the slope, to avoid hitting my head against anything hard.

I came to a stop with my left leg and foot dangling in a small pool of stagnant, warm water. The rest of me laid winded on a large slab of flat rock staring up at the quarter moon. I was more angry than hurt. I sat up and inspected myself. Bruised and scratched, I was lucky I had suffered nothing more serious.

I looked back up to where I was tossed off the top of the ragged rock wall that lined the creek bed. It didn't look that high or that steep. I started to stand up when I felt a sharp burning in my right leg just above the knee. After the incident earlier in the week, the first thing that came to mind were scorpions. However, a quick and not-to-smart brushing of the area with my hand helped me to realize I must have bounced against some cacti on the way down.

I sat there in the dim moonlight and extracted a half dozen cactus needles from my leg and one from my hand. I gingerly canvassed the rest of my body with my hands. No more surprises, so I stood up and again surveyed the route I would need to take to get back up to where I hoped my car would be waiting.

I heard something move further down the creek bed. A deer or coyote, I thought. I wondered if there had been mountain lion sightings in the area. I doubted it, but even if any lived in the area I imagined they were rare. Apparently not wanting to waste a good opportunity to further scare myself, I started to worry about rattlesnakes. They're nocturnal hunters and probably common in the area. I had a long hike in the dark ahead of me.

"Don't spook yourself, Jim, my boy. Just get back up to your car, and let's get out of this place." I murmured to myself.

Chapter 14

I started up the incline which turned out steeper than it appeared. Suddenly, I heard a rustling above. I stopped and saw a beam of light scan the area above me.

"West! West! Can you hear me? Are you out there?"

It took me just a couple of seconds to realize it was Bert Falls.

"I'm down here. Shine that flashlight on the ground in front of me."

I waited until the beam of light hit me in the face and then shot down to the area in front of me. I followed it up to the top.

"Jim, are you okay?"

"Yes. Thanks for bringing the flashlight. I could have used your help about ten minutes ago."

"I know, sorry about that. I saw that jackass drive you away from the house, and I knew there would be trouble. I followed but couldn't get here quick enough to prevent them from roughing you up."

"They didn't rough me up. They just tossed me off the side over there. I think they just wanted to make a point."

"I didn't think they would do anything serious. He's a worthless son, but you had just come from visiting his dad in his house. Even he's not that dumb."

"My guess, Bert, is that he listened at the door to the first minute or two of my conversation with his Dad and got the wrong idea as to why I was there."

"You're probably right. I saw your car when I was walking

back here. It didn't look any worse for wear. I'll walk you to it. It's hard to see in the dark."

I was grateful Bert had come to my rescue, albeit a little late. My guess was that he didn't want the son to know he was following them and rightly theorized that no real harm would come to me. I didn't blame him. I might have played out the hand the same way if our roles were reversed. Plus, he was right. In the darkness, I doubted that I would have found my car without his assistance.

"It's over here, a little off the dirt road. I only saw it because their headlights hit it for a second when they drove out. I parked a little past where they pulled in and walked in from there." Bert nodded towards the end of the dirt road.

We walked over to my Mustang. The keys were in the ignition, and the car looked fine. I drove Bert back to his vehicle which turned out to be an old jeep.

"I've had this old thing for ten years now. I simply can't get myself to part with it. My fiancé used to say if it came down to either the jeep or her, I'd keep the jeep. I guess she was right. We never did get married, and I still have the jeep." He laughed when he said this, but I got a feeling it wasn't a complete joke.

"Follow me out, and I'll get you onto I-10. From there you should be able to find your way back."

"Thanks again, Bert, I owe you lunch sometime."

By the time I got back to the hotel it was nearly ten. I walked through the lobby and had just pushed the elevator button when I noticed Lee making a bee line toward me. I smiled at her, but I wasn't sure if the look back at me was a pleasant one. The elevator doors opened at the same time she made it to me. She took me by the arm and walked me into the empty elevator.

"What's up?" I asked.

She started to say something and then stopped. She stepped back and gave me the once over. "What happened to you?"

"Long story, I fell down a river bank."

She looked at me skeptically. "We need to talk. You haven't been totally honest with me."

"What do you mean?"

"The police came here today asking about you. They didn't talk to me. I wish they had, but they didn't. They talked to my boss. Apparently, they said you've been messed up with a couple of killings and that you are trouble. My boss now thinks you know more about the scorpion incident than you let on and wants you out of the hotel."

"I wish I knew more than I do about the killings."

"What's going on Jim?"

"Come on up to the room and I'll fill you in. I haven't lied to you Lee. There just wasn't a good reason to break the confidentiality of what I've been doing for a friend. Maybe it's time I do. I could certainly use any ideas you may have."

When we got to the room, I offered Lee a drink, but she declined. I excused myself and went to the bathroom to clean up. My face looked a mess, but that just meant it matched the rest of my appearance. I had a nasty bruise forming above my right eye, and a small gash had excreted a small amount of blood, now dried on my skin. The skin on my right cheek had been scraped and showed off a red rash. I washed my face which removed the dirt and blood but seemed to brighten the red.

My jean's leg had dried but now had an ugly brown look to it. The right leg was torn at the knee. If Lee hadn't been waiting for me I would have taken a long shower to try to get my mind around everything. As it was, I just shed the jeans and put on the white hotel bathrobe.

"That looks better," Lee commented when I walked back into the room. "I'm sorry to trouble you, Jim. You look like you just want some sleep, but my boss is really pissed. He thinks you have played us all along, and, in the process, you may be putting our guests in danger."

I grabbed a beer from the refrigerator and sat down at the table. "Come over here and sit, Lee. I'll tell you what I can. There are just a few names I need to keep out of it, for now, but I'll tell you what I can, and you can share it with your boss. I'm also open to any thoughts you may have."

She came over and sat opposite me, looking official, like she was interviewing a prospective employee. I smiled at her, and I could see she fought the urge to smile back. At least she didn't grab a tablet and start taking notes.

I started from the beginning, the phone call from Ms. Cynthia Rich.

"Why did Randy think you could help?"

"He knew I spent twenty years getting to the truth, and he wasn't confident anyone local was going to make the effort."

She wanted me to elaborate, so I did briefly before moving on. I told her about the consensus everyone shared regarding Randy's guilt.

"How many affairs do you think she had?" She asked after I mentioned the few that I had confirmed. I hadn't given her any names, and she politely didn't ask.

"I have no idea. The whole thing is bizarre."

"I could never live a life like hers. I never fooled around on my husband. Looking back now, there were a few times I could have, maybe should have, but I didn't. She was playing with fire."

"She certainly was."

Lee asked again if I knew who put the scorpions in the bed. I told her I still didn't have any idea. I told her about the truck almost running me over, about being followed, and about the people dying or nearly dying around me. I mentioned my discussion with Royale without naming him and omitted my run-in with his son.

"Well, Jim, I'm no detective, but it certainly seems to me someone doesn't want you messing with this case."

"Me too, but who?"

"Maybe the real killers."

"The obvious conclusion, Lee, and I'm hoping the police will pick up on that. But, if they did, it would blow their current theory and cause them a lot more work. Two things no police department ever wants to happen."

"Aren't you afraid something may happen to you?"

A lot of things had already happened to me since my arrival, as I had just told her, but I knew what she meant.

"Of course, but my only other option is to drive away, and let Randy take the hit. I can't do that."

She looked at me quietly for a few seconds. I couldn't tell if her stare meant I was a fool for sticking around or that she admired me. I was hoping for the second.

Before either of us said anything, my cell phone rang. I went into the bedroom and picked it up off the dresser.

"Jim, it's Cynthia. Randy's been stabbed. He's been taken to a hospital, but they aren't confident he'll make it through the night."

"What? How did that happen?" I nearly shouted back through the phone.

She explained that she didn't have all the details, but she told me where he was taken and how to get there.

"And Jim, Randy insisted that someone get in touch with you. He wants to talk to you. I don't know what shape he is in, but I wanted to pass on his message to you in case you want to head over there. Nita is already heading there."

As soon as I hung up, I started getting dressed. I had to put on yesterday's slacks and the last clean golf shirt I had brought along.

"What's up?" Lee shouted from the table.

"Randy's been stabbed."

I was dressed and out of the bedroom in a flash.

"I need to go. Tell your boss that I don't think that my being here puts any of the guests in danger, but that I'll check out tomorrow. And Lee, thanks."

She looked at me like she wanted to say something, but I didn't wait. I was out the door and gone.

It took me fifteen minutes to get to the hospital, but I didn't need to rush. Randy was in surgery, and the staff figured it would be at least another hour before anyone could speak to him. I found a cup of coffee and a place to sit and wait. I hadn't seen Nita, so I called her. She was on a different floor. She told me to sit tight and that she would find me.

She showed up just a few minutes after we hung up. After our quick hello's, Nita squinted her eyes and asked what happened to my face.

"Nothing serious. Kind of gives me the rugged look, don't you think?" I knew what happened to me wasn't a joking matter, but I didn't want to get into my run-in with Royale's son at the moment. "More importantly, how in the world was someone able to stab Randy while he was in jail?"

"That's being looked at right now. Another prisoner did it, but which one is anyone's guess. It shouldn't have happened."

Now that was an understatement.

"I thought you all were working to get him bailed out of jail?"

"We have been. It's not that easy in a homicide case, you know. The judge's initial thought was to not authorize him bail. We delayed that, and there was a good chance we were going to get a favorable ruling tomorrow."

"What is known about the stabbing?"

"Only that there was a mistake made. He was given exercise time in a part of the jail that was also being used at the same time by a group of prisoners already serving sentences. There was a scuffle, and the next moment he was on the ground surrounded by a group of men. They started waving for help at the guard post and security cameras. You never see the makeshift knife on the security monitors, and because they swarmed over him, there is no way to see who stabbed him. Understandably, everyone in the group is claiming innocence and saying that he must have fallen on his own weapon."

"You know that's not possible. You learn how to make a 'shiv' in prison. It's not something Randy would have learned out in his world."

"I know. The problem with this for the cops is that, to the best of everyone's knowledge, none of the other prisoners knew Randy or would have any reason to harm him. The other problem is that everyone else there belongs to a tight knit prison gang. My contact at the jail doesn't expect any of them to change their story. If one of them did do it, it was a planned, well organized hit. They knew when Randy was going to be there and knew just how to get to him while avoiding the security cameras."

"Nita, the staff I talked to here wouldn't give me their opinion of Randy's chances. Have you heard anything?"

"Yes, I talked to one of the doc's who is in there right now.

Right before he went into surgery, he told me that Randy should pull through. Of course that statement came with the usual caveat they always say. But he seemed fairly positive."

Nita looked like she'd had a rough day. Her hair needed combing, and the faded yellow tee shirt she had thrown on over her jeans looked a couple of sizes too big. I offered to get her a cup of coffee but she declined.

"Jim, why would someone want Randy killed?"

"His death might let the police close out Julie's murder without doing much more work. If someone else did kill Julie, that person would benefit if the investigation was closed. But that begs the question, which one of Julie's lovers, or even just an acquaintance of hers, would have enough clout to order a hit inside a prison?"

Even as I was talking, Royale came to mind. I still didn't think he was involved, but he probably had the money and connections to make it happen. I would have to rethink his role in this.

"Maybe Randy was involved in international smuggling or something. He was flying routes in and out of Mexico City. Maybe they both were involved and they double crossed their partners."

"I doubt that Nita. It would help to explain everything, but it's a long shot, and I doubt it has any legs. When we get to see Randy, I'll ask him outright. At this point I don't think he'll lie to us. If he was participating with some smuggling operation, he'll tell us."

"If he dies, Jim, it would also put the end to our defense efforts and your investigation into the facts around Julie's murder. That may also be the goal of whoever is behind this."

"Sounds more likely to me as the motive."

"But they didn't succeed," Nita looked deep in thought as

she said this. "Do they try again or back off for a while?"

"I think they would almost have to back off now. The authorities will have to have someone keeping a close eye on Randy around the clock for a while. They'll get a black eye from this one attempt and certainly won't want anything else to happen to him."

Changing the subject, Nita asked me how my meeting with Royale went. I told her it went well and that I didn't think he was involved with her murder. I didn't bring up my joyride with his son.

"Jim, every time you discover someone new who could be a suspect and help get Randy off the hook, you keep saying that you don't think they are involved. What do you think is going to jump out at you when or if you do end up talking to the real killer?"

"Excellent question and one for which I don't have an answer. It's just none of them have given me any vibe at all that they may have done it or even know anything about why Julie was murdered. Nita, I realize I don't do this kind of stuff for a living anymore and that I could be wrong. I'm just passing along my opinions."

"I know," she said as she slid back in her chair and closed her eyes.

I got up and walked out of the room and down to surgery. The operation was still going on. I told the head nurse where Nita and I would be waiting and asked again for a shout as soon as we could speak to Randy.

By the time I got back to our waiting room, I could hear the steady breathing of a sleeping attorney. I moved over to a large cushioned chair and tried to get some sleep myself. Unfortunately, and not for the lack of desire, sleep was out of the question for me. My mind was full of questions and I knew there was a lot of work that needed to get done.

I still hadn't talked to most of the friends whose names Randy had given me. There were a dozen or so more newspaper and magazine photos that needed to be analyzed for possible other lovers. A dozen! Certainly she didn't have that many other men in her life. Some of the pictures were older so maybe some of the men had been involved with her in years past or had moved away. On the other hand, many of the photos had more than one man in them. Did any capture more than just one lover in the picture?

I would need a week to run down all the possibilities. In another day or two I would have to drive back to Clovis, check on things, repack some clothes and then return to San Antonio for the long haul. I figured Randy would be in the hospital for a couple of days. He would understand.

A vacuum was slowing working its way down the hall towards the room we occupied. The noise had not yet affected Nita's sleep.

What would make a women fool around so much on her husband? Silly question, I thought, as I had known a few men who thought every business trip or TDY was a free shot at sex with a stranger. I guess it was just in some people's genes, didn't matter if you were male or female.

My mind crept back towards my own failed marriage. Not a memory I enjoyed revisiting so I was happy when the vacuum and its master moved into the doorway of the room we occupied. Nita sat up with a start and the cleaning lady turned off the vacuum.

"Oh, sorry," she proclaimed, "I didn't know anyone was in here."

"That's okay," I told her and then turned to Nita. "What are we doing here? There's little chance we'll be able to talk to him before morning anyway. Why don't we call it an evening and try again in the morning?"

"Probably a good idea, but let's check by surgery again before we leave."

We strolled down to the nurse's station right outside surgery and checked back in. The place looked quiet except for the young blond nurse sitting behind the counter, giggling and talking to the young policeman leaning against the front of the counter.

Nita asked the nurse about Randy's status.

"I believe they are finishing up right now, let me see if I can get one of the doctors to speak to you." She jumped up with more energy than I've had for a while at this time of the day and disappeared behind the swinging doors that led into surgery.

The young cop glanced at me and spent more time looking at Nita. I was about to say something to break his stare when the young nurse popped back out, getting all of our attention.

"Doctor Vanderbilt will be right out."

As if he was listening for his announcement, the doors swung open and Dr. Vanderbilt walked through them. He looked at all three of us as though he was trying to discern to whom he should address his comments.

"How's Randy doing?" I asked.

"He'll pull through but he received a nasty wound. The ribs diverted the blade just enough to miss the heart and fortunately the major arteries and veins. Ripped up part of the lung and there was a lot of bleeding. That's what took so long. But we got to him in time and there should be a full recovery."

"When do you think we'll be able to talk him?" Nita asked.

"He's going to be fairly heavily sedated for the next twelve hours. We need to make sure all the bleeding has stopped. Until then he won't be able to talk to anyone. Early afternoon tomorrow is my guess, maybe later."

"Doc, any chance the wound could have been self-inflicted or caused by a fall?"

"Anything's possible, but highly, no, I should say very highly unlikely. In my opinion, the patient was very forcefully stabbed."

I turned to the young policeman. "Will someone be here with him?"

"Until I'm told otherwise. I get off at midnight but another officer is replacing me then."

"Thanks," I said to both of them and looked at Nita.

She turned to the nurse and told her thanks. Looking at the two of them, I realized Nita probably wasn't much older than the nurse.

I walked Nita out to her car. We didn't talk much. I wanted to ask her if I could buy her a drink but kept my mouth shut. Hell, I was old enough to be her father. Upon reaching her car, she turned to me and told me she would stay in touch with the hospital and give me a call as soon as it was practical to talk to Randy. I told her that was fine and thanked her for calling me earlier with the news of his stabbing.

I turned and began to walk away as she started the car but stopped when she spoke to me through the open window.

"Jim. You know, if your theory is correct that it was an ordered hit on Randy and not done because of some double cross, then I think you better be really careful. As we agreed, his death could have stopped further investigation into Julie's murder. But he's still alive and now will be harder than ever to get to. To me that means that the next logical target would be the person turning over the rocks trying to expose the true killer. And that person could only be you. We both know the police haven't done much since they focused on Randy."

"That thought has already occurred to me, Nita, but thanks for the heads up."

She nodded and drove off. She was sharp but her comments only reinforced what had been on my mind for a while now. Someone had been trying to scare me into leaving. That hadn't worked, so they tried to eliminate what had brought me to San Antonio in the first place. Now that had failed, too. The next logical step, if they decided to take it, was to get rid of me.

I looked around the dark parking lot. My car was way over in the west lot. Rather than walk around the building in the now ominous looking shadows, I opted to head back in and cut through the hospital to get to the other side.

I found my car without incident and headed back to the hotel.

Chapter 15

Once back in the hotel room, I sat back down at the table and began again what I had started hours earlier. It was late but I didn't feel like sleeping. I spread the pictures I had taken from Julie's file across the table. A couple had no identifying data with them. I set them aside. Two others had enough detail in the accompanying narrative to indicate they were taken nearly five years ago. I set those aside, too. Next, I created a separate pile for the pictures that depicted the men whom I had already checked into.

I focused on the remaining group. There was a newspaper clipping of a group of adults lounging around a pool with a couple of men throwing a beach ball back and forth in the pool. The clarity of the individuals in the picture was poor. I read the partial narrative that had not been clipped off below the picture and realized that the picture and narrative may have come from an advertisement for the LaMoe's condo complex.

There were a couple of women stretched out on recliners, but I couldn't be sure if either of them was Julie. There was no way I would be able to identify any of the men either. I started to toss it into the trash can when I realized there was a man sitting in a chair on the far side of the pool facing the camera. My first thought was that he was made to look like a lifeguard. A little bit of false advertisement, no doubt, since the pool had no lifeguard. But, if I were a betting man, despite the poor quality, I would wager a twenty that the man in the chair was Al.

I put the picture in the pile with the other resolved ones.

Three of the remaining photos depicted people mingling at functions for various charitable causes. The pictures did not appear to focus on anyone specific. The more I looked at the pictures the more depressed I got. I was initially excited by the thought that Julie had kept photo reminders of past loves. I still believed that was the case, but I was also now hit with the realization that her focus had nothing necessarily to do with the camera's focus. What this meant was any of the dozens of men on the pictures was a possible former lover.

"Damn, Julie, why couldn't have you been more like a teenager and circled in a red heart the men you conquered. That would have helped Randy and me a lot."

I stood up frustrated, walked over to the refrigerator, grabbed a beer and went back to the table. I stacked all the clippings and moved them to the center of the table. Staring at the pile of newspaper and magazine photos, I realized that I had to come up with a whole new approach. It would take me weeks to identify and follow up on all the men in the pictures.

After another thirty minutes of staring at the pile on the table, it was all I could stand. I went to bed.

The next morning I got up at seven and went out for my morning hike along the River Walk. The sky was already a bright blue and the sun reflected mirror-like off the taller buildings that looked down at the San Antonio River below. Still in the shade, the river had a deep, dark blue hue.

I maintained a quick pace, not so much for the exercise, but more importantly to facilitate my spotting anyone who might be following me. There was no one out there.

I had come up with a new plan, but I still needed to convince myself that it wasn't as dumb as I suspected it was. On the positive side, my new plan didn't entail a lot of hands on work developing new evidence and talking to more people. It was even one that could get quick results. However, it was also one that could ensure that I found myself in the crosshairs of the killer's sights.

The plan was really quite simple and was based on the reality that things started happening to me almost as soon as I arrived in San Antonio. Early on I had placed the occurrences in the nuisance category. The events had since escalated to the point where Randy was almost murdered. I was focusing on the events and trying to determine the "why" and the "who."

The "why" had become apparent to me, but the "who" behind the acts was still a mystery. I had been spending a lot of time trying to identify the person or persons and had come up with zilch. Julie's proclivity to collect lovers was beyond a doubt more effective than my ability to uncover them. And, I didn't think I had weeks to resolve the case.

Somehow, the killer had been aware of my arrival and purpose here from my first day in San Antonio. That had to mean that someone within the law firm, the police, or the county jail had to be the source of the information that reached the killer. It seemed implausible, but the killer could be someone within those organizations. Just as possible, it could be someone outside those organizations who had a seemingly innocent, close relationship with someone in one of them.

A spouse? Janitorial service? Drinking buddy? The press? I had to forcefully stop myself from wasting time on guesses. It seemed to me that the best thing to do was to set myself up by giving the killer more of a reason to come after me. I had already decided that with the failed attack on Randy, I had now become the main target, anyway. So how much more danger could I cause myself by just raising the killer's urgency. If he felt rushed maybe he wouldn't be as thorough. And then, maybe, I wouldn't be as dead.

Chapter 16

My plan was simple enough.

The first call was to Cynthia Rich.

"Jim, if you're calling about Randy, other than knowing he's stabilized, we don't have any other update."

"No, I wasn't calling about him, but thanks for the info. I'm glad he's doing better. I wanted to let you know I may have had a breakthrough with Julie's files."

"You mean you think you know who did it?"

"I think so, Cynthia, but it's too early to be sure and the last thing I want to do is make an allegation I can't substantiate."

"Well, you can tell me. I mean we're in this on the same side, maybe I can help."

"I know. But I want to sit on this for another day or so while I do some follow-up. Once I'm sure, you'll be the first to know."

"Jim, don't be silly. If you are correct and something happens to you, Randy may get convicted for something he didn't do."

"Nothing's going to happen to me. Look, I've got to run. I'll call you back."

With that I hung up. My next call went to Grisshof, their squirrely PI.

"What do you want West?" He didn't seem too happy to be hearing from me.

"Just wanted to let you know that you were wrong and I

was right. Randy wasn't the shooter."

"Then who was?" His voice took on a tone that indicated that I may have heightened his interest.

"Sorry, my man, you'll have to get that from your employer." I just wanted to rub it in a little. "You have a nice day." I hung up. The call made me feel good for about two seconds. I knew if my plan didn't work, Grisshof would do his best to make me out as a complete loser. His job would be an easy one.

The next call was more difficult to make, but it had to be done. I dialed the number to Detective Reynolds' office. Luckily he was in.

He, like Cynthia, thought my call was about Randy. We did talk about his attack for a few minutes. Like me, and probably everyone else, Reynolds believed Randy was specifically targeted in the attack. He said prison inspectors were already looking into how it could have happened.

"Don't expect much though, Jim. It is doubtful any of those involved will talk."

"I know, Frank. I was actually calling to let you and Nosh know that I may have a lead on who the real killer is."

"What? Who is it?"

"It's too early to name him. But I need you to let Nosh know I may be real close to being able to identify the killer. I just need a day or two to confirm my theory. By then I should have the name and will either let everyone know who it is or I'll pack up and go home. If he can't live with that, then I'm sorry."

"Damn, Jim, he'll blow his stack. He already wants you out of town or locked up. You can't play games like this."

"It's not a game. Believe me it's complicated. I can't be naming the individual without substantial evidence. I know Nosh will be pissed. That's why I called you. I do want you to tell him what I said. I need you to word it in a way that doesn't give him a heart attack."

"Jim, don't play it this way. Even if you are able to confirm your info, he'll have you locked up for withholding evidence."

"What I have now is a theory put together by a few comments scratched on a piece of paper and a group of pictures. Nothing that, by itself, would mean much. There are some loose ends that need to be tied up."

"All right, I'll try to keep him from exploding, but by tomorrow we need some answers. Understand?"

"Sure. Thanks, Frank. By the way, did you ever get an ID on the jerk that was following me yesterday?"

"Yeah. Name was Juan Moya. No record. He claimed he wasn't following you. We had to let him go."

"That's okay. Just curious. And, Frank, as soon as I know something for sure, I'll let you know."

I hung up again. I wanted to call someone at the Bexar County jail but didn't have a number or a contact. Hopefully word of my pending solution to the case would filter there from police headquarters.

I knew I needed to start moving. I wouldn't put it past Nosh to have a patrol sent over to pick me up. I left my room and headed down to the lobby of the hotel. One more hook to bait.

Lee was in her office. She looked worn out.

"Hey!" I half shouted from her doorway.

She looked up. Despite her haggard appearance, she looked good to me. She smiled at me, despite the trouble I had caused her with her boss.

"I think I may have gotten a break in this thing I've been working. Hopefully, I should be able to bring it to a close by tomorrow. If your boss won't let me stay in the room one more night, just have the cleaning crew throw all my stuff in a trash bag and leave it here with you. Okay?"

"One more night should be okay."

"Thanks. And can you arrange with the front desk or the operator to hold all messages for me. I won't be back until late tonight. There's a strong possibility that I'll be receiving a couple of calls and maybe even a letter. I'd like to be able to call the front desk and have the messages relayed to me."

"Easy to do," she stood up and walked over to me. "Are you going to be okay?"

"Sure. Tomorrow or the next day, I'm going to need you to show me the town. Think you could?"

"I would love to. Be careful."

She came in close. I thought only to hug me but she kissed me. My arms went around her and I pulled her back to kiss her. It was natural and made me feel years younger. For a few seconds we embraced and then she gently pushed me away.

"Whoa, big guy, let's continue this somewhere else where we have a little more privacy."

"Later." I winked at her as I backed away.

My mind was going in too many directions as I walked out of the hotel. I needed to get focused and fast. My body really wanted to go back into the hotel. Not because of any change of heart regarding my plan, but simply to go back to spend more time with Lee. Privacy wouldn't be hard to find in the hotel. I kept walking, my mind reassuring my body there would always be tomorrow. Reminding myself that women and I hadn't seemed to mix very well in the past few years, also made not returning to the hotel an easier choice.

It wasn't just the divorce either. While that had been devastating, the few times I had stuck my toes back into that emotional quagmire called a relationship, I just got hurt again. I once had a dog that kept biting at the occasional bee that flew around him. Despite getting stung on those rare times he managed to catch one, he never seemed to comprehend the relationship between biting at bees and getting stung. I hoped I wasn't getting to be like that old dog.

No, I thought. It was safer to play hide and seek with killers than try to find the solution to my absent love life.

My cell phone rang. Shoving the futile thoughts of my personal life out of my mind, I answered it. Detective Frank Reynolds was at the other end,

"Jim, I just wanted to let you know that I talked to Nosh. He was upset at first, but I was able to calm him down. By the time I left him I think he was okay with everything. He still thinks you are just blowing smoke, but the idea that you'll be out of his hair in two days, one way or the other, is what I think won him over."

"Thanks, Frank."

"No problem."

"And, Frank?"

"Yes."

"One more important favor, keep your cell phone close by and turned on for the next twenty four hours."

"Not a problem, always do."

I rang off. One last call to make and this one would be essential for my plan to work. It was to Bert Falls, the former OSI agent who had helped me with the Royale's. I knew I could trust him and that he would have the expertise I needed to make my plan work.

Bert was happy to meet with me but once I explained my plan to him I could hear his skepticism through the phone.

"If what you plan gets the initial results you want, Jim, you may find yourself dead before you know it. Let me try to get you some back up."

"No time for it Bert, I just need to know if you will help me get the stuff I need."

"Can do. But I still want to talk more when we meet."

We talked for a while before agreeing to meet at noon.

I needed to kill a few hours. I also wanted to make sure I was not being tailed. I didn't want anyone to have the advantage of knowing where I was and sneaking up on me.

This time I didn't take my route along the River Walk but rather stayed up along the road and headed to the Alamo. I wondered about my choice as the Alamo came into view. I hoped my last stand would turn out more successful than Davey Crockett and crew.

To most people, seeing the actual Alamo for the first time is a bit of a letdown. When portrayed in the movies, it is not surrounded by twenty first century San Antonio. In other words, it looks large. Today, however, the Alamo is dwarfed by the city around it and appears small. An unfair reality but that's what progress does.

Fortunately, the Alamo has the ability to recapture your imagination if you take the time to go through it. The long barracks, interior grounds, the mission and even the gift shop, all serve to bring the past to the present day visitor. Dozens of displays along with a volunteer staff that does periodic historical briefings on the grounds ensure that visiting Alamo buffs can get their fill of history.

Although I have always enjoyed my visits to the Alamo, my purpose today was to stay in a public place where I felt safe and could see if anyone was tailing me. At some point in the next 36 hours I hoped that the killer would make his move.

I knew it was a long shot but I needed word to filter back to whoever it was that was behind my harassment. That was the weakest link to my plan. As I still did not know who the killer was, I had no idea if I planted my bluff in the right places. But, if the killer got word that I was closing in, I felt pretty certain he, or she, would do whatever it took to stop me from sharing my information. Too much had already happened for me to believe he was anything but a person of action.

Three or four times before noon, I took steps to determine if someone might be following me but saw no one. I half expected someone to be out there but it appeared no one was. I didn't know what that meant. Ever since my arrival somebody had been keeping an eye on me. Had they lost interest? Had they been called off? Was I just wasting my time?

At noon I walked over to the Menger Hotel and met Bert. We climbed into the back of the van he had driven over with the items I had requested.

"You know, I don't know if you are just wasting both our time or if you're asking to be killed. I hope it's the former," Bert said as we sat opposite each other on the slat benches in the back of the van.

"It may sound funny but I really need it to be the latter, except for the part about my being killed. Were you able to get everything?"

Over the next thirty minutes, Bert and I sat alone in the van and further debated what I was doing. He did come through with the assistance I had asked for. In turn, I compromised to one of his requests. By the time I left the van, it seemed like we were old friends.

I walked into the Menger, one of San Antonio's oldest hotels. It's allegedly haunted. I wasn't hunting ghosts though and went directly to the restroom. Once there, and after finishing one of the reasons for going in there, I studied my appearance in the mirrors. I brushed some dust off my jeans that I had probably picked up from the back of the van. Other than that, I thought I looked okay. The large black golf shirt with a Spurs logo that I had purchased that morning at the hotel looked a little big on me. Better that than a little tight I thought. I ran a comb through my hair. Showtime, I hoped.

I went back to the Alamo. A few minutes after one o'clock my phone rang.

"Hello," I answered.

"Jim, it's me, Cynthia. Are you okay?"

"Sure."

"We had another meeting with the partners. Lieutenant Nosh called the boss again. He wanted to know what we knew. I guess really he wanted to know if we knew what you know. Both my boss and Nosh got themselves worked up again about your behavior. My boss wants to know where you are and what you are doing."

"Sorry about that. Like I said though, I need another twenty four hours."

"I know. Think you and I could meet later today or this evening and talk, Jim?"

"I guess we could."

"Good. Let me call you back when I come up with a time and place."

We hung up. Was that it? Could it be one of the lawyers in the firm? How stupid of me. Why didn't I ever ask Randy how Caruzzo and Dilbert had come to represent him? Was Caruzzo in one of the pictures? Was Dilbert? How would I know? I never made the effort to connect the dots.

I felt like an idiot. Once Randy was up and about, I could ask him. I should have done it before.

I dialed Cynthia back. She answered at once.

"Yes, Jim?" Caller ID no doubt.

"Cynthia, how did your firm come to represent Randy in this case?"

"The LaMoe's know a couple of the senior partners. I'm not sure exactly which ones. It may have been through the wives, though, I'm not sure." She paused for a second while the reason for my question may have sunk in. "Why would you ask?"

"Just curious at the moment, thanks, got to go." I hung up.

I contemplated heading back to the hotel to look again at the pictures. My thoughts were interrupted by my phone. It was Bert, checking in.

Once the call was over, I started walking back to the hotel. It made sense that the killer could be someone with the law firm. They had access to my whereabouts in San Antonio from my first moments in town.

The motive didn't have to be a simple love triangle. Could Julie have overheard a conversation that she shouldn't have between the lawyer and another client? A dangerous client who might have then given an ultimatum to the lawyer? Fix the problem or we'll fix you. Possible.

My phone rang again. It was Nosh.

"Where the hell are you West?"

"Downtown checking on a few things."

"Well, I want to talk to you now."

"Okay, fire away."

"No, not on the phone. I'll send someone to get you. Where are you?"

I really didn't want to talk to Nosh. I didn't have the time and wasn't about to say I knew who the killer was.

"How about tomorrow, Lieutenant?"

"No, damn it. Now! Where can one of my men pick you up?"

I looked around. "How about in front of Pat O'Briens? Street level."

"Okay, stay there, someone will be there in twenty minutes."

"Crap," I mumbled to myself after hanging up. This was going to blow half my afternoon.

I walked across the street and leaned against the wall of Pat O'Briens pub. I dialed the hotel's front desk. I only had one message. It was from Grisshof and the message simply said let's talk. No number to call, nothing else.

Was he just mad? Curious? Or did he have another theory now, too? Did he also come to the conclusion that the answer may be no farther away than his employers' office?

I called Bert and made sure he was aware of my situation.

The weekend foot traffic was heavy up and down the street. The day was going to get hotter. I hoped I wasn't going to have to wait too long.

Standing there I also started to think that I was pretty much an open target. If someone had been keeping an eye on me, it would be pretty simple for anyone to drive by, slow down and put a couple of slugs in me before driving off. I didn't like the way I was losing control of the day. This was the wrong day to lose control of, too.

A car backfired at the corner and I instinctively ducked. Two teenage boys walked by, looked at me, and laughed to themselves at my reaction. Let them laugh. I couldn't help but remember a couple former agents I knew a long time ago. They went to meet with a person they thought was a reliable source and were blown to pieces by a car bomb. But that was Honduras, not San Antonio. I just needed to relax and stay focused. Besides, it was more likely that someone would drive by and shoot me while I stood there.

Could the killer be a cop? After all, there was that one

picture with all the cops in the background. Nosh and Reynolds were in the picture. Who were the others? Possible I thought, but my money was still on the lawyer.

Twenty minutes came and went. No one came by to get me. Two patrol cars drove by but didn't seem to have any interest in me. I contemplated calling Nosh but thought that if no one came soon, he couldn't blame me for not being here. I really didn't want to talk to him anyway. Not giving him a name would only irritate him and make him believe I was either holding back information from the police or a liar. No good would come from that, and despite my hunch that the killer might be someone in the Caruzzo and Dilbert law firm, there was no way I would be able to prove anything. Besides, what if I was wrong and it was a cop or someone that had good access to the police?

Thirty minutes came and went. I started walking towards the hotel again. I hadn't gotten far when my phone rang again.

This time it was Grisshof at the other end. I was surprised by his conciliatory tone.

"West, can we meet somewhere? If you think you really have a bead on the shooter, then I owe you a beer. Not to mention I'd love to know what you've got."

Now maybe I was getting somewhere. How close was Grisshof with the firm? Despite Cynthia's disclaimers, maybe Grisshof did know more about my arrival into San Antonio than she thought he did.

"How about Pat O'Brien's? I can meet you there right now."

"Perfect, I'm on my way."

For my plan to work, it was critical that the killer would want to meet with me. So far I had a lawyer, a policeman, and a private detective all wanting to meet. In one way I felt like everything was working out, on the other I felt like a farmer wishing for rain, only to get a flood. I needed the killer to call, not everyone else.

I went back to O'Brien's hoping a policeman wouldn't be standing there looking for me. No one was there. I went downstairs to the level on the River Walk but stayed back, well away from the foot traffic. This time I only had to wait about five minutes before Grisshof showed up.

The place wasn't crowded and Grisshof saw me right away. He approached and despite his attitude on the phone, he couldn't seem to keep the smirk off his face. No offer to shake hands, he simply plopped himself down in the chair opposite me at the small table.

"Look, West, I came here to give you a chance to prove yourself. The first beer is on me. Convince me I'm wrong and I'll pay for the second, too. But, to be honest, I still think you are full of it."

"Fair enough, but if you want a name, I'm not prepared to give that to you right now. When you called, I was on my way to confirm my theory."

"Then you don't know who the killer is."

I stared at him for at least ten seconds. He met my stare. I did so for effect. My hope was that he would think I was considering how much I was willing to tell him. It was time to bait my first hook.

"When we first met, Gary, I was approaching this matter with the right answer but based on absolutely wrong assumptions. At that point I didn't seriously believe that Julie had a number of different lovers. I was wrong."

"I told you that."

"I know. At least you were right about that. I spent a couple days tracking down past lovers, thinking that maybe the love triangle motive was correct but that the killer was the lover, not the husband. In doing so, I came to realization that love may have had nothing to do with the killing. More likely, I think, Julie must have seen or heard something that she shouldn't have. But that only helps out with a motive and did little to identify the shooter."

I paused for a moment again. Grisshof sat there in silence.

"In LaMoe's house, I found a number of file folders Julie kept. She was fairly organized. She had one file folder full of business cards and hand written notes identifying points of contacts with all sorts of companies and organizations in town. She also had a folder full of press clippings. Each clipping contained a picture of an individual or individuals. This file also contained actual photographs taken at events. Julie might not have even been at all the events, but I believe in each picture or photo, one or more of her lovers were."

"Was I in any?" I couldn't tell if Grisshof was joking or serious. I couldn't believe Julie could've sunk so low as to have had any relationship with this worm.

"Sorry Gary but no. However, some people with Caruzzo and Dilbert were."

"Who?" I had definitely got his attention but I still needed to plant the hook a little deeper.

"Not yet, like I said I need to confirm my theory. As I was saying, the pictures enabled me to approach a handful of people and verify their relationship with Julie. One of those I approached, a guy named Al who worked at the condo complex, was killed shortly after I talked to him. That meant a couple of things to me. One, he had known the person who murdered Julie. Two, while he may or may not have known that the individual was the killer, he had information that the killer didn't want made public."

"Now that he is dead, how do you plan to prove that?"

"I think that information will be self explanatory once I identify the killer."

Grisshof just grunted.

Now for the big lie.

"Then I noticed some of Julie's handwritten notes that I thought at first were irrelevant, actually pertained to her concern about her safety. For whatever reason, the notes didn't come out and actually identify what she was concerned about or who she might be worried about. In fact, at first glance, the notes didn't make sense. Julie referred to a function she had attended. In first reading the notes, I thought she was having trouble figuring out some role she must have had in organizing the activity."

I looked around the room as if I was concerned someone else might be listening to our conversation. I took a sip of beer.

"Then it was like a light bulb went off in my head." A light bulb had never actually gone off in my head, so I wouldn't know what it would be like if one had. But, I thought Grisshof would eat it up. "What if Julie was writing about something that she witnessed with one of her lovers? Something she knew was wrong and, if exposed, could seriously cause trouble for him. What if her notes depicted her effort to resolve this dilemma? You know, like how a lot people will annotate various possible answers next to a logic puzzle, trying to get one that will work."

Grisshof looked a little confused.

"Okay, perhaps not the best example. But accept what I'm saying for the moment. Her notes led me to focus on two of the pictures in her folder. About a half dozen men were captured in those two photos. From there it was just a matter of narrowing them down and working on the motive. I did succeed, I think, in narrowing the suspects down to one. Now I'm simply trying to firm up the motive. Her notes allude to it but I want to try to verify it before I turn the name over to the police or anyone else."

"So you think this other man killed Julie?"

"I can't say that he pulled the trigger. He could have had someone else do it for him. But, there will be more than enough evidence to link him to it and force the police to look into it. Not to mention, the press will eat it up."

Grisshof stared at me and was about to say something when my phone rang again.

It was Nosh.

"Where are you West?" He snarled. I could almost see his lips curling through the phone.

"I waited way past the twenty minutes. Where were you?"

"I have a guy there now. He says you are nowhere to be seen."

"Send him inside. I got tired of waiting outside."

"You go outside and find him, West. I'm not playing any of your silly games."

"Then you'll have to tell him to wait a few more minutes. I'm talking to someone right now."

"Who?"

It wasn't any of his business but I told him.

"I'm talking with a guy who works with the law firm. His name is Grisshof."

There was a pause on the phone. For a second I thought I lost him.

"Okay, no problem, I'll have my guy come in. Just stay there."

I was going to say that wasn't necessary. That I would be out in a few minutes, but Nosh abruptly hung up.

"What was that about?" Grisshof asked.

"I originally came here to rendezvous with the police. They never showed up so I agreed to meet you here when you called. Now someone is up on the street level looking for me. They're pissed, but it's their fault."

"I thought you weren't ready to go to the police yet."

I wondered if I detected concern in his voice.

"I'm not, but they won't wait."

"What are you going to tell them?"

"I'm not exactly sure, Gary. I don't want to tell them more than I've told you. More than likely they won't settle for that."

I watched Grisshof closely. If he was involved with the killings, he certainly wasn't giving me any outward sign.

"Well, I guess I'll get out of your hair, West, and let you go to your appointment."

We stood up. He still made no offer to shake hands.

"I still think you're full of it, West. I'll pay for the beer, but I still think LaMoe pulled the trigger."

I was going to respond, but I saw a man in a suit coming down the stairs from the front street level looking around for someone in the pub. The man looked at us and started walking in our direction.

"Jim West?" He asked glancing back and forth between us.

"That's me."

"So you must be Grisshof?"

Nosh had briefed him well.

"Yes."

"Lieutenant Nosh wants to talk to both of you. If you'll please come with me."

It wasn't phrased like a question and Grisshof reacted.

"What does the lieutenant want with me? I thought he just wanted to see West."

"Apparently the lieutenant believes you are working

together on the LaMoe homicide. Since we have an official case open on the murder, he wants to ensure the department knows everything that you two know. Routine, you know."

Grisshof looked at me, angrier than before, obviously irritated by this further intrusion into his day.

"Officer, what's your name?" Grisshof asked.

"My name is Quisp, Detective Jarrad Quisp."

He looked at Grisshof like he was daring him to ask another question. Great, I thought, two bull headed men trying to stare each other down.

"Let's go and get this over with detective. But for the record, Grisshof is not working with me in this case."

"You can say that again. Detective, I think West is just wasting everyone's time."

"From what I understand, I'm sure he is, but let's allow the lieutenant to make that decision. My job is simply to get you two to the lieutenant."

"I've got my car here," Grisshof stated. "I'll drive to the station and meet you there."

"Sorry Mr. Grisshof, you'll need to come with me. Those are my orders – get you both to Nosh right now."

"As long as someone will bring me back to get my car."

"No problem, the lieutenant will probably have me do that myself."

We followed Quisp up the stairs and onto the street. His car was parked just a few yards from the door. Grisshof was quick to jump into the front seat so I clambered into the back of the unmarked, black sedan.

Quisp pulled out onto the road and quickly made two right hand turns that took us in a direction away from police headquarters.

"Where are we going?" Grisshof inquired from the front seat.

"To see the lieutenant, like I said."

"He's not at the station?"

"I thought he told you all. He's just finished with a community center function and wanted me to take you to him. I don't think he is planning to return to the office today."

Grisshof looked back at me and glared.

For my part, I was actually glad Grisshof was coming along. His presence would take a little of the attention off me. He could also corroborate that what I would tell Nosh was exactly what I told him. I knew it wouldn't be much help, but at this point I needed all the assistance I could get. The last thing I needed was to be tossed into some interview room at Police Headquarters, while Nosh and crew tried to sweat information out of me that I simply didn't have.

"Detective Quisp, I have a meeting this afternoon. I need to be back at my office by four. This won't make me cancel that, will it?"

"My understanding is that the lieutenant only wants to ask you both a few questions. No statements, just a conversation. He knows I have to be back at headquarters for a safety brief this afternoon. My guess, he needs maybe ten to fifteen minutes of your time."

"Well, I'd better be back in time."

Quisp looked over at Grisshof and smiled. "If you have a problem with all this, take it out on the lieutenant. I'm not familiar with the case. I'm just doing what I'm told."

"No problem," Grisshof mumbled.

I sat back and closed my eyes. I didn't think the ride would be that long. A power nap might be just what the doctor ordered.

For whatever reason, my mind drifted to thoughts of Ms. Valentine. I felt bad that my activities here in San Antonio had put her in a tough spot with her boss. I liked her and I was starting to think she didn't mind being around me. Life had dealt her a bad hand, just like it had done with me. We both had gone through tough divorces that we hadn't seen coming. Looking back, I could understand how I probably hadn't been attentive enough to my ex. Not on purpose but that turned out to be a lame excuse.

I couldn't understand why Lee's husband would leave her. Admittedly, there was a ton of information I didn't know about her and the relationship she had with her husband. She could have all sorts of strange secrets I didn't know about. Hell, for all I know she could collect cats.

But what I did know was that Lee was attractive, bright, had a very nice figure and a sexy smile. Those qualities, plus the fact that she was taking a few risks to help me, put her up pretty high on the short list of women with whom I could imagine spending a lot of time.

I felt she was over missing her husband. If he showed up wanting to move back in, she would likely toss him out.

That made us a little different. Even though I wanted like crazy to get over my ex, I knew deep down if she showed back up, I'd want her to stay. Very unlikely, especially now, as I had heard she was either engaged to or living with some guy somewhere. Probably both.

A friend of mine, who had done a lot of family counseling, told me that I had to let go. I didn't disagree with him. I just didn't know how.

The car bounced over some railroad tracks and brought me back to the real world. I looked around. We were outside the city somewhere on a two lane road. Nearly twenty minutes had passed since we climbed into the car. That could put us anywhere.

"I hope we're getting close." I yawned as I said this.

Detective Quisp's eyes met mine in the rearview mirror.

"A couple of minutes more."

He maneuvered the car onto a narrow, paved road that led into an area of trees. Not sufficient to be called a forest, but definitely an area that appeared to have not seen civilization for a while.

"What the hell?" Grisshof sat up straighter looking around.

"There's an old abandoned building just around the bend up here. It's reportedly been used by some gangs recently. The lieutenant was meeting some folks from the city and the county to discuss having it torn down at public expense."

"Seems like they could have just taken some pictures to city hall. Why get everyone out here?"

"Mr. Grisshof, you can ask Lieutenant Nosh that himself. He's right there."

Nosh was standing alone in front of an old wooden structure that had surely seen better days. It looked like a barn to me.

"I remember this place, now that I see it," Grisshof remarked with some interest. "This is the old Bracken Country Club. Used to be quite the roadhouse during the forties and fifties. With all the soldiers that came through San Antonio for World War II and then the Korean War, this used to be quite the wild place."

"You here back then, Gary?" I asked.

"No, but I would have liked to have seen it in its heyday." He didn't seem to mind my ribbing at all.

I guess you had to be a fan of old roadhouses. To me, I still thought it looked like a rundown barn.

"Is this in San Antonio city limits?"

"No, but it's in our extra-territorial jurisdiction."

We climbed out of the car and into the afternoon heat.

The parking lot was just a large open field that wrapped around the building. The field was bordered by the road on one side and trees with thick undergrowth everywhere else. I looked around and didn't see another person or car.

"Glad you two could make it out here. Sorry for the long drive. Come on in and let's get out of the sun. You too, Jarrad."

"Lieutenant," Grisshof asked, "wouldn't it be better to rebuild this place than tear it down? You know it has a lot of history." The idea of tearing down the place must have really bothered him.

"I know, I know."

The inside didn't look any better than the outside. There was no door, only an opening where the door once stood. On one side, the walls had started collapsing. There was a long counter that ran from one side of the building to the other which I imagined was once a bar. There was nothing else in the building.

We walked across to where the counter met the far wall. Grisshof leaned against the counter. I started to lean against the wall, but it looked rotten enough to collapse around me, so I just stood there. Deputy Quisp, apparently not wanting to intrude, stayed back a few paces.

"First, I need to see who you both have been calling today. Can I see your cell phones?"

I handed him mine without thinking. Grisshof was just staring at him.

I looked at Nosh. Suddenly I knew something wasn't right. The hairs on the back of my neck stood up as though a shot of freezing air had blown across me. But there was nothing, at all, I could do.

Chapter 17

The next thing I knew, Nosh had a gun in his hand and fired point blank into Grisshof's chest. Grisshof's body collapsed backwards slamming off the counter and then into the wall. The wall made a loud cracking sound as the body crashed against it.

I looked at Nosh and at the same time futilely moved backwards colliding with the wall. I saw that Quisp now had pulled out his handgun but was aiming it at me rather than Nosh.

Nosh had transferred the gun to his left hand and was reaching under his left arm with his other hand. I watched, stunned, as he pulled out a different gun, a 9mm semi automatic and pointed it directly at my chest.

Again, I almost involuntarily surged backwards into the rotten wood in the wall as the gun roared in Nosh's hand. The round hit my chest like a sledgehammer increasing the force with which my body crashed against the rotten wood. The wall splintered, and cracked, and collapsed around me, sending me tumbling the four feet to the ground just outside the building. Wood and dust fell on me.

I heard two more rounds go off while I lay there getting my senses back. Had Quisp and Nosh shot each other? Was Nosh the killer I was looking for?

"Go check West. I'm sure he's dead, but he needs to be brought back up here anyway."

So, they were in this together. The Kevlar vest that Bert Falls had acquired for me and helped me get into earlier that day had saved my life for now, but if I didn't think fast, I was sure the next shot would be to my head. I had no weapon. I had considered getting a small one but didn't think I would be able to conceal it on my person. Plus, I wasn't licensed to carry one and didn't want to have to explain it to the police, if noticed. That decision was now starting to look like a fatally stupid one.

I looked around and saw a two foot, rusty metal rod that may have been used to reinforce something in the old foundation to the building. I grabbed it and rolled over on it.

"He's right below us. Looks dead, but I would have thought that bullet would have gone clean through him." Quisp jumped down without thinking about what he had just said. I could hear Nosh dragging Grisshof's body above me.

I felt a hand on my shoulder. Quisp pulled me over. As he did so, I rolled with his effort and slashed at him with the metal rod. It wasn't a powerful swing, but I caught him on his temple and stunned him. His eyes stared at me trying to figure out what had just happened as he stumbled backwards. I leapt at him the best I could from my position on the ground and put all the force I had into a vicious blow targeted directly at the red whelp caused by the first strike. In his daze, Quisp was unable to block my swing, and the metal rod smashed solidly against him.

He fell to the ground and lay there motionless. I wanted to find his gun, as he most likely re-holstered before jumping down to check on me, but there was no time.

"What the ...?" was all I heard before bolting off in the direction of the woods across the road. Nosh must have seen us through the hole in the wall. Fortunately, he must have also holstered his weapon or the gunshot would have happen much quicker. As it was, I was a good twenty yards away and just across the road when the shot exploded behind me.

The bullet hit me in the back, but it was nothing like the slug I took to the chest. If anything, it simply sped me up a little. Make that two beers I owed Bert. Now if he had managed to follow us, was in the area, and still receiving data from the small microphone he had helped me place against the bottom button in my shirt, maybe he could call for help and I could still get out of this mess.

Another bullet whizzed by my left ear and slammed into a tree about two yards in front of me. Hoping he would correct by aiming right, I made an immediate zig to my left and dashed into the thick underbrush. I then zagged back to my right hoping Nosh didn't see me. I had only run about thirty yards into the woods, thorns tearing at my jeans, before I ran into a steep drop off to a dry creek bed about ten feet below me.

I jumped five feet down to a boulder that jutted out of the bank and then the other five feet to the creek bed. The sound of footsteps crashed through the underbrush above me. I ran to the right, away from the sounds. The far side of the creek bed, which was about twenty five yards away, looked steep. I contemplated running to it and trying to climb out, but thought that I would be out in the open too long. That would give Nosh too good of a shot. That last miss was a headshot. He must have figured out that I was wearing a vest.

The creek bed turned back to the right. Perfect, I thought, if he hadn't seen me before I made the turn he would have no idea where I was. I kept running fast along the side of creek bed as it meandered along its way. I must have run about a quarter of a mile when I came to a bunch of large boulders and rock formations that collected along the inside bend of the creek. Three large puddles of water had collected here, too. Could I be at the same spot Royale's kid had his thugs push me over the ridge? I had no idea.

I ducked in between a large rock formation that stuck out of the ridge wall and two very large boulders that had been pushed by the flood waters up against it. It was a good hiding spot, other than the fact that there was no escape route. Despite the possibility of getting myself cornered, I needed to stop. I was winded, and I needed to try to communicate with Bert. If the microphone was still working, I had to let him know what had happened.

"Bert," I whispered into the microphone. "It's Nosh, he's the killer. He killed Grisshof and tried to kill me. He has another person helping him. Identified himself as a Detective Jarrad Quisp. I hurt Quisp bad back at the old Bracken Country Club. Get the police here. Get in touch with Detective Frank Reynolds but be careful. I don't know who all is involved. Best get in touch with Cynthia Rich, too, and tell her everything before the police show up. We may need her to help substantiate our side of the story. Jesus, I hope you're out there Bert."

I stopped talking and started listening. There were sounds all around me but nothing I could discern as something that could have been made by a person. I couldn't believe I handed my cell phone over so easily. If I had hung onto my cell phone help would be on the way already. As it was, I just had to hope Bert was out there somewhere.

I took a peek around the larger of the two boulders. This one was a good six feet high. No one was in sight. I crouched back down in my small hiding spot and looked for a place to sit down. The semi-enclosed area was about twelve feet long and between five and eight feet wide at various points. Two or three large rocks could serve as a spot to sit. There was a large puddle of water in the far corner.

It was there, by the puddle, that I saw the snake. It was a big one, partially coiled, and luckily impervious to my presence. I wondered if I should look for a different hiding spot. At first glance the snake looked like it could be a diamondback rattlesnake. I kept my eye on the snake. It didn't move. Probably asleep or maybe dead, I thought. It was a good nine feet away from me.

If it started moving my way I would have plenty of time to leave but I didn't want to leave the hiding spot. A person would have to walk into it to see me. With the overhanging ledge above me, Nosh could literally be standing over me and not know I was here.

I sat down on a large rock as far from the snake as I could get without putting myself in view of the entrance. The snake hadn't moved. Despite its presence, I was glad I was in the shade and not out in the hot sun where Nosh was, no doubt, running around in circles trying to find me.

I looked down at my chest. The hole in the front of my shirt looked smaller than I thought it should, based on the impact of the bullet and the pain in my chest. I pulled out my collar and the Kevlar vest as far as I could and tried to see what damage the bullet had done to me. I thought I could see some bruising, but there was no blood. I didn't think anything was broken. I reached around to my back where the other bullet had struck me. I found the hole in my shirt. My back didn't feel sore.

As I sat there, I started thinking about the situation I had gotten myself into. While my theory regarding who could have known my whereabouts and activities in San Antonio as quickly as they did had included someone who was close to the police force, I never really suspected any specific person. That it was Nosh was certainly not part of any theory.

But it did fit. He was in the newspaper photo that included

Royale. Perhaps it was Nosh's presence in the picture, not Royale's that inspired Julie to keep it.

Nosh had known the staff at the condo complex from an earlier murder. The staff even mentioned his stopping by now and then. He may have even met Julie during the prior investigation. If not, they could have met at the charity event depicted in the picture.

It didn't really matter. There was no explanation for Nosh's murder of Grisshof and attempt at killing me, other than his involvement in Julie's murder. I looked down again at the hole in the front of my vest. It was a direct hit at my heart. The shot at Grisshof was also a heart shot. Just like Julie and just like the pool guy. Lieutenant Buzz Nosh was obviously the person who pulled the trigger on all those killings. Habits are hard to change.

He had changed weapons after he shot Grisshof. The only reason he would do so would be to indicate there were two shooters. That would explain the two shots I heard while I was laying there on the ground. I bet he had put the gun he had fired at me into Grisshof's dead hand and fired the rounds off to insure that gunshot residue would be found on Grisshof's hand. That may be why it took him so long to get a shot off at me. The gun he used on me may have been left in, or by, Grisshof's hand. He would have then left the gun he shot Grisshof with in my hand. If he had succeeded, the crime scene would appear as though we had shot each other

I thought I heard a sound above me. It sounded like someone or something walking. Suddenly the noise stopped. Whoever or whatever, it was right above me probably looking around. I imagined the spot allowed a good surveillance point up and down the creek bed and across the creek, since the incline over there was not as steep or as high as this side. Flood waters had repeatedly overflowed and flattened the bend in the creek over there. On this side, the fast moving water had cut deeper into the side of the rock face.

Something in the corner of my peripheral vision caught my attention. It was the snake. It had started to uncurl and move slowly in my direction. I leaned back as tightly as I could against the boulder. The snake would have a few feet of clearance to get by me, but it wasn't staying close to the fall wall. Instead, it was staking out a center path towards the exit which would bring it within a foot or two to me.

I looked around for a rock to throw at the snake. Not so much to hurt it but to turn it around. There was a softball-size one close to my feet so I picked it up. The snake seemed to know what I was doing and retreated a foot before curling back up. It dawned on me that so far he had not rattled his tail. In fact, I was beginning to think he didn't have any rattles. With the position it took on the ground I couldn't see its tail. I was aware that there were a few fairly harmless snakes that looked like rattlesnakes. But I was also thought it might be possible for a rattlesnake to lose its rattles in a fight with a predator.

Fortunately, the snake again looked like it had no interest in me. I hoped it would stay where it was for a while longer. The sound above me had abated and I imagined whatever it was had moved on. However, I couldn't be sure. I wanted more time to allow some space between whatever made the noise out there and me.

Suddenly everything got darker. My first impression was that something had moved by out front, blocking the sun, but it quickly became apparent that a cloud had just temporarily blocked out the sun. Between the snake in the hideout with me and Nosh out there with a gun, I was getting a little jumpy.

The sound of a train's horn pierced the relative silence. It sounded close. I could even hear the train as it moved over its tracks. It brought to mind another murder investigation I had gotten sucked into a number of years back. A young couple had learned how to jump trains and travel across the country. Modern day hobos, their travels led them into the grasp of a psychotic killer. I heard the train's horn again and wished it was right outside my hiding spot. I certainly needed something that would take me safely away from the killer, out there, looking for me right now.

I decided to give it ten more minutes before I would start moving. That would be approximately twenty five minutes after Nosh shot Grisshof and then tried to kill me. I could only assume that Grisshof was dead. I wondered about Detective Quisp. I had hit him hard with the metal rod.

One thing that was starting to nag at me was the realization that I had not heard any sirens. If Bert had managed to follow us out of town and was in range of the transmitter I was wearing, then he would have certainly called the police, and I would have heard the sirens. But I hadn't heard any.

I sat quietly, straining to hear sirens coming to the rescue. The ten minutes came and passed, and I didn't hear any. The cloud moved on and sunshine again brightened my surroundings.

I looked back for the snake, but it wasn't there. I tensed and took a quick step toward the exit before forcing myself to stop and look around. For all I knew, the snake could have moved quietly past me and be anywhere on the path that led out of my hiding spot. I did not want to step on it or anywhere near it.

Sunlight filtered in and provided plenty of light to see, but some areas were shaded. Between the shadows, dozens of large rocks, and a few sticks scattered on the ground, the snake could have been anywhere.

Finally, I decided I needed to move and crept cautiously out into the open. I crouched at the opening to let my eyes get used to the bright sunlight. I heard nothing, and looking around, I saw nothing. Not Nosh, not the snake.

I headed back toward the Bracken Country Club retracing my steps the best I could. I knew I couldn't be too far from civilization no matter which direction I took, but I needed to know if anyone had responded to the crime scene. Every now and then I saw a flicker of movement and stopped to hide behind whatever cover I could find. Each time I was able to identify the movement as wildlife in the area. Three times it was deer and once it was only birds. I slowly moved on.

When I was running from Nosh I didn't take time to get my bearings, so I wasn't sure where I jumped into the creek bed. I did remember that the creek bed had bends in it. I was happy each time I made one because they helped conceal me from my pursuer. I thought I ran by three bends and stopped at the fourth. I had only run a short distance on the dry creek bed before I encountered the first bend in the creek.

If my memory was right I was now near the spot where I jumped down. I looked around for the rock ledge, or was it a boulder, that I first jumped to on my way down. I saw a couple spots near me that could have been the right location. Close enough, I thought and clambered up the creek wall. It was fairly steep, so I had to go up the ten feet on all fours.

I peered over the top of the ridge but couldn't see anything because the bushes and trees blocked my view. I listened and thought I could hear voices coming from somewhere in front of me. Then there was silence.

I stayed still, hoping to hear the sound again. There was nothing more, but I was fairly certain that what I had heard came from people talking or shouting.

I walked slowly in the direction where I believed the people to be. In a few seconds I could make out the outline to the Bracken Country Club. I stopped and looked around. Nosh was nowhere to be seen. My view to the building was still mostly obscured, and I saw no one by the building. I also didn't see any vehicles. That startled me until I realized that from my vantage point, the far parking lot, where Quisp had pulled in, was blocked from view by the building.

A very thick area of underbrush was about twenty feet in front of me and a little to my right. It provided the last bit of good cover before reaching the road and the open area beyond. I looked around to make sure everything was still safe and sprinted to the thick underbrush. I half slid the last few feet, almost blinding myself on the limbs of a sage.

I rubbed my eyes to clear my vision and saw the last thing I wanted to see. About three feet into the shrubbery sat Lieutenant Nosh. He turned slightly, so he was looking at me with a 9mm pistol pointed right at my face. I instinctively closed my eyes expecting to be immediately shot.

The fact that nothing happened surprised me. I opened my eyes and looked into his.

"If you want to live a little longer, West, get in here and sit right over there." Nosh's voice was hushed making me realize there had to be other people around.

He saw my hesitation.

"I will shoot you, West. Make no mistake about it."

"They'll hear the gunshot. They'll know it was murder."

"Maybe, maybe not, but more importantly, there would be an inquiry, and I would rather there not be one."

He cocked the hammer back. Not the time to die, I decided, and moved to the spot he had picked out for me. The vegetation was especially thick, and the immediate area was replete with vines bearing large, sharp thorns. The spot he had pointed to was an open space barely a foot wide.

"Sit down."

I sat. It was uncomfortable and my view to the building was almost totally obscured.

"You know, you impress me. At least to the point that you somehow figured this out and had the foresight to wear a vest. That was smart. I have to admit, I didn't expect that."

"Seemed, at the time, it might be the right thing to do."

"I should have thought about that. You did say you were a former cop, or fed, or something."

I just nodded.

Suddenly I heard the voices again. I looked back at the building but couldn't see anything.

"Stay still West. I'm not warning you again."

I looked back at Nosh. The gun was in his right hand. Both the hand and the gun rested on his right thigh as he sat cross-legged barely five feet in front of me. Three interwoven green vines full of nasty looking thorns were all that separated us.

"Why don't you just march me in and tell them I killed Grisshof? That would be the smartest thing to do. It would discredit any allegations I might make against you. They would just think I was just trying to save my own skin."

"I'm still debating that option, so don't do anything stupid."

The way he said it made me doubt seriously that he planned to let me live but I had little option but to play along. Dying immediately is never a good choice.

"Who's over there?"

He stared at me for a few seconds. "I saw Reynolds and two other cops. Someone must have called about the shootings. I expect reinforcements will be here any second."

As if on cue, I heard the sound of sirens in the distance.

If Reynolds was there it meant Bert must have called him. He must have heard at least part of what happened when we arrived. That was the only time anyone specifically identified our location. Of course there was a different possibility. Bert was following us. He may have only seen us arrive. The transmitter didn't need to be working.

"Could you tell if Quisp was all right?" I was worried what role Quisp could yet play in this situation.

"I wish I knew. He's not on the ground where I last saw him. They wouldn't have moved him if he was dead. So, he either crawled back into the building himself, or they moved him in to make him more comfortable."

"I was worried I may have killed him."

"If I knew you had, I would have shot you by now and taken my chances. He's family you know."

Of course I didn't. Nor did I really care at the moment.

"What did you hit him with? He looked awful bad when I saw him."

"A metal rod, probably an old reinforcement rod. It was just lying there in the debris."

"Lucky for you."

I didn't respond. We sat in silence for a few minutes as more emergency responders arrived.

"Aren't you afraid they'll see us over here?"

"There's only one car parked by the building. They'll know it belongs to the department. The logical explanation is that any other persons who were there, are gone. Their attention will be the crime scene and the immediate area around it. Plus, they'll start losing daylight in an hour. Someone will come out here tomorrow and walk this area, but they won't be interested in it this afternoon."

Nosh was a making a rational argument, based on the cards

he thought he was dealt. Under normal circumstances, I would have to agree with his analysis of the situation. What he didn't know was that I still had a wild card in my hand, the transmitter. I certainly needed to get out of this situation alive, but I also wanted to find out why Nosh had killed Julie. If the transmitter was working and if Bert was out there somewhere with a functioning receiver then, even if I didn't make it, the authorities would know who the real killer of Julie LaMoe was.

Two more police cars and an ambulance pulled into the crime scene. I stretched my head to get a better view, but Nosh signaled with his 9mm for me to stay still. He had the better angle to see the building and probably the better view. He could watch what was going on and still keep an eye on me.

The ambulance pulled off the road and up next to the spot where I fell through the wall. An awkward spot to get in and out of the building, I thought, but closer to Grisshof and to where I had last seen Quisp. The police cars must have parked on the other side of the building.

The ambulance's engine was left running, muffling the voices that now permeated the air. I couldn't recognize any of the voices. What if Bert wasn't there and the police responded, as Nosh thought, because of someone calling in gunshots in the area?

Chapter 18

Nosh seemed to be intrigued with the activity. "Here comes the Medical Examiner."

"Nosh, why did you kill Julie?"

He looked at me with hatred in his eyes. My question had brought forth all the blame for his current predicament, and that blame was now focused at me.

"Maybe I should shoot you now." He raised his gun and pointed it at me. I watched his trigger finger. It kept my eyes off the open end of the barrel of the 9mm which, if you've never had the opportunity to look down as it is being aimed at you, can be quite terrifying. He wasn't ready to kill me. The trigger finger never moved toward the trigger, and his gun hand slowly went back down to his leg.

"She saw something she shouldn't have. I could have forgiven her but my partners couldn't. I had no choice. I really liked her. How well did you know her?"

"Not as well as I thought," I answered truthfully.

"She was one classy dame. LaMoe was a lucky guy to be married to her."

I assumed from his statement, that he didn't realize that he was just one of several men who had shared her bed in the last few years.

"Hell, West, I even tried to talk her into leaving that feeble husband of hers and marrying me, but, for whatever reason, she wouldn't hear of it. I guess those pilots make a lot of money.

No other reason I could think of."

I wanted to tell him that Julie might not have been as impressed with him as he was with himself but kept quiet. I wanted him to keep talking.

"You know he was gone as often as he was at home, and Julie was a hot blooded woman. You just can't leave that type of woman alone like that. Hell West, she was amazing in the sack, and I simply gave her what she needed. You know there are a lot of women who like cops. They know we're real men, and that is still attractive to a lot of women. You're not married, are you?"

"No, I'm not."

"Ever been married?"

Not an area I wanted to get into. He realized this right away.

"You have been, haven't you?" He asked this with a nasty grin. "She left you right? Ha! She probably ran into a cop like me who could give her something you never could. It's called satisfaction, West."

I wasn't going to let him get to me. But it wasn't easy.

"Hell, I've been divorced twice. But it wasn't because they ever fooled around on me." He had a big grin on his face. "Women have always been attracted to me, and I've never been able to disappoint them. My former wives just weren't as understanding. God, did they ever turn into real witches. They get most my paycheck and still want more."

"I still don't understand why you killed Julie. Did she threaten you or try to blackmail you?"

"No, nothing like that. She's not that type. I tried to tell them that, but they wouldn't listen. To them she was a loose end that had to be fixed or their whole operation could unravel. Hell that was BS. I told them my neck was out as much as theirs and that I could handle her if she ever showed signs of being a threat to us. But they didn't buy it. The real problem wasn't that they were worried that the operation would be compromised."

I started to shift my position to alleviate the stiffness in my legs. Nosh instantly raised and pointed his 9mm at me. I settled back down and he started talking again.

"What messed up everything was that big fat Manny Falcone," he stressed the long 'o' in cone, "personally showed up at the drop with a couple of his goons. It was only supposed to be a simple drop off of my money. A waiter at the steakhouse did it all the time - low key, no fanfare. But this time out of the blue, Falcone walks in and sits down. He personally passes me the money, barely covered by a folded piece of paper, and wants to talk about a problem he is having with the police in Uvalde."

"Who is this Falcone character?"

"Somebody you never want to meet. He runs half of Texas."

I figured he didn't run it legitimately.

"Before he got too far into telling me about his problem in Uvalde, I asked Julie if she wouldn't mind excusing herself for a few minutes. She was cool. She said she would go to the bar, get a drink, and wait there until the meeting was over. Hell, she just thought it was police business. Falcone stayed for only a couple more minutes. I told him I would handle his problem in Uvalde. Before he left, he asked me who Julie was. I told him. No big deal, I told him. They got up to leave, and Falcone talks to one of his guys. Spoke in Spanish, but I got enough of it to know I wasn't going to like it. The one guy stays and the rest leave. This guy comes up to me and says that Falcone wants me to get rid of her. I told him she was no threat to us, but he said she was. He said she was a loose end now, and that loose ends had a habit of getting one killed. There was no doubt in my mind that he was now threatening me."

"So what did you do?"

"Nothing right then, I still thought I could convince Falcone that Julie posed no threat. We finished our dinner and I drove her back to her condo. I made an excuse that I had to get back to the office. In reality, I didn't think I could make love to her knowing I may have brought a death sentence down on her. I tried a number of times to call Falcone the next day, but he wouldn't take my calls. Finally, one of his deputies talked to me. I pled my case but he said that if I couldn't fix my own problem that they would. I knew how they fixed things."

Nosh stopped talking for a second. I waited quietly until he started talking again.

"You know what they do to make an example out of those men who are disloyal or maybe just hesitant in not following their orders?" He looked at me.

"I'm not sure who they are Nosh, but I imagine they could do all types of different things that I'd rather not become too familiar with."

"I'm talking about what they do to their women or even girls. They go after the men's wives, sisters and daughters. It's much more persuasive, and they don't just kill them. No, what I did for Julie was a mercy killing. What they would have done is far worse. They would have grabbed her off the street and taken her to one of their camps in Mexico where the cartels would have kept her alive for a while. When they got tired of using her they would kill her in whatever fashion was most entertaining for them at the time. I couldn't let them do that to her. She didn't deserve that. My dilemma was that they didn't give me a deadline, which meant I had to move fast – at least before they made their move."

"I guess putting her under police protection was out of the question."

"Don't be a fool. I had no choice. I made it as quick and painless as I could for her. One shot in the heart. She never knew what happened."

"How about Al, the pool guy from the condo? You killed him, too?"

"Yes, the fool saw me at the complex that day. I came and left from the gate by the pool. Went into the building through the dressing room. You avoid the security cameras that way. He called to warn me that you were asking questions, trying to find out who Julie might be having an affair with. He somehow knew that I was popping in there now and then to see her. I don't know how. I never saw him. He told me he didn't tell you about me, but he still thought it was important to warn me."

"So he was another loose end?"

"Yes, I guess you could say that. I didn't think anyone knew of my connection to Julie. Once I discovered he knew I was seeing her and had been there that day, he had to go. I told him to meet me so we could discuss the murder. Can you believe he didn't have a clue that I killed Julie? He showed up as oblivious as Julie."

"Nice touch, using a different gun."

"Yeah, I thought so, too. Easy to get your hands on guns when you're a cop."

We heard voices again coming from the building and diverted our attention to it. A stretcher was being carried out to the ambulance. I couldn't tell who was on it but imagined it had to be Quisp. I was sure that Grisshof was dead.

"Quisp?" I asked.

"Yeah, has to be."

"That may be a problem for you, Nosh. His story may be different from yours."

"Think I'm stupid? I won't go near anyone 'til I know what his story is. Besides, he may yet not make it."

The way he said it gave me the impression that Nosh believed he had the ability to affect the detective's recovery, and not in a positive way.

"It can't be that easy for you, can it?" He knew I was talking about taking another person's life.

"Don't kid yourself. The only reason you are alive is that those people are still over there. Once they are gone, so are you."

I again started my inner debate whether or not I should make my move now. Not that I had a move, but waiting didn't seem like a better option except that for the moment I was still alive.

"Like I said, it would just be more of a hassle for me if I killed you with them around." He opened his sport coat displaying the gun he used on Grisshof. "One bullet between your eyes with my gun then I put the gun used to kill Grisshof in your hand and fire one shot in the air. I would just claim we sat out here, as we have, but you held the gun on me." He grinned at me as though he was just announcing checkmate. "It's not a bad tradeoff. You get to live a little longer and I get to do less paperwork. It's your call."

I didn't answer. The ambulance started its u-turn heading back to the city cutting on its siren as it did. Two men whom I assumed were police officers looked around the area for a moment and went back into the building. I didn't know how long we had been sitting there, but the shadows from the trees were now shading the building some forty yards away.

"I'm surprised you didn't get called about this."

"I did. I told them I was heading down to Corpus. My uncle has been sick and took a turn for the worse."

I almost said I was sorry for him.

"They said that Reynolds had responded. I told them he could handle it. Pretty easy when you're the boss."

Although I hadn't seen him, this reminder that Reynolds was out here somewhere was still about the only good piece of news I had heard all day. I wondered again if Bert had called him or was it just by chance that he got the call? I sure hoped it was the former.

"How did you get in so deep?" I was still hoping the conversation was being recorded. However, in the back of my mind I couldn't help but wonder why, if someone was hearing our conversation, there wasn't anyone out looking for us? They would have to know we couldn't be too far away.

Bert and I had tested the transmitter at fairly close proximity to each other. I didn't know its true range. I began to wonder if it was damaged when Nosh shot me. As subtle as possible, I glanced down at the bullet hole in my shirt and estimated that its effect on the transmitter should be minimal at worst.

Nosh had not responded to my question. He seemed focused on the building.

"I wonder why they haven't sealed off the crime scene yet?"

"I guess they just want to be thorough." I was hoping that Nosh wasn't starting to get antsy. "Nosh, how did you get in so deep with these guys?"

"Oldest and most legitimate reason in the world – money."

I doubted his logic but kept my mouth shut.

"My ex's were squeezing me. Those two bloodsuckers wouldn't quit. I was going bankrupt. One day I was approached at a bar off Alamo St. A young lady wanted my help in getting her uncle out of a jam. Someone had told her I was a cop and that I could help her. The uncle was being held on a minor burglary charge, but it was his third one. They knew the judge would throw the book at him this time. She offered to do anything I wanted if I just helped her uncle. Hell, I said to myself, just the week before I helped a local politician get his son out of trouble, drugs not burglary, for nothing more than a pat on the back and a promise that 'he wouldn't forget it.' Whatever the hell that's supposed to mean."

"Did you help her out?"

"Sure. I told the burglary guys to give him a break. I claimed he had helped me out on a recent homicide and we owed him one. It was easy. So, as she agreed to do, she came to my place to make good her offer. I just expected sex, which by the way was pretty damn good. But when she left she handed me an envelope. Said it was personal from her uncle. It contained five thousand dollars. I told her to take the money back, that she had more than held her side of the agreement. She told me no, the money was her uncle's, and she would be in trouble if she didn't leave it with me. Then she turned and left. I was stuck with the money."

"Too bad."

"Yeah, looking back it was probably a mistake."

"That wasn't enough to hook you, was it?"

"Not just then, but I developed a weakness for that young lady. She, coincidently, developed a habit of finding me at my favorite bar. After a few more favors, she introduced me to her boss. Later, I met Falcone. By then I was in way too deep to get out. The money is good, real good, but I don't get to see my little lady friend anymore." He paused for a minute while another police car pulled up to the building. It parked on the far side, so I couldn't see who was in it.

"How long do you figure we'll be sitting here?"

"Why? Are you in a hurry to die?"

"No, my legs are just getting cramped. I need to stand up for a second."

"Move and I will shoot you."

My legs were getting stiff, but, more importantly, I had to get out of the semi-cross legged sitting position if I was going to make any move to try to reach him before he could shoot me. Even with a running start my chances were low, but sitting like I was, across from him, I had no chance at all.

"Don't worry, West. We won't be here much longer. Unless they bring out a set of lights they'll have to close up 'til tomorrow. Once the main group of them leave so can we. They'll leave someone here to make sure the crime scene stays secure but that won't bother us."

"It can't be that easy for you to kill people, Lieutenant. Was Julie your first?"

"No, but she was the first that didn't deserve it. I shot a punk or two before when I probably didn't need to. But they were bums. Hell, the first one threatened me with a knife. You should have seen his eyes when I pulled out my gun. I guess he didn't realize I was a cop. He dropped his knife like it was burning his hand. When I heard it clang on the pavement I just couldn't resist putting a bullet in him. I didn't need to shoot him but I bet if I wasn't carrying, he would have stabbed me. The other guy, maybe a year later, had recently beaten up a prostitute. He was her pimp and apparently he didn't think she was trying hard enough to bring him money. Maybe she wasn't meeting the goals he had set for her." He chuckled to himself when he mentioned goals. "Anyway, I don't like guys beating up girls. I don't like pimps and I have soft spot for the women that have to work the streets."

I felt like making some sarcastic remark, like "you don't

sound like such a bad guy after all." Instead I stayed neutral. "I don't think those two really rate as being that bad, Nosh. They're a long way from shooting Julie in cold blood."

"Yeah, I know it. I never felt bad about those two. I still regret shooting Julie. Hell, I should've shot Falcone and dared the rest of them to do anything about it."

"I kind of wished you had, too."

That comment brought a grin to his face.

"Lieutenant, why don't you simply turn yourself in? With the info you have on Falcone and the rest you can work a deal with the DA. Maybe just get ten years. You keep killing people in this state, and they will give you the death sentence."

"You're crazy, West. They won't deal with me. No way. Besides, if they get too close I have my escape plan. I'd be in South America before anyone would miss me."

I imagined he did have a plan to disappear. At that moment I wished I had one too. I decided to quit talking. If the transmitter was working then Nosh had said enough to convict himself. But if it was working, the same thought came back, where was the cavalry?

"How did Quisp get hooked?"

"He didn't. He came into the force already on Falcone's payroll. Scary, isn't it, to know that they send their guys in to join the force? The jerk is actually related to me in a roundabout way. He's the son of my sister's husband's cousin or something like that. He's been on Falcone's payroll since he was a teenager."

I wanted to ask him if that made Quisp any worse than he was, but I was too busy looking around, hoping to see someone closing in, but there was nobody. The shadows continued to lengthen. The sun started its disappearing act in the western horizon. I imagined we would be moving within another thirty minutes or so and I would be dead shortly thereafter, unless I came up with my own disappearing act.

I needed to get my hands on something I could use for a weapon but there was nothing within reach. I saw a large rock about four yards to my right that would do a good job, if it only had a chance to smash against Nosh's head. Behind Nosh a stout cedar branch had fallen from the tree he was leaning against. Both were useless, too far away.

There was a large fire ant mound built up against a live oak that split the short distance between us and about three yards to my right. Too bad he wasn't leaning against that tree. The ants were active on the mound and fortunately not moving in my direction. They were aggressive and could both bite and sting. I didn't like them.

The wind started to pick up. A pair of doves took flight from the trees overhead. Something must have spooked them. I looked around again.

"Relax, there ain't nobody out there."

I had the advantage of looking past him. I thought I saw movement about a quarter mile to my left. I was sitting too low in the underbrush to see anything clearly. However, for just a moment, I was sure I saw something moving. I strained to get a better view without success.

Somehow my anxiety affected Nosh. He took a quick look behind him. Too quick for me to do anything, and my legs were too stiff to allow me to move fast.

"Maybe it's time for us to move on."

"I thought you said you wanted to wait 'til dark. That'll only be another half hour." I was in no hurry to die and I wanted to give them more time to find us – assuming what I saw was a person, and that person was looking for us. "Besides, I have one more question for you?"

He looked at me in silence.

"Were you responsible for someone following me around and harassing me these last couple of days?"

"Not directly." His face broke into a genuine grin. "How'd you like those scorpions?"

"I didn't."

"That was all Falcone's doing. I told him we might have another issue when you showed up. I let him know you weren't going to be able to affect the results of the LaMoe case, but he thought it wouldn't hurt to try to scare you out of town. I told him to have fun. I didn't care what he did to you."

"Thanks a lot."

"That scorpion thing, I thought that was great. I tell you what, West. That would have probably been enough for me to high tail it out of town – friend or no friend. I guess because nothing seemed to bother you, Falcone escalated matters. I never knew that they were going to hit LaMoe. You're lucky there. I imagine, by that point, they decided he was the easier target."

"They should have just waited a day."

"Yeah, that's the funny thing. After all they had done, last night I get a call from one of Falcone's lieutenants telling me that they were backing off. The problem was now mine to resolve. I told them that I was happy with that. Last night I didn't think I had a problem to solve. Then this morning you raised your lousy head and created a big one. For both of us, I'd have to say right now."

"What caused them to back off?" I already thought I knew the answer – Royale.

"No idea. Not that it matters now." Nosh focused back at the building.

I wondered what Royale's role in everything was. He

seemed genuinely interested in my success. I didn't think he was involved in anything that had happened so far. Someone had mentioned to me that he had come from a large family. Maybe there was a family connection somewhere that gave him access to Falcone. There didn't have to be a business or criminal link.

"Nobody has come out of that building for a while. My guess is that we should be able to get back to that creek bed without being seen. If you want to live at least that long, you better be quiet and do just what I tell you."

If he insisted on our moving, I knew I would have to do something, and quick, if I wanted to have any chance at all.

"Now I'm going to stand up. You stay where you are until I tell you to get up." Nosh uncurled his legs and got up slowly. He looked as stiff as I felt. He stretched his back first to the right and then to the left and then worked one leg at a time to get the circulation going.

"Your turn."

I leaned to my right to push myself up with my arms and half collapsing, half falling further forward toward the fire ant mound. I turned my head to face Nosh.

"Sorry, I'm getting up." I said in a hurried whisper hoping to sound as nervous and afraid as I was. At the same time, my right hand grabbed a large piece of oak bark that had fallen off a nearby tree.

Fortunately, as my feigned slip was diagonal to our positions, it put me no nearer or farther away from Nosh. More importantly, it didn't result in any rash action by him, like shooting me in the back of my head.

I put my left hand back down as though I was going to push myself back up. Instead, I lunged forward toward the fire ants. At the same time, I jammed the bark into the base of the large mound and, spinning around, threw as much of the mound as I could at Nosh. I was aiming at his face. I just needed a distraction. The dirt, debris and ants from the mound scattered in the air as it approached him, fortunately distracting his aim. The shot, when it came, slammed into the tree just inches from my face. I scrambled, crawling, rolling and stumbling up and away from the tree. A vine grabbed my right ankle, and I sprawled face first into a thicket of sharp thorns. As I struggled to continue my escape, I looked back and saw Nosh not eight feet from me with his gun raised and aimed at my head.

They say when you are about to die your whole life flashes through your mind. Well, not in my case. I staggered another step or two away from him and tripped over a log. The only thing that went through my mind was how lame my escape attempt had been.

Nosh stood there sneering at me. He looked half way back at what was left of the Bracken Country Club and yelled.

"Stop! Police. Stop or I'll shoot!"

He aimed the gun back at me.

Chapter 19

Detective Frank Reynolds voice was loud and forceful. It sounded like music to my ears.

"Drop your gun, Lieutenant. Now! Don't make me shoot you."

I watched as Nosh turned his head and looked at Reynolds. He obviously was bewildered at Reynolds' sudden appearance and his threat to shoot him.

"What?" Nosh asked in feigned amazement. "After what he just did to those two in there?" Nosh motioned with his head back toward the building.

"Sorry, Lieutenant, please drop the gun."

Still no movement by Nosh. No doubt he was trying to figure out why everything in his plan was unraveling like this.

Reynolds kept his gun leveled at Nosh. I could see another person closing in on us from about thirty yards behind Reynolds. I hoped he was on our side.

"Lieutenant, it's over. West is wearing a wire. We heard your whole conversation."

The scene stayed quiet for about five seconds. I thought Nosh was going to drop his weapon. I was wrong and the silence was suddenly broken by a guttural roar that came from somewhere deep inside Nosh's maniacal soul. The sound was unnerving but what was worse was his focusing back at me and again firing his gun at my face. I fought the urge to stare back into his hate filled eyes when he pulled the trigger.

I rolled to my right, instinctively raising my hands as I did so to protect my face. I heard the blast of the gun being fired and felt a searing burn to the top of my head. I kept rolling, or at least in my mind, I kept rolling. Everything started going hazy. I thought I was going to black out. My eyes focused on my right forearm resting inches away from my face. There were things crawling on it. Fire ants, I thought. They must have gotten on me when I scooped part of the mound up and tossed it at Nosh. I blacked out.

The sounds of people talking and then of someone lifting me up brought me back to consciousness. My eyes began to focus and I could see that while I hadn't been moved, I was now surrounded by a group of people.

"Where'd everyone come from" I mumbled to myself.

"Are you back with us?" I looked to see who asked. It was the same young, good looking female medic who fixed me up after the joker with the knife sliced me.

She and a young guy I didn't recognize had just moved me to a stretcher. She was doing something to the top of my head. It didn't hurt, but I could see red on the sponge or cloth she had in her hand.

She noticed my looking. "You just got grazed. You may need some stitches but most likely not. Better let your doctor make that decision tonight or tomorrow."

"I thought you were my doctor." She smiled at my comment.

"While you were out I looked under your vest. You were fortunate, the vest stopped both bullets. They aren't always as effective as they claim to be. Do you feel like anything is broken?"

"No, I'm pretty sure I just have some bruises, nothing broken."

I looked over at the guy. He was rubbing something on my right arm.

"You caught some nasty thorns and about a dozen fire ant stings and bites. Nothing serious, unless you're allergic to insect bites. Are you?"

I told him no. An ambulance had pulled in close to us and two other first responders were hustling a stretcher to it. Nosh was on it and he didn't look good. I sat up.

"Are you sure you feel good enough to do that?" The young lady asked while still trying to clean up and bandage my head.

"Actually, right now I feel pretty good. My arm bothers me more than my head. I think I also have some scratches on my right leg."

The male moved from my arm to my right leg pulling up my slacks to the knee. Two nasty scratches ran from a few inches above my ankle to just below my knee.

"These aren't serious either but I'll clean them up for you. Only take a second." He reached back in his black bag that was sitting at his feet and pulled out some more cloth and some kind of liquid that he poured over it.

"How are you feeling?"

I looked up. Detective Frank Reynolds was standing there looking rather pallid himself.

"I'm fine, thanks to you. How are you doing?"

"Not very well at the moment. In all my years with the force, I've never shot anyone before. To make the first one your boss, your friend and a fellow cop all rolled up into one – that's not right. I actually feel a little sick."

Both medics were listening and moved quickly from me to Reynolds. The young man took the lead.

"Here, sit down, sir."

He half dragged Reynolds to the stretcher I was on and sat

him next to me. I moved over. Reynolds started to protest but then just sat down.

"I was all right a minute ago. I called the chief and told him how things ended up. I did that just fine."

"It's normal," I told him, not really having any idea what was normal after what he just went through. For me, I was the mouse that got away from a cat. A cat I didn't know very well. I only felt immense relief.

Frank had shot and probably killed someone whom he had been close to since coming on the force. Someone with whom he had likely shared many meals, drinks, stories, and even the occasional departmental picnic; someone who had backed him up on the street , maybe even saved his butt a few times. I had no idea how he felt. I was awful glad I wasn't in his shoes, and I was very glad he had done what he did.

"You did what you had to do, Frank. You did what you took an oath to do. I know it doesn't feel right, at least not now, but it will."

"I know, I know." He stared at the ground.

I could hear another siren coming closer. I looked around. There were at least six other officers nearby. Back by the building in the near darkness I could see two more taping off the building. Off to the side, I could see a lone man standing on the other side of the road and about twenty yards away from the building. It was Bert Falls. He saw me looking at him and waved. I gave him a thumbs-up.

"West, one thing I got to know. Give it to me straight. Did you know it was Nosh?"

"No. I did not know who it was. My whole plan for today was to try to bluff the real killer out. I was simply going with the knowledge that it had to be someone who was real familiar with my movements once I got into town. I was shocked that it was Nosh. If I wasn't wearing this vest," I tapped my chest, "he would have killed me. I was completely surprised."

Reynolds smiled. "Good. All hell was going to break loose if you knew it, and didn't tell anybody."

"If I knew it, would I have driven out here to the middle of nowhere without a weapon to meet him?"

"No, I guess not."

The two medics finished up with me and started to pack up.

I looked over at Reynolds again. He stood up, looking better and then let out a deep breath.

"Guess I better get back to work." He walked off to talk to another officer.

What I didn't tell Reynolds was that I should have been more suspicious of Nosh. I should have at least exercised more caution. While I never really believed it was him, I should have realized that he had to be on the short list. What did they say in the military? A good tactical plan with terrible strategic implications - win the battle just to lose the war. I could have discovered who the killer was just in time to get myself killed. I could blame it on the expediency of the moment, but it was a short sighted plan that nearly got me killed.

"Are you going to be okay? We can take you to the hospital if you'd like." My attractive lady medic said this while smiling at me like a school nurse.

"I'll be fine."

"I think you just blacked out. More like fainting than being knocked out. Too much stress and the body shuts down. That's not uncommon. The bullet barely grazed your head. I don't think there is any internal damage and only minimal swelling. I had to cut a little bit of your hair off. I hope you don't mind."

"Not at all, I feel like I owe you a steak dinner."

"Then give me a call." She turned as she said this and

walked away.

I watched her go. As she crossed the road, a number of portable lights went on around the building and nearby, lighting up the area around me where the gaggle of policemen were inspecting this shooting location.

"Too young for you old man."

I looked back to see Frank Reynolds approaching me.

"I know."

"You and I need to leave this area now. I understand you're okay?"

"I'm fine. I'll have a bit of a headache for a while but I'm fine."

"Listen, you can go now. Bert can give you a ride back to your hotel. But first I need the transmitter you are wearing."

I reached under my shirt and with some degree of difficulty managed to remove it. I handed the transmitter to him.

"We already have custody of the receiver. Tomorrow morning, be at my office at nine. As you can imagine, you won't be seeing me. Get a good night's rest and a good breakfast. You may be at the station for a while."

"Will do, Frank. Are you going to be all right?"

"Procedurally, yes, a lot of people saw what went down. Personally, I don't know. They've got a table set up for me in the building. There will be an inquiry, that's automatic, so I'll be over there for a while. But you better take off before someone changes their mind and decides they want to keep you here, too."

"Okay. Hang in there." We shook hands and I looked around for Bert. He was leaning against the far corner of the building.

"Hey, Bert," I said as I approached him, "thanks." Not much of a greeting but I didn't seem to know what else to say.

"You okay?"

"He just grazed me. The fire ants got me worse." I held out my arm to show him the small blisters.

"You know they took the receiver and all the data."

"That's to be expected. I was going to give it to them anyway to prove our case no matter who the killer was. With it being Nosh, I'm sure the department doesn't want any loose copies of the audio falling into the hands of the press."

We walked over to the van and climbed in.

"Where to?"

"I guess back to my hotel if you don't mind. I'm sorry I tied up your whole day."

"Think nothing of it. I haven't had this much excitement since leaving OSI. You had me rather worried for a while. The range on the transmitter wasn't as good as it should've been."

"How so?"

"Luckily the poor reception caused me to move in close to you when you were at O'Briens. You were breaking up. But that allowed me to get a visual on the car you left in. That was important because otherwise I wouldn't have had any idea where you went. Following you out here wasn't easy. When you all pulled into the parking lot, I had to stay behind the bend right there."

We had just pulled out of the lot and were approaching the bend in the road that Bert was referring to, about three hundred yards from the Bracken Country Club.

"I tried to listen to what was going on inside the building, but the receiver wasn't picking up anything. Then I heard the shots. The first one startled me and then came the second. I jumped out of the van to look around the bend. I could see the side of the building but nothing else. That's when I heard two or three more shots so I ran back to the van. Still nothing was being picked up by the receiver. I called Detective Reynolds and told him what was going on. He told me to stay put - that he would be out as fast as he could. I watched the building from the tree line but never saw another body or heard another sound."

"How long did it take him to get out here?"

"I didn't keep track. Maybe twenty minutes. I heard nothing on the receiver the whole time. When Reynolds arrived with another cop I followed them out to the building where we found one guy dead - Grisshof. Then we found the cop, nearly dead but still had a pulse. At that point, Reynolds called in the reinforcements. The place was soon crawling with cops and the county medical examiner's team. Before they got here Reynolds had his partner do a quick look around for anyone else. I saw the guy walk through the area where you were later found, but he never saw you."

"We weren't there then."

"Well, we initially figured there must have been a car on that other side of the building, where I couldn't see it. We figured the driver took you and left before we arrived. Later, sometime after everyone arrived, I went back to the van and there you were as clear as day. I got Reynolds over and we both listened for about a minute. We heard Nosh admit to killing Julie. It was obvious he had you somewhere close by, but where?"

"No one thought it would be wise to fan out and start an obvious search. That would give us no chance to surprise Nosh. So Reynolds called in more reinforcements. That was after he called the chief and told him what was up. They had a team drive in from the other direction and stop about a half mile on the other side of the building. Their job was to sweep the woods on that side. Reynolds left with another cop in one of the Crown Vic's and met up with a couple other officers just round the bend, out of sight, near where I had been waiting earlier. They started the sweep on the side of the road, where you were eventually located. The rest you know."

"How much did you all hear?"

"A lot, enough. Once we heard what was going on, Reynolds had one of his guys stay in the van with the receiver taking notes and passing on key stuff."

"Everything recorded all right, didn't it?"

"Just fine. Once they had you and we heard Nosh was down we checked the playback. It was just fine. They got a lot on Nosh - if he survives."

"How bad was he Bert? I missed that part."

"Real bad, I think. They had an ambulance staged around the bend, along with some other emergency responders. Their being so close may be what saves Nosh but I doubt it."

"I kind of hope he survives."

"Well, don't get your hopes up too high. I only heard what happened from here in the van. From what I was told, Reynolds caught him from the side under his right arm. The bullet must have torn up his whole chest cavity."

I watched the countryside turn into city outside the van's windows. The lights in the city were on. It had been another long day.

Chapter 20

I thanked Bert when we got back to the hotel. I told him I owed him big time and was going to pay him back big time. He just laughed and drove away.

I walked into the lobby of the hotel. A number of people stared at me, looking guiltily away when I noticed them. Catching myself in one of the lobby's mirrors, I saw what was catching everyone's attention. I looked quite frightful.

Perhaps the worst part was the portion of my head had been shaved and bandaged. One of the bandages had come loose and was curled upwards. It was stained red and orange. I patted it down into place and continued up to my room. The hole in my shirt wasn't that obvious.

Once in my room, I went straight to the fridge and grabbed a Bud Light. I popped the top, took a big swig and sat down on one of the large comfortable chairs. I reached for my cell only to remember that Nosh still had it. I wanted to check on Randy and let him know that it was over.

I went to the bedroom and found my notes with all the phone numbers I needed. Sitting down on the bed, I started making my calls. The first was to Randy. Actually it was to the nurses' station by Randy's room. They told me Randy was doing well, and that he should have a full recovery. However, at the moment he was sleeping and that I would have to call back in the morning or come by during visiting hours. I told the nurse I would stop by in the morning, but if Randy awoke to please give him the message that everything was successfully resolved. I emphasized the significance of the message to Randy's stress levels. The nurse reassured me she would pass on the message.

The next call went to Cynthia Rich. I would have preferred talking to Nita again but my ego made me call Cynthia. I wanted to tell her that I was right, Randy was innocent, and that my plan to uncover the killer worked. Luckily, the press had not caught wind of the incident yet and my story was news to Cynthia. Her reaction was what I expected.

"What? You say that Nosh was the killer. I can't believe it. I'm watching the news right now. They haven't made any mention of it."

"Trust me, it's true. I imagine this is the type of story the police department and the city would like to keep quiet as long as possible. Have your boss call the police chief or you can call Detective Reynolds, although Reynolds may be tied up at the moment with the case."

"You're serious, aren't you? Have they arrested Nosh?"

"I guess you could say that. He was shot and may be dead for all I know."

"Jesus! I just talked to him this morning. Who shot him?"

"Detective Reynolds."

"No way!"

"If he hadn't, you wouldn't be talking to me right now."

"Are you okay?"

How about that? She cares. "I'm fine."

"Let me go, Jim. I need to call Nita and the boss to fill them in. I may need to call you back. If I don't, can I see you in the morning?"

"Better than that Cynthia, I'm supposed to meet with the police tomorrow morning. I was thinking you or Nita could tag along and hear everything first hand from them and me."

"Sounds great, Jim, but do you mean you might need me as your lawyer?"

"No, not at all, I just thought it would be beneficial to both of us since you are representing Randy. You could kick me on the shins under the table, though, if I say something I shouldn't."

"Okay, I'll be there."

The next call was the most awkward one. It was to the hospital where Jack Wilson was taken after he was shot by the Comal County deputies. It was a long shot that I would get to speak to anyone but I wanted to know how he was.

The hospital operator transferred me twice before I got someone on the phone.

"Hello," a woman's voice came through the line.

"Hello, I'm calling to check on the status of Mr. Jack Wilson."

"Who is calling?"

"I'm Jim West. I was there when he got shot –"

The voice cut me off.

"I know." There was a pause. I waited, somewhat confused. "I'm his wife."

"I'm sorry, ma'am. How's he doing?"

"It may be a miracle but they say he's going to make it."

"That's great, ma'am. That's really all I wanted to know."

"Wait a minute. Jim, is that right?"

"Yes."

"I want to thank you."

"Me?"

"Yes. Everyone was mad at you at first. Some at the office still are, but they don't know the whole story. The deputy told me that if you hadn't jumped in and knocked my husband down to the ground, the shots may have killed him. He also said you stayed and helped out with the first aid. My husband told me this morning, that was the first time he could talk, he had wanted to die. He didn't blame the police. He said you tried to talk him out of it."

"Yes, ma'am. I tried to tell him he hadn't done anything bad enough to kill himself."

"I know. Did you know this woman, Jim?"

"Not as well as I thought. But I do know that your husband was only one of many that fell under her spell. I know that may sound funny but, believe me, she had some kind of power over men. Your husband never had a chance."

"A bit overstated and I don't necessarily agree with you. But I believe we can work this out. I just want my Jack back. And I could see it in his eyes yesterday and today. He wants things back like they were, too."

We talked for a few more minutes then hung up. I needed a shower and a good night's rest. I stood up but the door bell interrupted my thoughts.

I opened the door to find Lee standing there with a bottle of Champagne and a big smile on her very lovely face. Upon seeing me, her expression changed to one of surprise.

"What happened to you?"

"Long story, come on in. Why the Champagne?"

"You have apparently made a good friend since you arrived here in San Antonio."

"A few enemies, too," I mumbled, half to myself.

"Well, you must have impressed a Mr. Royale. You do know him, don't you?"

"Yes. Did he send the Champagne?" I looked at the bottle. The Champagne was from France. "The real stuff, I'm impressed. Did he leave any note or explanation?"

"Not much of one."

She handed me a small card that simply read, "Glad you made it back safely. Thanks." I wondered how he heard about what happened so quickly. As far as I knew, the incident had not yet been made public.

"And that's not all. He also paid for your hotel bill."

"The whole thing?"

"Yes, through next weekend."

"Next weekend? I need to head back home. I was thinking about leaving tomorrow afternoon if I can."

Lee looked at me. I could almost see her mind working on something.

"What's wrong?"

"Nothing, nothing at all. But seriously, Jim, what happened to you?"

"A bullet grazed my head and a few thorns and fire ants played havoc with my arm. More importantly, the real murderer has been identified and is in the hands of the police. Randy will be set free and have a chance to heal."

"Is that what I think it is?" She asked pointing to the hole in my shirt.

"A bullet hole."

She reached hesitantly to the hole and put a finger through it feeling the damaged Kevlar.

"And is that what I think it is?"

"A bullet-proof vest."

"So I guess we're really due for a celebration." She took the bottle from my hand and walked into the kitchenette.

"Need help?"

"Nope," she grinned and with the skill of a true professional she had the bottle open in no time.

She poured us both a glass and we toasted Royale.

She came in close and we kissed.

"If we're going to finish this bottle together, I'm going to need a shower."

We embraced again for a longer kiss.

"You know, Lee, I may be leaving town tomorrow."

"I'm counting on it. I don't want a relationship. I don't want any strings on me. Been there, done that and it hurt too much to let go."

I held her close and we kissed with more passion. I reluctantly stepped back.

"I really do need a shower."

"Go ahead."

I went into the bedroom and tossed my clothes and the vest on the floor.

"Are they going to miss you at work?"

"I called them and told them I would be taking my lunch hour early."

That brought a smile to my face. I walked into the bathroom and into the large shower. The hot water came fast. The wound on my head burned but I didn't care. I started wondering, as I washed my face, if I shouldn't yell out that there was plenty of room in here. I rinsed the soap off my face and realized I didn't need to. She was standing there, wearing nothing and looking beautiful, just out of the spray of the shower.

"Like to join me?" I reached out with my hand.

"Oh yeah," she extended her hand and I pulled her in.

Chapter 21

The next morning at the police station was long and tough. I was glad Cynthia was there. The two, and sometimes three, policemen interviewing me weren't thrilled about her presence, but I insisted and they gave in. I didn't have the advantage of having Reynolds handling the interview and the two detectives who spent the most amount of time with me were not friendly, to say the least. I didn't really blame them. They were trying to get their hands around a multifaceted, major investigation which included three murders, maybe more, one cop shooting another, police corruption, and a tsunami of press interest that began around seven in the morning when the news hit the streets.

They wanted to know what I knew and when I knew it, what I saw and when I saw it. What Nosh had said, despite having most of his conversation with me already recorded, and when did he say it. They then wanted to know what I had told Reynolds and when had I told him. The facts were there, but they weren't ready to accept them. Perhaps, they simply wanted to put possible conspiracy theories to rest. They even wanted to know if I knew Falcone. Whatever their strategy was, they attacked the shootings from all angles. They were thorough to the point that twice Cynthia stepped in and asked them if I needed to be advised of my rights.

As the interview ended, the word came in that the hospital had taken Nosh off life support and he had died. Except for the anguish Reynolds would go through, I didn't care. I also was told Quisp was going to be fine. He had a serious concussion and had spent the night in the hospital. He had refused to make any comment once he found out Nosh had been arrested.

When the police let me go, they told me that they would need me when, and if, the matter with Quisp went to trial. I assured them I would be available.

"Will you let me buy you lunch?" Cynthia asked once we were outside.

"No thanks. I want to see Randy and I still need to get back home today."

I knew she was just trying to make amends. I was sure that she really wanted to get back to her office to fill everyone in with the latest.

"There's one thing that grates on me, Jim, now that I have the full story."

"What's that?"

"Why didn't Julie answer or return any of Randy's calls?"

"I guess we'll never know. Randy did say she was not very reliable with her cell phone. That was one of the reasons he wasn't over worried."

"I remember, but if she had taken any of those calls she might still be alive today."

"Possibly, but more likely it would have only delayed her murder. Nosh felt like he had to act fast."

"Maybe so."

She gave me a hug and was gone.

I swung by the hospital to check on Randy and was happy to discover he was doing a lot better. He told me the fact that he was no longer a suspect in his wife's murder was the best medicine anyone could have given him. He offered to pay me or, at least, cover my expenses. I told him someone else already had. He looked at me quizzically, but didn't ask who.

We talked for about an hour. When he asked about what I had found out about Julie and other men, I told him I could only confirm that she had one other lover, and that was Nosh. I told him she had paid for her transgression and there would be no good in dwelling on it. He needed to grieve her passing and move on. I think he believed me.

Epilogue

I wanted to do something to pay Bert Falls back for saving my butt, regardless of his refusal to let me. The least I could do was to buy him a nice dinner, but I needed a way to get him to attend the dinner despite the fact that I would be long gone from San Antonio.

My ploy was simple. I set up the meal at Ruth's Chris Steak House and paid for everything ahead of time. I then coordinated what I was trying to do with Mr. Royale to make sure Bert got sufficient encouragement to go. I invited my little Florence Nightingale, whose actual name was Karen Law, and asked Detective Reynolds to do what he could to encourage her to attend. I also invited Reynolds and his wife, but he said he couldn't accept. I didn't push him.

I never followed up to see if either Bert or Karen went to that dinner. I had made my effort. I knew it wouldn't pay back the huge debt I owed to Bert.

The letter came three months later. The letter was from Bert and said very little, "Thanks for the dinner. It was a great idea, life's been good."

What said more was the photo inside that captured Bert and Karen smiling, holding hands, and walking along the beach. Maybe Mexico, I thought. They were in swimming attire, and there wasn't much to Karen's bikini.

Studying her closely, with my dog doing likewise from my lap, I couldn't help but remark, "Damn, Chubs, I think I overpaid him."

--- Jim West

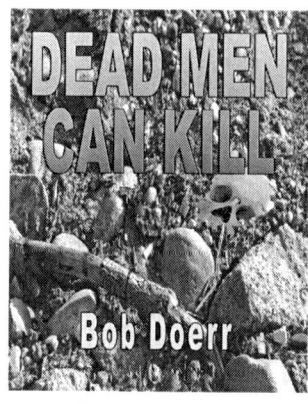

Dead Men Can Kill

- Author: Bob Doerr
- Price: $27.95
- Publisher: TotalRecall Publications, Inc.
- Format: HARDCOVER, 6.14" x 9.21"
- Number of pages: 320
- 13-digit ISBN: 978-1-59095-758-5
- Publication: December 8, 2009

When Jim West, a former Air Force Special Agent with the Office of Special Investigations, moves back to New Mexico, his goal is simple: start an easy going second career as a professional lecturer on investigative techniques to colleges and civic organizations. He never envisioned that his practical demonstration of forensic hypnosis on stage with a state university student would stir up memories of an 18-year old murder mystery. When the student is murdered three days later, West finds himself ensnared in a web of intrigue that pits him and the small town's authorities against a ruthless, psychotic killer.

An aggressive reporter for the town newspaper seeks out West for help with the story, but after one of her co-workers is murdered, she quickly aligns her efforts with West and the Sheriff. As West works closely with her, he begins to wonder if this could be the first real relationship for him since his devastating divorce a few years earlier.

The killer, though, has other plans for the reporter and the story takes fascinating twists and turns, leading to an inevitable, riveting confrontation.

Praise

Look out for a new hero on the mystery/thriller landscape! Jim West, retired military investigator, is resourceful, intuitive, pragmatic and always competent. All of West's abilities are tested when he matches wits with psychopathic serial killer William White, a man whose appreciation for murder is surpassed only by his delight in domination. Bob Doerr has crafted a must-read addition to the genre in *Dead Men Can Kill*, which evolves from absorbing story to absolute page-turner as West closes in on a killer who is supposedly dead. Highly recommended!

--Dallin Malmgren, author of...
The Whole Nine Yards   The Ninth Issue   Is This for a Grade?

A Jim West™ Mystery/Thriller

Cold Winter's Kill
A 2010 Eric Hoffer Award Finalist
- Author: Bob Doerr
- Price: $27.95
- Publisher: TotalRecall Publications, Inc.
- Format: HARDCOVER, 6.14" x 9.21"
- Number of pages: 288
- 13-digit ISBN: 978-1-59095-762-8
- Publication: Dec 8, 2009

Cold Winter's Kill is a fast paced thriller that takes place in the scenic mountains of Lincoln County, New Mexico and throws Jim West into a race against time to stop a psychopath who abducts and kills a young blonde every Christmas...

It was one of those phone calls former Air Force Special Agent Jim West never wanted to receive--an old friend calling to ask if he could drive down to Ruidoso, New Mexico to help locate his daughter who has disappeared while on a ski trip with friends. Jim found himself heading to Ruidoso even though he believed, much like the local authorities, that if she had gone missing in the mountains in December, her survival chances were slim. He didn't want to be there when they found her, but still he drove on.

Once in Ruidoso, Jim discovers a sinister coincidence that changes everything. It appears that someone is abducting and killing one young blond every year around Christmas. The race is on--can Jim locate his friend's daughter in time? But why is this happening and who's doing it?

Jim can't wait for the local authorities to raise the priority of their search, or for the pending blizzard to pass. In his haste he puts himself in the killer's sights. Will he, too, suffer from a cold winter's kill?

Praise

"GREAT SUSPENSE! In *Cold Winter's Kill* Bob Doerr grabs your attention from the beginning and holds it until the last sentence. Hard to put down!"
>--Shelba Nicholson
>former Women's Editor, *Texarkana Gazette*

Author Bob Doerr Uses his special knowledge to provide authentic details in his novels about how law enforcement agencies do their work.

A Jim West™ Mystery/Thriller

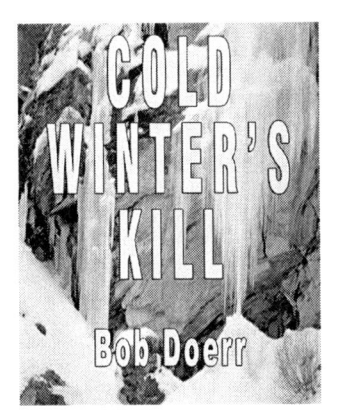

LaVergne, TN USA
04 March 2011
218704LV00002B/89/P